"I keep my word."

"Implying that *I* do not?" demanded Margot indignantly. "I was not seeking to escape, Sir Thomas!"

"Even so," he pointed out icily, "you gave your word that you would not escape, but neglected to inform me of a secret entry that could have led to my defeat. If the stronghold has fallen, a rescue is not an escape, is it?" he demanded harshly.

"You did not ask about such things! And I had forgot—"

Sir Thomas's steely gaze seemed to pierce right through her. She met it boldly, having nothing to hide.

"And are there other secrets you have forgotten? More hidden passages, mayhap? A concealed sally port that has escaped your memory?"

"No, there is not. At least—" she hesitated "—none that I have ever heard of. But my husband did not tell me all his secrets...."

"Convenient." His tone was scornful. "Go back to bed. I will sleep in your bower, across the door to this chamber. I shall take no more chances on your honor or your memory."

Sarah Westleigh

Set Free My Heart

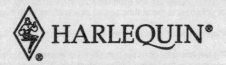

HARLEQUIN®

TORONTO • NEW YORK • LONDON
AMSTERDAM • PARIS • SYDNEY • HAMBURG
STOCKHOLM • ATHENS • TOKYO • MILAN • MADRID
PRAGUE • WARSAW • BUDAPEST • AUCKLAND

ISBN 0-373-30327-0

SET FREE MY HEART

First North American Publication 1999

Look us up on-line at: http://www.romance.net

Printed in U.S.A.

SARAH WESTLEIGH

Since leaving grammar school, **Sarah Westleigh** has enjoyed a varied life. Working as a local government officer in London, she qualified as a chartered quantity surveyor. Having married a chartered accountant, she assisted her husband in his Buckinghamshire practice, at the same time setting up and managing an employment agency. Tired of so hectic a life, they moved to Brixham in Devon, where she at last found the time to indulge her long-held ambition to write, publishing short stories and articles for magazines, and a number of modern romances. In writing historical novels, she has discovered a new and enchanting world for her future characters to inhabit.

Chapter One

1367

"*D*oña! Doña! Holy Mother of God! There are soldiers at the gate demanding entry!"

Margot's tiring-woman burst unceremoniously into her chamber with news she had been expecting since hearing the flourish of trumpets at the gatehouse a few moments earlier. She quelled her growing panic and rose slowly to her feet.

"Calm yourself, Inés," she instructed the girl sternly. "Whose are they? Do you know?"

"No, *doña*."

"Then mayhap 'twould be better to find out before descending into abject fear! They may belong to Don Roberto. Your master may be home!"

Inés's smooth, olive-skinned face dropped into mutinous lines. "You know that cannot be so, *doña*. The sound was not of his herald's horn—"

"I know nothing, girl, except that Don Enrico of Trastamara's army was defeated four days ago, that he has failed to hold Castile." Fear had been festering in her mind since the news arrived. But she must not show it before her servants. Without her strength the household would disintegrate into an unruly rabble, fighting among themselves for survival. She spoke encouragingly. "Don Roberto may have escaped capture, or he may have returned on parole. Mayhap he has been brought back under guard."

Whatever the circumstances of his return, he would be in a temper which he would take out on her. Unconsciously, she hunched her shoulders defensively.

"*Doña,* I do not think—"

Margot forced a repressive note into her voice. "You are not supposed to, girl!"

At that moment an urgent knocking on the heavy wooden door brought both women to a momentary stillness.

"Enter!" Margot schooled her voice with difficulty, tense with dread. When she saw who had come, the anticlimax left her shaking. "What is it, Juan?"

"The English, *doña!*" The youthful servant's lips worked in agitation as he tried to form his words. "A great English Duke and dozens of soldiers, *doña.* He asks if you will be so kind as to grant them entry so that he may speak with you."

"He did not demand?" queried Margot, astonished and relieved. She had expected enemy forces to storm the castle and rampage unceremoniously into her sanctuary to pillage her beautiful rugs and hangings, and probably rape her. Her heart began to beat less fiercely.

"No, *doña.* They come in peace."

"We could not deny them entry, even if we wished. There are not enough of us...the few soldiers left behind by Don Roberto are not enough to defend the castle. Go and instruct the gate-ward to lower the drawbridge. I will join the Duke in the Great Hall directly.'' She turned to Inés. ''Bring me my azure surcoat and the matching head-dress. I shall not need to change my kirtle.''

The youth disappeared. Inés brought the things with shaking hands. Margot slipped the sideless garment on, and the girl began to fumble with the small buttons down the front.

Margot settled the richly ornamented head-dress over the white coif already covering her head and framing her face. She wanted to look her best for this encounter. She would not meet these strangers as a supplicant for mercy, but as Marguerite, Doña Sedano, Châtelaine of Castillo Sedano and, in her husband's absence, its castellan.

Her fine, nondescript brown hair hung from beneath the cap almost to her waist. It would not grow longer. She wished she had beauty to charm these foreign invaders. But her thin face, with its over-long nose and too-wide mouth, her skin, neither the smooth olive of the Spanish women nor the fresh pink and white of the English, and her eyes, neither velvety brown nor sky-blue, but an unattractive pottage of brown, grey, blue—and even, on occasions, green—gave her no claim to the kind of looks which could move men to deeds of valour or chivalry.

She tweaked the soft folds of her silver-grey gown into position, lifted her trailing skirts, squared her slim shoulders under the wide, cape-like yoke of the blue surcoat, and prepared to face her captors—for what else could they be, since Roberto had fought against the deposed King Pedro of Castile in the army of his half-brother, the usurper Don Enrico of Trastamara?

She walked steadily down the winding, difficult stone staircase with its uneven steps, familiar to her but placed deliberately to foil invaders, and entered the Hall quietly, at the dais end.

Flashing steel, a swirl of peacock colours met her eye. Her visitors were striding around inspecting the rich tapestries with which the vast chamber was hung. Before long, she fumed impotently, the priceless treasures would doubtless be decorating some English castle's walls.

Hearing the soft swish of her skirt against the rushes covering the flagged floor, a tall man swung round with a jangle of golden spurs. His jupon quartered the lilies of France with the leopards of England.

This must be the Duke, a royal Duke, judging by his heraldic emblems and the coronet-like roll edging his helmet. She curtsied low, as she would to any noble, refusing to be intimidated by those piercing blue eyes into dropping to her knees in supplication.

"Margarita del Sedano?" He bowed with knightly courtesy. "You speak French, *doña?*"

"*Oui,*" replied Margot in that language. "And my name is Marguerite, not Margarita. I also speak English, if you prefer. My mother was of your nation."

The Duke bowed again. "My apologies, *doña.* Your father is the Chevalier Bertrand de Bellac, Comte de Limousin, I understand, one of my brother of Wales's vassals." He threw back his head. "I am John, Duke of Lancaster," he announced in English, his voice ringing through the Hall with royal arrogance.

"Your Grace." Margot swept another curtsy. "Will you and your men take refreshment? I will send for wine. Juan!" She issued her orders in Spanish.

The boy darted away. Margot settled herself in a chair near the dais, indicating that the Duke should seat himself, too. But he shook his head in refusal.

"I bring you bad tidings, Lady Marguerite," he said curtly. "You know of the battle which took place near Nájera four days ago?"

"Yes, lord. Don Enrico's army was defeated. Was he killed?"

"We did not find his body. However, we did find the body of Don Roberto of Sedano among the dead."

"Aahh!"

Margot's already pale skin went parchment-white as the blood left her face. She clutched the arms of her chair and drew a deep breath.

At that moment her servants arrived carrying earthenware flagons and silver drinking vessels. She accepted a brimming cup of wine and drank gratefully.

"I had feared such news, Your Grace."

"So I imagine. Your husband's lands are forfeit to King Pedro. You will remain here until the King decides what will be done with you. I will leave enough men to guard you. Thomas!"

A man stepped forward to take his place beside his lord. A couple of inches shorter than the tall Duke, and of about the same age, he made a lithe, compact, forcefully masculine figure in an azure jupon slashed by a broad red diagonal band on which was embroidered a golden castle surrounded by a dusting of the lilies of France. Margot guessed what that charge implied. The man was a bastard, the arms of his noble father kept within the confines of a band.

His challenging grey eyes were fixed on her with a faintly puzzled expression in their depths. Perhaps she had not managed to hide the relief sweeping through her at the news of her husband's death. Almost nothing the future held could be worse than spending it as Don Roberto's wife.

The Duke introduced him. "My Lady, this is Sir Thomas d'Evreux, my most trusted knight. You can rely on him to see that no harm befalls you or your servants. He will protect this castle from pillage on behalf of Pedro, the rightful King of Castile."

The young man bowed as Margot inclined her head.

"You are most kind," she said tightly, addressing the Duke, while her eyes narrowed on the undeniably handsome features of the man he had just appointed her gaoler.

Now that the immediate relief had passed, anxiety began to nibble at her mind again. Pedro had no reputation for clemency. Her fate could be to rot in some dungeon. She lifted her chin defiantly, refusing to allow these English conquerors to see the fear growing in her.

"Thomas, you will remain here with thirty men while I return to Burgos. Keep the castle against raiders and prevent the lady's escape. I rely on you."

"Your Grace, I will do my best, if that is your wish. But what of your own safety? I would prefer to remain by your side, to guard your person as is my normal duty."

"I am quite capable of looking after myself, Thomas! Think you I cannot command my own retinue?"

"Nay, lord, but its numbers will be much reduced. The journey back to Burgos will be fraught with danger—"

"God's nails, man!" The Plantagenet temper was being sorely tried by Sir Thomas's persistence. The blue eyes blazed from their deep sockets, the wide nostrils flared, the chain-mail, dependant from his helmet to protect his throat, clanked as he jerked his head in irritation. "Do you obey me, or do I take you back to Burgos under guard?"

Sir Thomas looked not one whit abashed. He grinned, an unrepentant grin that brought creases to radiate from the corners of his impudent eyes and deepened the furrows slashing his lean cheeks.

"I do but remind you of the dangers, lord. Lady Blanche would not thank me if I neglected my duty," he returned mildly, gazing fearlessly into his Duke's irascible face.

The Duke's temper dissipated as quickly as it had flared. "Aye, my wife." His whole aspect softened. "It must be about her time. Mayhap I am a father once more!"

"For her sweet sake you will take care?"

"Aye, Tom." The Duke clapped Sir Thomas on the shoulder. "I'll take care of my precious carcass! I'll send instructions as soon as may be. Enjoy your comfortable quarters!"

"Aye, lord. Lying here will be an improvement on our encampment on the Ebro plain!"

"My brother resides in comfort in Burgos, where he treats with Pedro. Pray God he soon recovers from this plaguey attack of dysentery." The Duke frowned, concern etching new lines on his still youthful face. "Meanwhile, I must return to the army." He turned to Margot and executed a courtly bow. "Farewell, Lady Marguerite. Mayhap we shall meet again under more favourable circumstances."

"Mayhap, Your Grace," she returned with an inclination of her head. "I thank you for your courtesy to one you must regard as a defeated enemy."

The Duke swept out, Sir Thomas and the others with him. But Margot knew that most would go no further than the inner ward. She must arrange accommodation for thirty or so extra men.

She barely had time to direct her servants before Sir Thomas d'Evreux returned, accompanied by his squire, a youngish man wilting under the weight of his master's weapons and accoutrements. Margot drew herself up to her full height and faced the young knight with all the dignity she could muster.

"Sir Thomas. I have arranged for your men to be quartered in the barracks. You will no doubt wish to remain in this part of the castle. I have instructed my servants to prepare a guest chamber—"

"I thank you, *doña*, but I must lie near you. Where is this chamber?"

"On the other side of the Great Hall," Margot admitted a trifle breathlessly. The man didn't look like a rapist, but one could never tell.

"Your husband had his own chamber?"

"Aye, sir."

She clasped her hands together in agitation, but met the scrutiny of cool grey eyes fearlessly. Hers were but a hand's breadth below his, the inner ring of flecked brown iris almost green, a sign of her nervousness.

"Where?"

She swallowed. "It adjoins our bower, as does mine."

She spoke in a slightly husky, engagingly accented voice, in which he could detect strong evidence of her Limousin upbringing. But what made her intonation so fascinating was the way certain Spanish nuances of pronunciation had become mixed with the French. She hid it well, but she was rigid with fear. He spoke more gently than he had intended.

"You will not mind my using it? I do not think your sensibilities will be offended. I fancy you do not mourn your husband, *doña*."

He was astute. He *had* seen her relief at the Duke's tidings. She drew a deep breath and spoke honestly.

"No, Sir Thomas, I do not. Don Roberto could be a cruel man when thwarted. I confess his death is a relief to me. Or would be, were my own future more certain."

Thomas frowned, his grey eyes reflecting instant distaste. "He was unkind to you?"

"I would rather not speak of it."

He scrutinised her afresh. "You do not look cowed," he remarked at last.

"I have tried to preserve my dignity, sir. I may be merely half French and half English, but my pride is as strong as that of any Spaniard. Will you follow me?"

She turned before the man could see the tears gathering in her eyes, and led the way up her private stair to the suite she had shared with Roberto—a bower and two bedchambers, with adjoining wardrobes and pallet-chambers for their body servants. Her stomach clenched as she led Sir Thomas and his squire into the room she had left less than an hour previously. It remained unchanged. Yet everything had changed.

"My bedchamber is there." She swept an arm towards a door to the right, and then turned to her left. "This was my husband's room."

She thrust open the door, revealing a chamber hung on every side with heavy tapestries depicting scenes of brutality, depravity and war. Armour and weapons vied with them to find space on the walls. Yet the sumptuously hung bed was soft, and looked inviting within the purple velvet drapes. This was where Roberto had so often dragged her to violate her body, and Margot could not repress a shudder.

"Hmm." Sir Thomas looked around with ill-concealed disgust. "This will have to do. *Doña*, I must

be on hand to defend you if we are attacked. I have no
lewd reason for wishing to lie near you. You understand
this?''

His level gaze met hers without guile. Despite his
overwhelming aura of male virility, a strange sense of
security overtook Margot. She nodded.

''You need have no fear that I shall try to escape, Sir
Thomas. I have been brought up in the finest traditions
of chivalry. I give you my word of honour.''

''Then we shall be comfortable together while we are
thrown into each other's company, *doña,*'' he said, his
eyes smiling into hers. ''Ned!'' He began to remove his
gauntlets. ''Relieve me of this armour! Then I must see
that my men are comfortable.''

The boy dropped his load on the floor and sprang
forward, sinking to his knees to unbuckle the knight's
greaves.

''Supper will be served in an hour,'' she informed the
preoccupied Sir Thomas. ''The kitchens have been
warned to provide extra food.''

He looked up from unbuckling his sword-belt. ''Again
I thank you, *doña.* I see there is a door to the gallery. I
shall not intrude on your privacy. You have no need to
bolt your chamber door. My word, too, is honourably
given. My men obey me. You are safe from them, as
are your servants.''

Margot's shoulders visibly relaxed. She managed a
brief, stiff smile before retreating to the bower. But she
closed the door firmly in her wake.

Margot retired at her usual time, but knew sleep would
be hard to find. Supper had been a boisterous and rowdy
meal, but the men had been neither destructive nor un-
reasonably bawdy. Sir Thomas had taken Don Roberto's

seat at the high table as of right, which had nettled her at the time, but sitting beside her on the high-backed bench he had controlled his men with the authority of a born leader.

As the level of drunkenness threatened to cause a brawl, d'Evreux called a halt to the meal. Once grace had been said he sent his soldiers back to the barracks.

"They can do little harm there," he'd shrugged. "I will post guards to make sure none come back into the Hall. I promised you safety, *doña*, and you shall have it. But the men have fought a hard battle, and have been short of rations this few weeks past. You must forgive their over-indulgence now that opportunity presents itself."

"Indeed, Sir Thomas." She had inclined her head in acknowledgement of the truth of his statement, and stood up. "Is there aught you require further?"

"Not this evening, *doña*."

"Then I will see you on the morrow, sir."

He had bowed, taken her hand and, in a courtly gesture, carried it to his lips. Colour had flowed under Margot's skin, turning it a dull pink. She didn't know why. Sir Thomas's quizzical gaze had held hers for a moment before he'd smiled and released her hand.

"Until the morrow, *doña*," he'd said briskly.

His hair was brown, she'd discovered, the torchlight bringing out bronze lights which ill-matched his black brows and the long, thick, dark lashes fringing his lively grey eyes. How many women had envied him those lashes? wondered Margot, only too aware of the shorter ones surrounding her own indeterminate orbs. His hand had been cool and lean, strong and sinewy as a swordsman's hand must be, his firm lips dry as they touched her skin.

She was dozing when she heard a soft tap. It was repeated, and she realised it came from the door leading to the gallery. She sat up sharply, her heart thudding as she reached for her chamber-gown.

"Who is it?" she whispered urgently.

"*Doña?* May I come in?"

The low voice was thick, male, and spoke in Spanish. Margot's bare feet made no sound on the soft Persian carpets covering the floor. She lifted the bar, opened the door a crack, and peered anxiously into the torch-lit corridor.

"Domingo!" Her soft exclamation brought a grim smile to the face of the dirty, bearded man standing there. His livery was tattered and filthy, but recognisably that of her late husband. "What do you here? How did you enter the castle?"

Domingo waved his arm and two more dirty, unkempt figures joined him in the gallery. They filed past Margot, who closed the door and dropped the bolt into place. Her chamber was in darkness apart from a glimmer of moonlight slanting in through an open shutter and the flickering, dancing flame from a votive candle on the prie-dieu.

"You have forgotten the secret entry, *doña?* The one which leads from the round tower to the cellars beneath the kitchen?"

"I had! But how...?"

"We passed behind the screens, *doña*. There are no guards there, though a few foreign soldiers keep watch in the Hall." He paused. "You have heard the news?"

"That the battle is lost and Don Roberto dead? Aye, I have heard."

"We knew the castle is held for Pedro, we saw the

English banner flying from the battlements. But Don Enrico is alive, *doña!*"

"He is?" Margot was not certain whether she considered this good news or bad. It probably meant more fighting.

"Aye! There are others of us waiting outside. We go to join him, but thought you might need our help. We can take you with us, if you will but call Inés and don your garments—"

"No, Domingo! You must all escape, and quickly. I am glad to see you alive, but I must remain. I have given my word. And the other servants and retainers need me here."

"But, *doña—*"

"Do as I say, Domingo! Go at once! Else you will be caught, and mayhap killed! You know King Pedro's liking for revenge!"

"Aye, *doña,* that is why you must come with us! If Pedro has his way with you..."

Domingo's voice had risen in his anxiety. Seeing no relaxation of the determination written on her face, he tried again.

"Everyone in Sedano adores you, *doña,*" he pleaded. "Man, woman and child. Any one of us would die for you! We do not want to leave you to the mercies of a cruel tyrant!"

The others joined their entreaties to Domingo's. Margot hushed them desperately.

"Softly, Domingo! Go, all of you, before you are caught!"

"Hold hard there! What goes on? Who are these men?"

Despite the hangings, his voice rang around the stone chamber. Thomas d'Evreux stood in the doorway to the bower dressed only in hose and shirt, sword in hand. Full armour could not have given him a more aggressive appearance. Behind him, young Ned held a torch aloft, his own weapon poised.

Domingo reached for the hilt of his sword.

"Nay! Do not resist, Domingo! You will be killed—"

"I doubt not we'll suffer that fate in any case, *doña*. Allow us to die like men—"

"Answer me!" interrupted Sir Thomas sharply. His eyes no longer laughed, they were hard as the tempered steel in his hand.

"These are my husband's retainers," retorted Margot frigidly. "They believe that they may as well fight for their lives, since they are likely to die in any case. I was attempting to dissuade them."

"Light a wall-torch, Ned!" ordered d'Evreux, and waited until the light flickered over his captives. He eyed them coldly. "An they can raise a ransom, they can go free," he told her tersely.

"Ransom?" scoffed Domingo bitterly as Margot translated. "Where would the likes of us find a ransom?"

"I will pay it." She faced Sir Thomas fiercely, her taut features lit by a sudden flare from the lighted torches, determined that these men should not suffer for their loyalty to her. "I will pay it," she repeated in English. "Name your price!"

"*You, doña?*" His voice held a note of interested wonder. "How will you pay, since all Don Roberto's goods and lands are forfeit?"

"I have jewellery! It was my mother's! Here!"

She ran across the chamber to fetch a small carved coffer from an ambry by her bed. She opened the lid and held it out to the knight.

"Take what you will! All of it! But allow these men to go free!"

D'Evreux eyed the glittering contents of the coffer with hooded eyes. Eventually he picked out a gold filigree necklace studded with sparkling precious stones, the most valuable piece there and a particular favourite of Margot's.

His lean fingers closed around the delicate adornment. "This should suffice. Provided I am told how your churls gained entry to the castle. I had thought it impregnable."

Margot eyed the angry knight and then transferred her gaze to Domingo as she translated the demand.

"Do not tell him, *doña!*" protested Domingo.

"Defiance will do no good, my friend. We have no choice but to tell him."

Domingo's reproachful look pierced her heart, but Margot knew resistance was useless. She repeated what Domingo had told her earlier.

"Instruct them to show me!" ordered Thomas imperiously. "Then they may depart the way they came!"

Ned relieved the men of their swords and daggers while D'Evreux laced on a pair of leather shoes before shepherding his prisoners from the room.

"Await my return!" he instructed Margot grimly. "I shall not be long."

"Oh, *doña!*" Inés had been woken by the sound of angry voices, and appeared from the pallet-room smoothing down her rumpled gown. She crossed herself quickly, "Praise to the Holy Mother! They are safe, *doña!*"

"Aye, and as long as we obey the English knight we shall all remain so! See that you do nothing to anger

him, Inés. Do not attempt to speak with the men outside.''

''But it was Domingo! We were to marry! I must go
to him—''

''I forbid it, Inés! You would only be a trial to Domingo and the others; your presence would probably
lead to their capture again. What would you do then?
Besides, I need you here! Would you desert me in my
time of need?''

''No, *doña*. Forgive me.'' Inés shuffled her feet, her
face lowered in shame.

''Then go back to your pallet. I must await the return
of the English knight.''

Throughout all this exchange Margot had been sub-
consciously listening for sounds of conflict. To her profound relief Sir Thomas returned showing no sign of
recent battle, and his sword was sheathed. She smiled
nervously.

''They departed safely?''

''Aye, *doña*. I keep my word.''

She caught the edge on his voice. ''Implying that *I*
do not?'' demanded Margot indignantly. ''I was not
seeking to escape with them, Sir Thomas! Despite all
their arguments I told them I must remain behind!''

His eyes narrowed, but his expression did not soften.
''Even so,'' he pointed out icily, ''you gave your word
that you would not escape, but neglected to inform me
of a secret entry that could have led to my defeat. If the
stronghold has fallen, a rescue is not an escape, is it,
doña?'' he demanded harshly.

''You did not ask about such things! And I had forgot—''

''A likely tale!''

''But true! Had you been listening sooner and able to

understand what was said, you would have heard me tell Domingo so! I could not imagine how he had gained entry to the castle!''

Sir Thomas's steely gaze seemed to pierce right through her. She met it boldly, having nothing to hide.

"And are there other secrets you have forgotten, *doña*? More hidden passages, mayhap? A concealed sally port which has escaped your memory?"

"No, there is not. At least—" she hesitated "—none that I have ever heard of. But my husband did not tell me all his secrets..."

"Convenient." His tone was scornful. "Go back to bed, *doña*. I will sleep in your bower, across the door to this chamber. I have posted a guard in the gallery, and, of course, at the secret entry. I shall take no more chances on your honour or your memory. Sleep well, *doña*."

Her small, pointed chin lifted. He saw the hurt and anger in her eyes, and wished he could trust her. But trust came hard to Thomas since his brother had betrayed it. Stephen had escaped the consequences of his crime, though retribution had caught up with him in the form of the plague, but Thomas had lived ever since with the knowledge that his childish love and trust had enabled Stephen to introduce poison to their father's wine. No, he did not find it easy to trust or to love anyone now.

Certainly not Marguerite Sedano, recently wife to a traitor to Castile. At first sight he had thought her a plain, skinny woman with nothing but pride and a certain bravery in the face of defeat to recommend her.

Now he knew that she could command intense love and loyalty from those who served her. Why else would those men have risked their lives to save her? Besides, he had seen their devotion on their faces. And her un-

usual eyes, like turbulent seas dappled by sunshine and
hiding mysterious depths and shallows, were quite beautiful in their own way. The long, pale oval of her face
could have been fashioned from ivory, her rounded forehead, high cheekbones and patrician nose carved by the
finest craftsman. Her mouth was too wide, of course, but
the full, shapely lips held a hint of unconscious sensu-
ality, and what he had thought to be a skinny body
showed subtle, tender curves under the clinging folds of
her chamber-gown.

Thomas wondered whether her husband had ever been
able to awaken the passion implicit in these things.

He decided not. There was an innocence about her
which roused in him an unwelcome desire to protect, a
feeling to which he was not accustomed.

He spun away and strode through the bower, shutting
the door behind him with a forceful bang.

Chapter Two

Margot had quickly realised she could not remain at Sedano, even had she wanted to. The noisy garrison of foreigners, shouting, swearing, jousting, drilling, consuming the last of the winter's stores, drinking wine by the tun and demanding scarce fodder for their horses, were a constant reminder that the castle and its manor were no longer hers to hold. Would Pedro revenge himself on her, since Roberto was dead? Or might he rid himself of her presence by returning her to her father in Bellac? And, if he sent her there, did she wish to go?

Years before, her father had killed all the affection she had felt for him when, despite her anguished protests, he had insisted on her marriage to Don Roberto del Sedano.

Why Don Roberto had been so insistent on having her as his wife Margot had never fully understood. She was neither beautiful nor particularly attractive. He did not love her. Yet for some unfathomable reason he had desired her with a fierce, consuming passion which had scared her sixteen-year-old immaturity into total unresponsiveness.

Not that he had ever seemed to want more than a

shrinking body on which to vent his lust. Of course he had wanted an heir, and when his frantic couplings failed to produce one he had blamed her and begun sneering at her inability to bear him a son, asking cruelly what use a barren wife was to a man with an ancient line to carry on.

But few things in life lasted forever, good or bad, and eventually Roberto, a fierce and dedicated fighter, had departed on a long campaign against the Infidel. One campaign had followed another. He had returned at irregular intervals, loaded with booty and demanding his marital rights. The news of his death had signalled her final release from a bondage which had left her with a body knowing nothing but shrinking numbness in the face of passion, and a mind set against enduring such misery again at the hands of any man, ever.

She was a widow now, and older—a mature woman who had seen five and twenty summers. Life had to go on, and for her people's sake she had to make a show of normality. Thus she was in the dairy up to her elbows in buttermilk when a commotion outside heralded the arrival of strangers.

Having hastily wiped her arms and pulled down the sleeves of her gown, she hurried to the Inner Ward. There, she found Sir Thomas d'Evreux greeting a new arrival with every sign of enthusiasm. The two men clasped arms with whoops of joy.

"Dickon!" exclaimed Thomas exuberantly. "You look well, and survived unscathed!" He held the youngster off for a moment, taking in the mailed hauberk covered by a jupon displaying the red cross of Saint George coupled with the Prince of Wales's feather badge. His eyes dropped to the golden spurs attached to the boy's mailed chausses. "By Peter! You've been knighted!

Greetings, Sir Richard d'Evreux!'' he cried, executing a bow of mock reverence before clapping the youngster on the back. ''I see your jupon is not charged with your own arms yet!''

''There has been little time!''

''True,'' admitted Sir Thomas with a laugh. ''Did you see much of the action?''

''Aye.'' The handsome young face, the clean lines partially obscured by a silky golden beard and moustache, broke into a grin. Pride in his own achievements shone from beautiful grey eyes. ''The Prince of Wales himself knighted me on the field! And how fare you, Tamkin? Well, by the looks of it!''

Sir Thomas grinned affectionately and said, ''Aye, well, nephew! Though I would rather not be stuck in this benighted place!''

Nephew? Margot scrutinised the two men curiously. Sir Thomas could not be many years older than the new knight, and they behaved like brothers. In her curiosity she barely registered his disparaging reference to Sedano.

''You don't know when you're well off, Tamkin. You would not enjoy being camped out on the plain while Prince Edward and King Pedro argue over our just reward! But it's early days yet. Mayhap they'll come to terms soon enough.'' He sobered. ''Meanwhile, dysentery still runs through our ranks. I have Uncle Cedric with me. He is seriously ill. I brought him here hoping he might receive better care.''

''Where is he?''

Anxiety filled Sir Thomas's voice. He strode off with young Dickon, and Margot hurried after them. Sickness was her preserve. She had ministered to the people of Sedano for many long years.

Sir Thomas hurried over to a litter already lifted from the horses between which it had been slung and placed on the ground. As he approached the occupant struggled to rise to his feet. Sir Thomas held out a hand and helped him up.

"Cedric! I'm sorry to see you so distressed. Come inside. Mayhap we can help you."

"God's greetings, Thomas. Cock's bones! But I'm as weak as a kitten! And I needs must remain within close reach of a privy!"

The man's hair, the colour of ripe corn in the April sun, was sprinkled at the temples with strands of grey. The wry expression on his weather-beaten face caught at Margot's compassionate heart. Despite his evident sickness, his blue eyes contained more than a hint of laughter.

Sir Cedric staggered up the steps, helped by Sir Thomas and Sir Richard, with a young man she presumed to be Sir Cedric's squire following closely behind. She had run up ahead, and greeted them in the entry behind the screens.

"Welcome to Sedano, sir. I am sorry you are indisposed." She glanced at Sir Thomas for approval. "Mayhap you would like to use my late husband's room? The privy is just beyond his private wardrobe."

Sir Thomas nodded his agreement to her suggestion. "Cedric, Dickon, this is Marguerite, Doña Sedano, daughter of the Comte de Limousin, whom I have been ordered to—" he paused only slightly "—protect, and who is our hostess. *Doña*, Sir Richard d'Evreux is my half-nephew, though we grew up together as brothers. Sir Cedric de Clare is the brother of my half-brother's wife."

So these were legitimate members of his family. Sir

Cedric wore a jupon charged with a golden dragon on an azure background, though he wore no armour. He looked rather older than the others, but his illness could account for much of his apparent age.

Sir Cedric acknowledged the complicated introduction with a remarkably cheerful smile, and indicated the young man hovering behind. "I trust your hospitality will extend to Guy Woodley, my squire? I should not like to be without his services."

"Of course. Will you follow me?" she invited quietly, and led the way through the Hall and up the stair.

Sir Cedric at once saw Sir Thomas's things scattered around the bedroom.

"I'm turning you out of your bed, Tamkin! I do not wish to inconvenience you—"

"I will sleep in the bower," interrupted Sir Thomas quickly, not looking at Margot. "There will be no inconvenience."

"Where he will be able to ensure that I do not stray in the night," she explained calmly, and was rewarded by the sight of dull colour staining Sir Thomas's cheekbones.

She left the men to settle Sir Cedric in Roberto's bed while she went in search of medicines and wine.

"I've kept nothing inside me since some time before the battle," Sir Cedric informed her weakly when she reappeared at his bedside.

"Yet you fought?"

He grimaced ruefully. "Aye, after a long march through the Sierra de Cantabria, which brought us to the rear of the Bastard's army. The Prince of Wales is a brilliant commander," he enthused, his tired eyes shining with admiration. "We were short of rations, and many of us had this cursed disorder of the bowels. Since so many were ill, no one could be excused. Everyone was exhausted by the march, but Edward had to force the battle before the army disintegrated before his eyes!" He grinned. "Mayhap you would rather we had turned tail and retreated to Gascony!"

Margot made no comment. "Drink this," she instructed.

Sir Cedric pulled a face but made no move to take the draught she had prepared. "And bring on more gripes? Even milk causes me pain."

"This potion should not. 'Tis a remedy handed down by the Moors through many generations. Dysentery is not uncommon here. Do not drink water unless it is boiled. I have been told it is small creatures in the water which gnaw at the gut. Sip this, instead."

He glanced suspiciously at the ruby-red liquid she was pouring. "Wine? That will surely cause me pain!"

"Not if you swallow it very slowly. It may be all the nourishment you can take for a few days. You must avoid solids, and cannot tolerate milk. The wine will keep you alive."

On impulse, she stroked the matted hair from his hot brow. He had a low fever, another symptom of his complaint.

"There is soap and water in the wardrobe," she told him quietly. "Be careful to cleanse your hands when you leave the privy. We have found this essential to a speedy recovery."

A sudden spasm of pain convulsed Sir Cedric's face. Regardless of her presence, he leapt from the bed and stumbled towards the privy.

Thomas, who had been standing by, torn between suspicion and the thought that if Marguerite Sedano treated all her patients with the apparent tender care she was lavishing on Cedric it was small wonder she was loved by all, sprang forward to assist.

When they returned, Sir Cedric's face was grey with exhaustion. He sank back on the bed and Sir Thomas instructed Guy to bring the bowl of water.

Under the thin linen of his shirt, Margot could see that Sir Cedric's normally stalwart body was already wasted. Once his hands were washed, she presented him with the medicine again.

"Drink!" she ordered firmly, thrusting a small goblet towards him.

"Wait!"

Suspicion had won. Thomas's barked command startled everyone in the room.

"Let me see *you* drink some of that concoction!"

Margot gazed at him blankly. Dickon frowned. Sir Cedric roused himself to shake his head.

"Nay, Thomas. I trust Lady Marguerite!"

He grasped the silver vessel and carried it to his lips. Before he could drink, Margot snatched it from him.

"You think I would poison Sir Cedric?" she enquired haughtily, her eyes flashing such scornful fire that Sir Thomas looked abashed for the second time in a very short while. "Then let me prove my good intentions, sir!"

She drank down the draught without hesitation. Then she refilled the cup from the flask. She smiled at Sir Cedric.

"Here, sir. My only desire is for your speedy recovery."

"I know it, lady."

Sir Cedric drank and lay back to await the inevitable consequences of allowing anything to pass his lips. Marguerite refused to look at Sir Thomas. What did he think she was? Then she brushed all thought of him aside, smiling secretly to herself. The remedy, infused from a mixture of tart herbs, had never failed her yet. She waited confidently for the knight's symptoms to ease.

After five minutes without further discomfort, Sir Cedric relaxed.

"What magic potion was that, lady?" he grinned, lying back among the soft down pillows.

"Take a cupful every four hours," she instructed him with an answering smile. "You are not cured yet, but things should improve within a few days. I will see that more wine is brought. Meanwhile, try to rest."

She left him and went through to her bower, followed by the other two knights.

"Thank you, my lady," smiled Sir Richard, his fair young face wreathed in grateful smiles. "My mother would be much obliged to you if she knew the care you have taken over her brother. She is much attached to him."

"As are we all," inserted Sir Thomas. "I apologise for my distrust, *doña*. But...." He shrugged.

"I am an enemy," she supplied quietly.

"But even enemies can be honourable! Come, Tamkin, cast off your suspicions! The lady would be our friend!"

Sir Thomas compressed his shapely lips into an uncompromising line. "Not so easily done, Dickon! However—" his grim expression relaxed into the ghost of a smile "—for the moment I trust Doña Sedano to tend Sir Cedric with every care. As you say, your mother will be full of gratitude if he recovers. As shall we all."

"You are a close family," observed Margot, unaware of the hint of wistfulness in her voice.

"Thanks to Dickon's mother, the lady Eleanor. We

all adore her, so can do nothing else but please her by looking out for each other,'' explained Sir Thomas, his smile grown more warm then he realised in response to the envy in her expressive eyes. It occurred to him that she was lonely. Not for the first time, he wondered about her childless state. A barren woman could only be pitied.

''I must return to my duties,'' declared Sir Richard ruefully. ''The Prince gave me permission to visit Chandos's camp to see how my uncle did. I had not expected to be absent for so long. But I could not leave Cedric there in such grave discomfort. I knew you were safe and had been sent here. I heard Lancaster telling Prince Edward.''

''You did right. I am awaiting new instructions from the Duke, but meanwhile Cedric can rest here. Does John Chandos know where he is?''

''Aye, he gave his blessing to his departure. He said Cedric should return to England, he has been abroad for too long.'' Sir Richard turned to take his leave. ''Farewell, Lady Marguerite.'' He bowed over her hand and raised it to his lips. ''I leave my uncle in your kind and capable hands. My thanks, and may God bless you.''

Margot noted that he, like Sir Cedric, had used the English mode of address. Only Sir Thomas stuck rigidly to the Spanish, despite the fact that they spoke in the English tongue. Reminding himself that she was the enemy? she wondered fretfully. His distrust and thinly veiled hostility irked her. But it hardly mattered. Their ways would shortly part.

For the next couple of days Margot barely left the bower, where she was on hand if Sir Cedric needed her. Guy remained with him most of the time and helped him to the privy whenever necessary. Margot was relieved to note that the visits were becoming less frequent.

On the third morning she made her normal visit, to find her patient sitting up in bed.

"Good morrow, Lady Marguerite!"

"Sir Cedric! You are looking better." She placed her hand on a brow furrowed by time and weather, and was delighted to find it cool to her touch.

Sir Cedric captured the hand and carried it to his lips. "And feeling it!" he grinned. "Think you I could try a little solid food, my lady? I confess I'm feeling starved!"

"We might risk some bread soaked in milk, I think. I will order it sent up. Would you like to come through to my bower? I have a chair you could use." She moved to take a long velvet robe from a perch on the wall. It had been Roberto's. "You could wear this."

Sir Cedric came through ten minutes later, leaning heavily on Guy and wearing Roberto's purple robe, which, being too short, revealed several inches of the yellow hose in which he had arrived. A shaggy, straw-coloured growth covered his cheeks and chin. But even with an ill-kept beard he was a handsome man.

"Are you married, Sir Cedric?" she asked impulsively, once he was settled in her chair. No one had mentioned his wife, only his sister.

"Nay, lady. I was betrothed once, many years ago. But I have never wed."

"What happened?" she enquired gently.

His smile was self-mocking. "My betrothed preferred another."

"There must have been other women since?"

"Aye, plenty, but none I wished to wed. I took to soldiering, and joined Sir John Chandos after leaving my brother-in-law's service. I was with Chandos at Poitiers.''

"Telling your life story, Cedric?"

Sir Thomas's teasing voice from the doorway made them both turn. Margot reluctantly abandoned the further questions hovering on the tip of her tongue.

They looked cosy, thought Thomas, sat close together and obviously sharing confidences. He felt an unaccustomed sense of being shut out. He strode over and perched on the sill of a window embrasure, eyeing Cedric critically.

"You look better, brother. Have you eaten?"

"Not yet. Lady Marguerite has ordered paps for me. I'm still weak as a kitten."

"Hardly fit to travel, then."

"Travel? Where?"

"I am ordered to the Duke of Lancaster's camp on the morrow. Doña Sedano goes with me. I fear you will have to return to the plain."

"I am ordered to the Duke's presence?" asked Margot faintly.

"Aye, *doña*. For what purpose, he does not say, though he orders you to take all your own possessions with you. King Pedro is in Burgos. Mayhap the Duke wishes to see you before sending you to him."

Margot stood, drawing herself up with unconscious pride, though her stomach was churning like buttermilk. "I must instruct my steward. I assume you wish the castle and estate to be under his control in my absence?" At Sir Thomas's murmur of assent, she went on, "I will tell Inés to begin packing when she returns with the food for Sir Cedric. I may take her with me?"

Sir Thomas pursed his lips thoughtfully. "The Duke said nothing either way about servants." Making up his

mind, he nodded briskly. "You will need a woman with
you. Bring her along if you will."

She turned to Sir Cedric and said, "I am sorry I
cannot offer my personal hospitality for longer, sir. But
if you would prefer to remain in the care of my servants—"

"Out of the question!" Sir Thomas spoke decisively.
"They are not to be trusted. Do not forget we are foreign
usurpers to them! I am to leave a small force to defend
the castle if need be, but I think you will be safer if you
accompany us back to the Ebro plain."

"It seems I have little choice. But my stay here has
improved my health so much that I doubt I shall die! Is
this my sustenance?"

He took a wooden bowl from Inés, who returned at
that moment, and began to eat hungrily.

Inés gazed apprehensively at her mistress's taut face.
Sensing trouble, she muttered, *"Doña?"*

"Inés, we are to go with Sir Thomas to the English
camp on the morrow. You must make ready to accompany me. Pack as many clothes as possible, and all the
tapestries and rugs in my bedchamber. They belong to
me," she added in English, with a defiant look in Sir
Thomas's direction. "I sold some of the jewels I inherited from my mother to pay for them," she told him
coldly. "I must take those, too."

"Do not fill too many coffers, *doña*. We have few
pack-horses."

"Our stables hold mules bred for the purpose. I have
an excellent mount—"

"You will ride pillion, *doña*. That way I shall know
exactly where you are."

"I shall not flee!" she spat fiercely. "Sir Thomas,
why must you insist on humiliating me? I have always

ridden my own horse! I have an Arab palfrey I love more than anything else on earth! You *must* allow me to ride her!''

Her vehemence caught him by surprise. Thomas looked again into those strange, stormy eyes, and was lost.

"Very well," he agreed reluctantly. "You may ride your own animal. But I shall hold a leading rein."

Margot compressed her lips, but did not argue further. She had gained her main point. Fleurette would go with her.

"What a stern guardian you are, Thomas! By my oath, I'd not treat the lady so harshly!" chided Sir Cedric.

"But you are not answerable to the Duke of Lancaster for her safe-keeping," retorted Sir Thomas grimly.

Sir Cedric had consumed his bread and milk and looked quite cheerful. "Do you know, I believe I am better? By morning I shall be strong as a lion!"

"You will return in the litter," Sir Thomas told him uncompromisingly. "It will be some days before you are fit to sit a horse!"

"Thomas, I really don't know what has bitten you," sighed Sir Cedric mildly. "Has the responsibility gone to your head?"

"For God's sake, Cedric! You know I'm right!"

Sir Cedric grimaced. "Perhaps. I could almost wish I were back in England."

"At Wenfrith?"

"Aye. My manor in Suffolk will be cheerless."

"Eleanor would be glad to welcome you. Mayhap it can be arranged."

"If news of the battle has reached them, she will be anxious about Dickon. Perhaps I could carry a message?"

"Humph! We'll have to see. You've no pain?"

"Not so far!"

"Thank God for that!"

"And my fair physician," responded Sir Cedric softly.

"Aye. Mayhap she should minister to all our men on the plain!" said Sir Thomas wryly. "*Doña,* I hope King Pedro deals gently with you. I will tell the Duke of your service to Sir Cedric and, I believe, to several of the men who were suffering similar distress."

He had been talking to his sergeant-at-arms, and discovered some thought-provoking things about his hostess.

He eyed her afresh—her quiet face framed by white linen, the hair flowing unconfined down her back in the Spanish way; her slender figure, masked by the garments she wore, the tight lacing at the sides of her tunic flattening any swelling at her breast. He imagined her tender body unconfined, as he'd once glimpsed it. Again that desire to protect swept over him, warring with an instinctive distrust it could not quite conquer.

He would plead with John not to hand her over to Pedro! The decision came to him suddenly, surprising him. He had not considered the possibility before, but he would keep to it. And John would listen.

Thomas knew he would never be able to claim the Duke as friend—John's royal blood precluded such an avowal. Yet the understanding and intimacy between the two men was such that at any other level of society friendship was the way their relationship would be defined. They were of an age. He lived close to the Duke, was with him almost daily. And the Duke respected his opinions. Yes, he would speak for Marguerite Sedano.

He did not like to think of her at the mercy of a vengeful despot.

He stirred, a shaft of sunlight burnishing his hair as he moved. He ran a hand round his smooth-shaven jaw and stood up, his eyes suddenly bright, his lips curved in a smile.

If only he would always smile! thought Margot, admiring anew the lithe grace with which he moved. He wore no armour that morning, merely his russet padded gambeson over long green hose, a combination which emphasised his broad shoulders and shapely limbs. A jewelled belt spanned his lean hips. An unaccountable tension gripped her as she looked at him, his sheer male beauty causing the breath to catch in her throat. She quickly lowered her eyes.

"The winter has quite disappeared," said Sir Thomas gaily. "The ride tomorrow should prove pleasant exercise. We set out at dawn."

"I shall be ready, sir," responded Margot quietly.

Chapter Three

Thomas's expectations were more than justified. Even Margot felt a stirring of her senses as the fiery disc of the sun began to creep above the horizon to gild the day with promise.

She glanced back only once. Nestled on the hillside and dominating the valley, the Castillo Sedano already appeared remote, its square, embattled towers and sturdy walls merely part of a romantic tapestry, not the place where she had lived for so many years. Silently, she said a final farewell. She had no desire to return.

The soldiers rode jauntily, singing and shouting bawdy jokes she was glad she couldn't catch. The pennon fluttering from Sir Thomas's lance was charged with the red rose of Lancaster. The same emblem appeared on all the men's tunics in addition to the huge red cross of Saint George, worn back and front for easy identification in battle. They were part of the English army, the Duke of Lancaster's retinue, and everyone would know it.

Sir Thomas's gauntleted hands rested on the rearing pommel of an extravagantly decorated, high-backed, padded war-saddle designed to protect his body and to hold him secure, allowing him the use of both hands in a battle without losing his seat. He was in full harness, his chain-mail hauberk covered by the colourful jupon. The polished steel of his helmet and the plate armour protecting his legs and arms threw fiery shafts of light as it caught the sun's rays. His horse's trapper glowed blue and white in the bright light, the red cross of Saint George and red roses of Lancaster appliqued in crimson velvet on the damask. A fringe of gold tassels six inches deep danced around the chestnut destrier's shaggy fetlocks. The engrailed leather headstall and reins gleamed with copper studs a few shades darker than the charger's flowing golden mane.

Margot rode at the head of the column beside Sir Thomas, who held the leading-rein. Neither Margot nor Fleurette liked the arrangement, and the bay mare snorted angrily, tossing her head and setting the little bells with which her headstall was decorated jangling in protest every time Sir Thomas pulled on her bit. Margot soothed her palfrey with a quiet word and reassuring pat, herself resigned to enduring the man's distrust.

Inés and Juan rode pillion behind two of the grooms. Juan had begged to accompany her. Margot was fond of the boy, an orphan from the village, who had served her since he was a small child. He was now about twelve years old. He knew how to look after Fleurette, and could be useful in other ways. His loyalty verged on devotion. To leave him behind would have seemed like desertion.

Last evening she had approached Sir Thomas, who had subjected the boy to a close scrutiny. As Juan had stood beside her in an almost protective attitude, his brown eyes desperate with pleading, a strange expression had flitted across Thomas's face. Not quite a smile, but a look of almost tender understanding.

"Aye, he may accompany you." A curving smile touched his lips, but it was in no way mocking. He spoke with wry conviction. "You may need his protection, *doña*. Even one so young can be a lion in defence of one he loves."

"Thank you, Sir Thomas." Margot had returned his smile, and for a moment sympathy had flowed between them. But it hadn't lasted. This morning the knight seemed as remote as her castle.

Sir Cedric travelled on his litter at the rear of the column, between the pack-animals and the rearguard, where, if his ailment forced him to stop along the way, he could easily be passed. He had improved vastly overnight, had eaten quite a substantial dish of groats before setting out, and had allowed his squire, Guy, to trim his beard. Margot believed he was well on the way to recovery, though he would remain weak for some time. With the beard tamed he looked much younger, less than the forty years he owned.

The jingle of harness, the clop of hoofs and the chorus of hearty voices precluded much conversation but, with Sir Thomas so withdrawn, communication would have been difficult anyway. His eyes were everywhere, anticipating danger at every turn.

"You are fearful of attack?" ventured Margot, in an interval between raucous songs.

"It is possible." He brought his attention to her, the frown of concentration still slashed between eyes which searched hers with sudden, hostile intensity. "Your husband's men are free," he pointed out. "They may attempt rescue. Any band of defeated soldiers may attack, looking for revenge and needing our supplies and equipment. We are a small company in a strange land. Vigilance is essential.''

"I see," said Margot coldly, wishing she had not asked, and relieved when his eyes left hers to scan the countryside anew.

She adjusted the light mantilla she wore over her head and shoulders for riding, and scanned the surrounding terrain herself. There was not much shelter now they had left the valley, but she supposed there was cover enough for an ambushing party. She tightened her grip on her useless reins, and hoped Inés's predictions of disaster did not come true.

Persuading the girl that they would not be murdered on the way or in their sleep, once they left the doubtful safety of the castle, had not been easy.

"You will be safer under the Duke of Lancaster's protection than here on your own! Having preserved us so far, he will not lightly allow anything untoward to happen to us! Neither do I believe Sir Thomas would willingly see us ill-treated—''

"Him!" spat Inés spitefully, her scornful face emerging from the protection of the cloth. "He would have no say!"

Margot remembered the way he had addressed the Duke, the friendship she had sensed beneath the surface of their relationship, and for some unaccountable reason her own fears lessened slightly.

Accustomed to Spanish ways, Margot would have rested during the heat of the day, but the Englishmen were not prepared to bow before uncomfortable conditions.

On they toiled, crossing the plain on which Burgos stood, a plain which would burn with the heat in a few more weeks. The tender growths springing up in the sun after the winter rains would soon shrivel without moisture.

At last the forbidding walls of Burgos appeared on the horizon, the shimmering spires of its cathedral catching the eye long before anything else could be distinguished.

As they drew nearer Margot realised that a new town had sprung into being on the plain outside the city walls. A huge encampment of tall, bright pavilions over which brilliant banners and pennons rippled like colourful plumage ruffled by the slight breeze.

As the column approached the palisade guarding the tents from surprise attack, the herald blew a flourish on his trumpet. The huge gates swung open.

Margot gazed in wonder. Such a vast array of men and beasts! Near the main stockade were other, smaller ones, where the farrier's hammer struck sparks from red-hot iron, where horses neighed and pranced as they were curried or exercised, watered or fed, where mock battles were fought with sword and halberd, where horses and their riders, lances levelled, charged at quintains. Not far away archers practised their skills in the butts.

Men, milling around undertaking the multitudinous duties required to sustain such a host, stopped to gape as they passed through their midst. Sir Thomas guided his destrier among the silken pavilions, leading Margot towards his own. Somewhere out of sight minstrels practised their art, the strains of pipe and tabor, lute, viol and timbrel, gittern and shawm rising intermittently above the general din.

Sir Cedric and most of their party quickly dispersed to their own quarters, leaving only a tight knot of Sir Thomas's personal retainers, squire, man-at-arms, archer and horse groom to accompany them.

Banners and pennons bearing the cross of Saint

George flew everywhere. Margot felt she was in a foreign land. She noticed no one thing with any clarity, confused by the myriad new sights and sensations clamouring for attention; but suddenly her eyes focused on a tall man, in the garb of a sergeant-at-arms, standing by a white pavilion. Why she should notice him above all the others was something she could never afterwards fathom. Yet she did, realising on the instant that his brooding gaze was fixed on the man riding at her side.

An uneasy tremor shook the reins in her hands. She glanced quickly at Sir Thomas, but he seemed quite unaware of the other man, quite oblivious of that concentrated stare which Margot found somehow threatening.

She glanced back to the stranger to meet the cold gaze of smallish grey eyes set in a tough, lean, weathered and bearded face under greying brows. She knew she would not forget those calculating eyes easily. They seemed to sink a shaft of cold steel in her heart before the man moved out of sight.

"Whose pavilions are those?" she murmured hoarsely.

Sir Thomas glanced at her, puzzlement contracting his brow at the anxiety in her voice.

"They belong to Sir John Hawkwood's White Company. Why?"

Margot's face paled. "They are ruthless mercenaries, are they not?"

He pursed his lips, shrugging. "They fight for whoever pays them best, where the pickings are richest. Their only true loyalty is to England, and all such companies flocked to the Prince of Wales's banner when he called. But why do you ask?" he demanded again.

"No real reason." She would sound stupid if she

voiced a fear based on nothing more than a glance. "I saw a man..."

"And he frightened you?"

"A little."

"Forget him. The camp is full of tough, brutal soldiers, but you have no need to fear. You are under the Duke of Lancaster's protection," he reminded her with a proud lift of his chin.

Only partially reassured, Margot could do nothing but trust she had been mistaken. She could hardly tell Sir Thomas that it was for him she feared.

He finally reined in before a large, circular pavilion made from layers of azure satin. From the high pinnacle of the pointed roof fluttered his own pennon—red, bordered azure with his golden castle and lilies fluttering like butterflies sipping from an exotic flower. The valance, striped in blue and red, had castles and lilies set in alternating sections. His shield hung above the door, repeating the arms with which his jupon was charged.

In that tented city there were brighter, larger, more elaborate pavilions than Thomas's, and near by the red rose of Lancaster and the leopards and lilies of England rippled over a shimmering silk, castle-like edifice. Looking round, Margot realised that her escort's pavilion was one of a number forming a defensive ring around the Duke's.

Sir Thomas dismounted and turned to help her from her saddle. He still wore his gauntlets, and the steel bruised her tender skin through her garments. He bowed slightly and swept an arm to indicate where the satin had been rolled back to form an entrance.

"*Doña*, my pavilion is at your disposal. Please ask for anything you require."

Margot stepped into the welcome shade, though the

interior of the tent was far from cool. A couple of folding stools, a trestle-table, a coffer or two, were its only contents. Spare armour hung on wooden perches attached to the central post, and a clutter of rusting weapons lay waiting for Ned's attention.

A section of the space had been curtained off. She presumed that was where Sir Thomas slept. A curious sense of apprehension mixed with excitement threatened her calm and swept away her memory of that other, intangible dread of the stranger.

How would he arrange their sleeping quarters? Opportunity for privacy would be even less here than in the castle. A curtain was but a flimsy barrier compared to a solid wooden door.

Yet, in reality, what protection did she have except the knight's word? And, strangely, she trusted it.

"I go to report to the Duke now," he went on. "When I return, I hope to have news for you. Meanwhile, a couple of my men will stand guard." Seeing Margot's expressive eyes fill with anger, he made an impatient gesture, though he hastened to explain. "You cannot hope to escape from here, *doña,* even if you wished it; but you will be safer with a guard. I cannot answer for every man in the army, be he English, Gascon, or of any other breed."

"I see. Thank you."

Her words came with difficulty from a tight throat. Only Sir Thomas stood between her and some lecherous brute brash enough to try his luck. A pair of cold grey eyes rose in her mind to haunt her, and she shivered.

"Ned!" Sir Thomas called his squire, who came in carrying an armful of impedimenta. "Remove my pallet from behind the screen, and obtain three others. See that the straw is fresh."

"Aye, Sir Thomas. Where shall I put your things?"

"Out here somewhere, with yours and a pallet for the boy." He turned to Margot. "I'll leave you now. Order things as you wish, *doña*."

Her skin cooled and cleansed, wearing a light silk kirtle, Margot sat on her coffer while Inés brushed and combed her hair. Being so fine, it easily tangled, and the girl was used to teasing out the knots without pulling at her scalp. Margot stopped her as she reached for a clean coif.

"A band will do, Inés. That silver circlet set with lapis-lazuli."

"Will you not wear a head-dress?" asked Inés doubtfully.

"No. Just the circlet."

Inés stared. "But *doña*—"

"I know, a simple circlet isn't suited to a mature widow! Nevertheless, that is what I will wear."

What others thought no longer mattered! Inés could not know how her inmost feelings had begun to unfurl like a tight bud bursting into flower. Although she was physically a prisoner and surrounded by men she didn't trust, she was essentially free for the first time in eight years! For the moment no one could tell her what to wear, even how to behave! If she wished to be a girl again, who could say her nay?

It was as though she had only this moment realised the full meaning of Roberto's death. He would never return! The certainty burst over her like a shower of golden stars and, as Inés finished her work, Margot sprang to her feet and pirouetted past the curtain, her small feet, shod in dainty leather slippers, dancing lightly over the uneven turf in a spirited imitation of the wild dancing favoured by the Spanish gypsies.

She laughed aloud, twirled around, and came to an abrupt halt.

He stood in the tent opening, a startled expression on his handsome features. He still wore his hauberk, but had shed the rest of his armour. The lowering sun lit his clean-shaven face and burnished his hair to copper.

"Sir Thomas!" gasped Margot, wondering what he must be thinking of her abandoned display, her indifference to the opinions of others quite forgotten. "Forgive me! I did not realise you were there!"

Sir Thomas's eyebrows lowered again and a slow smile stretched across his face, bringing the attractive gleam back to his eyes. "So I imagined. Why such exuberance, *doña?* Can it be that you have forgotten your fears, that you are happy to be here?"

"I am not happy to be a prisoner, how could I be?" gasped Margot, struggling for self-possession in the face of his potent masculinity. "Yet I have just realised that I no longer have responsibilities, that I am free! I want to be gay while I may, while I am safe!"

"Then you do think yourself safe, *doña?*"

"Aye, I do. While I am here under your—" she hesitated "—the great Duke of Lancaster's protection, what ill can befall me?"

She laughed, a light yet throaty laugh that set Thomas's pulses racing. A dignified, serious, compassionate but prideful woman had suddenly turned into a maid of about eighteen. Her body moved freely under the simple saffron kirtle and her hair swung in a brown cloud down her back. She would never be beautiful, her figure was scarcely voluptuous, yet her appeal reached out and took him by the throat.

He fought down the surge of desire which gripped his loins, swallowed hastily, and cleared the obstruction in his throat with a short cough. "If you continue to behave in such an abandoned manner, not even Lancaster's protection will save you *doña*," he told her repressively.

Margot's breath caught. She had read the momentary flare of desire in his eyes and her whole being shrank. Facing his dormant masculinity was quiet enough for her to deal with. What aggressive demons had she released by her stupid behaviour?

She composed her features and drew herself up in an attempt to resume her cool, dignified manner. "I apologise, Sir Thomas. I will assume my coif."

"There is no need for that," protested Thomas gruffly. "I am here to collect you. We sup with the Duke, who still awaits the Prince of Wales's final decision. Since the evening is fine, we eat in the open. If you are ready?"

"I must bring a mantilla," said Margot stiffly, "there may be a chill as the sun sets. Where are Inés and Juan to sit?"

"They will join the Duke's servants at a trestle near by. Inés need have no fear."

"I will tell her."

Margot made her escape, heart pounding. Behind the curtain she told Inés to find a softly woven woollen mantilla. By the time it was unearthed from the coffer and draped over her arm, she had her breathing under control. Then, followed by her servant, she lifted her chin and returned to face Sir Thomas.

Fires burned in all quarters of the camp. It seemed that each company was responsible for its own rations. The smoky blaze before the Duke's pavilion had a deer roasting over it, while several great cauldrons bubbled on iron tripods set around the edges. Catching a whiff of the drifting aroma, Margot realised she was ravenous.

Even as they walked towards the trestles, already set with trenchers of coarse bread baked in field ovens, and a number of wooden or silver spoons, the venison was lifted from the spit and the carver began his work, setting the joints on a huge silver platter. A fanfare announced the arrival of the Duke and his immediate entourage.

Margot wondered whether, but for her, Sir Thomas might have been among the privileged few to accompany the Duke from his pavilion.

Perhaps not. The Duke was entertaining Sir John Chandos, the High Constable of Aquitaine, and several other high-ranking officers.

Supper was well under way when a messenger came running up to drop to one knee beside the Duke.

"From my castle of Bolingbroke!" exclaimed John of Gaunt, so loudly that all the chatter around the trestles died away. A hush descended on the company as Prince John ripped open the seals and began to peruse the message. Noise continued in the background, but those gathered around Lancaster's boards held their breaths, watching.

A broad smile lit the narrow, handsome face and the Duke sprang to his feet, blue eyes blazing with joy.

"Praise God! A son!" he exclaimed. "The Duchess has been delivered of a strong and healthy boy! Let us drink a toast! To my son! He is to be called Henry! Henry of Bolingbroke! And to the Duchess Blanche, my fair, sweet wife!"

Margot drank the toast, her imagination caught by the undoubted joy on the Duke's face. Congratulations and cheers rang around the camp. While rejoicing to see such happiness, Margot knew that same sense of regret she always felt when a baby was born. Why had the Holy

Mother not sent children to fill her days with love and joy? To ease the burden of Roberto's scorn?

She glanced up, her strange eyes green as the deep shadowy depths of a bay tree, reflecting her pain. With a small shock she realised that, although Sir Thomas was smiling and shouting congratulations with the best, his grey eyes were bleak. As their gazes locked that strange flow of understanding surged between them once more. Then Thomas tore his eyes away and drained his cup.

The meal resumed and, once he had eaten his fill, Sir John Chandos entertained the company with a song. His pleasant tones had barely died when another messenger arrived at the Duke's side.

Margot recognised Sir Richard d'Evreux at once. She glanced at Sir Thomas, wondering whether he had noticed the young man's arrival. He had. His eyes were fixed on his nephew, no longer bleak but warm and smiling.

While Lancaster read the missive, young Dickon strode round the trestles, greeting them both with a bow.

"I bring the Prince's decision concerning Lady Marguerite."

"Oh!"

Margot's exclamation brought Sir Thomas's eyes to her suddenly taut face.

"Courage, *doña*," he murmured. "I do not think any evil will befall you. My lord Duke would not allow it."

"Could he prevent it, if Pedro so willed?" asked Margot tightly. For a few hours she had managed to forget the threat hanging over her head like a pall. Now it returned, threatening to smother her. Her former sense of safety under Sir Thomas's protection deserted her. She trembled.

The Duke read swiftly, then sent a page to summon them.

Sir Thomas dropped to one knee, Margot curtsied low, crushing the fragile silk of her gown in cold, clammy hands.

"You have news, Your Grace?" enquired Sir Thomas.

"Aye, my brother has agreed something with Don Pedro at last! Pedro has released Doña Sedano into his keeping, to dispose as he wills."

"I am the Prince of Wales's hostage?" gasped Margot faintly. She wasn't sure whether this was entirely good news, but at least it was better than being handed over to the mercies of Pedro. He wasn't known as "the Cruel", for nothing. "The Prince requires a ransom?"

"Nay, lady, he requires no ransom, but a declaration of loyalty from Bertrand de Bellac. You will be held in England as hostage for your father's good faith. My brother wants no traitorous lords in Aquitaine, especially when their lands lie close to the French King's. Your presence in England as hostage will ensure Monsieur le Comte de Limousin's acceptance of my gracious brother's rule as Sovereign Prince of Aquitaine."

Margot's mixed emotions were reflected in the changing colour of her eyes. Relief seemed to be uppermost, together with a dawning curiosity to see the land of her mother's birth. But apprehension still had a sizeable place, and resentment, too. Where would she be sent, under what conditions would she live? And for how long? Would she ever be a free person again?

"It seems, then, that I have no choice to obey his command," she said quietly. Was it only a short hour or so ago that she had been dancing for joy? Her sense of freedom had been short-lived and illusory. She was still a chattel, a mere pawn in these men's political manoeuvres. "When am I to go?"

The Duke smiled indulgently, reducing Margot's apprehension slightly. "I am to travel to England myself. I am eager to see my son, as you may imagine, and I have need to replenish my purse. We will share an escort." He turned to Sir Thomas. "Thomas, you will detail fifty men to accompany us. You will lead them, naturally."

"Of course, lord. I will see to it immediately."

Sir Thomas bowed, half turned to go, but the Duke stopped him with a gesture.

"Wait, Thomas. You will continue to be responsible for Lady Marguerite's safety. My brother requests that she be held in one of my castles." He eyed Margot consideringly. "Leicester should prove a pleasant place in which to wait, my lady. Once your father has sworn an oath not to take up arms against the Prince, you will be free to leave. Until then I appoint Sir Thomas to be your guardian."

Margot's heart sank. Was she never to be free of the man's suspicious presence? At the same time she heard a sharp intake of breath beside her.

"I am not to return here with you, lord?" asked Sir Thomas, his voice taut with anxiety.

"No, Thomas. Lady Marguerite's comfort and safety are of the utmost importance to my brother. I can do no less than put my most trusted and able knight in charge of both."

"And if my father will not swear this oath you require?" asked Margot faintly.

"Then you will remain our guest until he can be persuaded."

Margot did not press the point further. She knew the

probable consequences of any defiance on the part of Bertrand de Bellac. She would be taken to some remote, uncomfortable castle, and left to eke out her days in lonely despair. And she had little hope that her father would allow her fate to influence his actions.

Her eyes lifted to meet those of Sir Thomas, seeking sympathy.

Instead, she read in his bleak grey gaze resentment and rebellion to match her own.

Chapter Four

Fleurette tossed her head angrily, jibbing against the unfamiliar leading-rein.

"Quietly, now," soothed Margot.

The cavalcade had made good progress, covering more miles than Margot had ever travelled in a day before. The Duke of Lancaster, a splendid figure mounted on a huge black destrier at the head of his men, was anxious to press on.

Immediately in front of her rode the Duke's banner-bearers, one carrying the emblem of England, the other of Lancaster. Sir Thomas rode beside her on the chestnut charger he called Rasmus, holding the leading-rein. Even in this company he would not relax his guard.

Margot straightened her tired shoulders, refusing to let him see that she found the long hours on horseback exhausting. Glancing over her shoulder, she saw Inés clinging to the waist of Thomas's lanky groom, Edwin, with whom she was riding pillion. The weight of the two together would not exceed that of a stalwart man, and the horse kept up without difficulty. Juan, to his delight, had been found a spare hack, and rode easily beside the man-at-arms, holding his leading-rein. Sir Cedric she could not see, since his litter and the men detailed to escort him had fallen some distance behind. She curbed her concern, knowing that camp would have to be made shortly; the sun was setting and the horses were tired. The others would soon catch up.

"We should enter Navarre on the morrow," said the man beside her abruptly, breaking a long silence. "I believe His Grace will camp in this valley, by the river. 'Tis not far from Nájera."

"We shall not cross the battlefield?" asked Margot with a shudder.

"Nay, but close by. 'Twas fought beside the road from Pampeluna to Burgos."

Margot's fists clenched on the reins. "I suppose there will be little to see? The bodies have been buried?"

"Upwards of sixteen thousand of Trastamara's men strewed the field afterwards, and the task may not yet be complete. Doubtless the horse-flesh will have been taken for meat."

Roberto had gloried in the butchery of battle. It had been his just reward to have been slaughtered in his turn. But still... She composed her voice with an effort. "I do not look forward to that part of the journey."

Thomas heard the strain she was desperate to hide. "Shut your eyes. I will lead you," he told her quietly.

"You will lead me in any case," she retorted stiffly.

"Still resentful, *doña?*"

His voice teased, and Margot glanced across to see him regarding her with roguish eyes. Despite herself, a small grin tugged at her lips.

"Wouldn't you be?" she demanded, her composure restored.

"Aye." Thomas breathed a silent sigh of relief, sensing her tension broken. He did not want a hysterical female on his hands.

As Margot had anticipated, Sir Cedric caught up soon after they'd dismounted for the night. He looked fatigued, but had some colour in his sunken cheeks. While Inés flirted with Edwin, Juan rubbed Fleurette down, the pavilions were erected and the fires lit, Margot administered more of her remedy and warned Sir Cedric again to be careful of what he ate and drank.

"I am feeling stronger every day," he informed her cheerfully. "I shall be on horseback before we cross the mountains, never fear! The purging has almost stopped, and the griping is less painful."

Margot smiled affectionately. "You'll be quite recovered by the time your sister sees you!" she told him encouragingly.

"Aye, it seems he will!"

Sir Thomas had strolled up, and stood looking down at Cedric, who had flung himself on the ground. "Are you as much better as you look, brother?"

"I believe so! But my physician tells me I must continue to be careful of what I eat and drink."

"Otherwise you will bring back the flux and the pain!" warned Margot.

"And that I do not want! You seem to be able to eat and drink exactly what you like, Thomas. How do you do it?"

Sir Thomas laughed. "I was never a fussy eater, you know that. Besides, my guts became tough at an early age!"

"Aye, kitchen scraps, wasn't it?"

They exchanged a meaningful chuckle which aroused Margot's dormant curiosity.

"Kitchen scraps?" she echoed. "Why did you eat them?"

A shadow passed over Sir Thomas's face. "I didn't want to starve," he told her abruptly.

"But that is all in the past," interposed Cedric quickly, as though he knew the other man would not wish to pursue the subject. "Lady Margot, I believe your pavilion is ready. You will be glad of a rest before we sup."

Intrigued despite herself by this glimpse into Sir Thomas's past, Margot hid her disappointment at Sir Cedric's intervention behind a smile.

Lancaster's was the only other tent erected. Since it was a fine night, the men slept in the open, stirring before dawn to make an early start.

Next day Margot passed by the scarred battlefield with her eyes fixed on the road ahead, her mind closed to the sight of men dragging what looked like bundles of rags towards the mounds of earth which marked the huge common graves being dug by dozens of sweating men, to the buzzards circling lazily overhead, to the stench of death. She swallowed hard, barely aware of the tears streaking her ashen cheeks, determined to deny her heaving stomach, to pass the place where so many men had died without making a spectacle of herself.

The soldiers behind her were gleefully exchanging individual tales of valour and chivalry, of danger and victory. Sir Thomas chatted about inconsequential things—the weather, the state of the road, the condition of the horses, the kind of ship they would take from Bordeaux, where they might rest that night. Margot responded in mindless monosyllables until they were past Nájera, but even when the scene of victory and defeat was left far behind she found it difficult to respond to Sir Thomas's remarks.

He seemed to understand. Just as he'd picked up her relief at Roberto's death, so he had sensed her unease at passing the scene of so much carnage. No doubt he thought her just a foolish woman, but she was grateful for the unexpected tact shown to someone whose presence he patently regarded as an unwelcome burden.

They forded the Ebro and made camp. Thomas did not insist on sleeping across the door of her pavilion, but joined his lord in his. Not that this meant he had abandoned his mistrust or his care. There were, after all, upwards of fifty other men ready to see that she didn't stray or come to any harm.

The days began to blur in her mind. By evening her body was a mass of aching muscles and all she wanted was to find her pallet and sleep. Once they reached the narrow pass at Ronscevalles, the high, snow-clad peaks and wild dark slopes demanded her interest. As they climbed and wound and dropped down again to splash through tiny streams, she kept a sharp eye open for bears, but not one put in an appearance, though an abundance of deer and small game scrambled over the rocky terrain of the lower slopes and provided them with fresh meat each day.

Sir Cedric, mounted now, sat his Great Horse easily. When there was room, he rode at her other side, when the way was narrow, he followed closely behind. He and Sir Thomas laughed and talked together, and Margot joined in, feeling less like a prisoner each day, despite the loathsome leading rein.

This feeling of ease was largely due to Cedric's presence. His was an easy friendship which she enjoyed. Yet it was to Sir Thomas that she turned for information and advice, and Sir Thomas she instinctively trusted to keep her safe through every hazard.

Inés, riding pillion, kept her eyes firmly closed whenever the forest pressed in close, eyed the mysterious, misty hills warily, and fiercely clutched Edwin's waist. He didn't seem to mind, Margot noticed with amusement. And, since leaving the encampment at Burgos, Inés had gained so much confidence that each evening she treated the men to a flood of orders in Spanish which they interpreted as best they could. Most obeyed with good-natured chaffing. Inés at her fiery best was an attractive girl and, although Margot's comfort benefited, she became concerned for her tiring-maid's virtue.

"Inés," she warned, "don't tease the men beyond their endurance! If one of them thinks you ready to give him a reward for his services, you cannot blame him if he claims it! Be more circumspect, girl!"

"Pooh!" snorted Inés complacently, "I can handle those buffoons! Do not fear, *doña*, I will see to your comfort and keep my virtue! One day I intend to marry a better man than any of these spineless English dolts!"

"Not so spineless, Inés," frowned Margot. "They won the battle, remember! Almost the entire Spanish chivalry was either killed or captured, and most of the Spanish men-at-arms and bowmen were killed!"

"But those that are left will regain the throne for Don Enrico! These English, they do not know how we suffered under Don Pedro! They do not realise that most of Spain was behind Don Enrico! Why could they not leave us to settle our own affairs?"

"I do not know," sighed Margot.

She had often wondered, and the next day she asked Sir Thomas, choosing a moment when they were momentarily isolated during the midday halt.

"Don Pedro asked for Prince Edward's help," he explained, surprised that she should even need to ask. "How could he deny it to the anointed King of Castile? The Prince did not consider it Christian for a rightful heir to be disinherited by force of arms by a bastard. He saw the campaign as a righteous one, an act of chivalry to deliver the King and his daughters from exile. King Edward, his father, approved his decision, and the Duke, his brother, came hot-foot with a thousand archers to support him."

"Yet Castile was relieved of much tyranny during Don Enrico's short reign."

"Don Pedro is God's anointed. It is God's will that he reigns."

"Then God has chosen ill!"

The words were out before she could stop them. She coloured hotly and hastily crossed herself. "Sweet Jesu, forgive me," she murmured hurriedly.

"Blasphemy ill becomes you, *doña*," said Sir Thomas repressively, but his eyes were thoughtful.

"I only hope the Prince of Wales is never forced to regret his action."

"From which I gather you supported the Bastard's claim?" surmised Sir Thomas, the frown between his eyes deepening.

"I neither supported nor opposed. I am not of Castile. My husband chose his own path, for his own reasons."

"And is dead."

"Aye."

There seemed no more to be said. In silence, Margot rose from the bank on which she'd been resting and moved to join the throng of men and horses preparing to resume the journey.

That night Margot awoke abruptly from the deep,

dreamless slumber of exhaustion to hear such a commotion outside that her heart thudded uncomfortably against her breastbone.

"Inés! Are you awake? What is happening?"

"I don't know, *doña!* Mercy on us, we'll all be killed!"

Inés rolled from her pallet, moaning, and buried her head in the blanket, while Margot threw off the wolfskin covering her, and felt around for her shoes.

As she fastened the latchet she heard shouting and confusion followed by the ring and teeth-grating scrape of steel on steel. Fighting! Sweet Jesu! They were being attacked!

Her hand went instinctively to the haft of the dagger hanging from her girdle and concealed in the folds of her gown. Sir Thomas had never searched her, never asked whether she carried a weapon. With that intuition of his he'd probably realised that she would never use it on him. She had brought it for just such an occasion as this.

She crouched in the darkness of the tent, straining her eyes towards the flap. She would see if it was opened. A glimmer of light, a start, the flash of a blade...

Her palms sweated. She rubbed them on her gown. Waiting was intolerable! She had to see what was happening!

As she jumped up the flap moved. A swirl of mist caught damply in her throat. She froze.

"Stay where you are!" she warned hoarsely, instinctively using Spanish. "I am armed!"

A coarse laugh preceded a gloating voice answering her in a patois difficult to decipher. "A woman, eh? Fight all you will, my little dove. I shall enjoy your struggles."

A lewd chuckle sent a shiver of fear down Margot's spine. The bulky shadow moved forward. "Come to me," he coaxed evilly.

Inés screamed. Margot clutched the dagger in her hand, ready to die rather than be taken.

The pavilion was small, and one stride brought the noisome bandit close enough to touch. His stench made Margot retch. She took a shuddering breath and lifted her arm, striking out at a point below the pale blur of his face.

He forestalled her, catching her wrist in a huge fist. The knife dropped from her nerveless fingers.

Another throaty chuckle made her flesh crawl. "So my little dove! What a treasure! You will come with me!"

He reached forward with greedy arms and swung her over a broad shoulder. Margot beat at his filthy leather brigandine. The shoulder-buckle stuck into her stomach and her hair caught on others fastening the sides. Vaguely, she heard Inés's screams. Heard the man curse as he shook off an assailant like a bear shaking off a terrier and kicked it aside. Heard a moan followed by new shouts drawing closer. Then the pain, the stink, the blood rushing to her head took her senses.

She felt herself hit the ground with a thump. Feet trod near by and she huddled into a ball to escape them. Dark figures loomed from the lightening mist and steel clashed and rasped overhead. She lay shrinking, waiting for a cold blade to rend her apart. "Sweet Jesu," she prayed silently, "save us!" Then she heard a scream, cut off short, and the sound of blood bubbling in someone's throat.

"Margot! Are you all right?"

A man bent anxiously over her, and she knew it was

Thomas. She stirred and sat up with the help of his arm around her shoulders. He was on one knee. As she rested back against his raised thigh, he brushed the wild mess of hair from her forehead.

His touch sent a shiver through her. "Aye," she whispered.

"Thank God!" His voice shook slightly. "*Doña,* I apologise! My protection proved worthless!"

"You saved me!"

"Not from the fear of death and worse! I had thought to give you some semblance of freedom, but from now on I guard you day and night!"

She laughed shakily. "Is that a threat, or a promise?"

"A promise!"

For a fleeting moment his lips touched hers, and Margot thought she must be dreaming. For a moment she dwelt in some place where nothing mattered but pleasure.

Struggling to dispel the inexplicable lethargy which had overtaken her, "Have they gone?" she demanded briskly. "Who were they?"

Thomas lifted his head, shaking it slightly as though to clear his thoughts. "Mountain bandits, roving soldiers—who knows? They were after plunder, and it seems they succeeded in getting away with some of our supplies and a horse or two before we were roused."

His thigh felt comfortingly solid behind her, but she was too aware of him, of the warmth of his hand penetrating the silk of her gown, of the fact that in an unguarded moment he'd called her Margot and then kissed her. Her nerves tightened in instinctive withdrawal, and she was relieved when they were interrupted.

"Tom! Is that you?"

Thomas lifted her gently as he got to his feet and faced his master. "Aye, lord."

In the flickering light of a torch held by his squire, she saw the Duke, hair rumpled, bloodied sword in hand. Margot fought for dignity. Not only was she emotionally upset, but her gown, already travel-stained and slept-in, was now torn. She felt unwashed and almost as filthy as the man lying dead near by.

"Lady Marguerite! I regret my men were engaged elsewhere when you were attacked. You and your maid are unharmed?"

"Your Grace." Margot curtsied, twitching her hem away from a dark stain on the ground which might have been a pool of blood. "I am quite safe, thanks to Sir Thomas." She shot him a swift smile as he picked up his sword and wiped the steel on a tuft of grass. His hair was boyishly rumpled like his master's; they looked like two schoolboys caught out in a midnight romp, and her gratitude was suddenly swamped by tenderness.

She brought her mind back to the Duke's query with an effort. "Inés was not molested, but..." She suddenly remembered the leaping figure, the moan. "Where is Juan?"

"Juan?"

"Yes! He tried to save me, and that brute kicked him aside— Juan!" she called anxiously.

A muffled moan from near the tent sent her hurrying towards a dark form lying in a huddle of clothing.

"Juan! Are you hurt?"

"Not too badly, *doña*," gasped the boy. He struggled to sit up and held his head, then hugged his arms around himself. "But he kicked me and my ribs hurt and I hit my head..."

Margot knelt on the chewed turf and began to examine

the lad's broken head by the light of a flickering torch.
The wound looked angry, he had a large bruise, but it
would heal. He must have caught his scalp on one of
the wooden tent-pegs sticking out from the ground. As
for his ribs...

"What did he say? Is he badly hurt?"

Thomas dropped to his knees at her side, inspecting
the damage for himself.

"His head will mend, but he was kicked in the ribs.
I hope they are not broken."

"He's breathing easily enough."

"Yes."

"Your servant is badly injured?"

Margot lifted a face streaked with dirt to answer the
crisp voice overhead. "I do not believe so, Your Grace.
I can tend him. Do any of your men need my care?"

"I think not, Lady Marguerite, thank you. My own
physician can attend to the minor cuts and bruises they
received. He can attend your servant, an you will."

"I thank you. I will call him if I think it necessary.
Was much stolen?"

"Too much, I dare say. Two of the guards will not
see the dawn."

"They were killed?"

"Aye. Taken from behind. Their vigilance was at
fault," said the Duke frostily. "They deserved to die.
Such slackness must not occur in the future, else we will
all be killed as we sleep. The guard must be doubled."

"The men will have learned their lesson," said
Thomas grimly, rising to his feet. "They will have eyes
in the backs of their heads tonight."

"Aye, Tom. I hope you're right," rejoined the Duke
briefly. "Come, we have work to do."

Margot called to Inés, who appeared reluctantly,

crossing herself, staring into the shadows with dark, frightened eyes.

"Devil's spawn!" she muttered fearfully. "Did you see him, *doña?* Huge, and black, and he had horns on his head!"

"Nonsense, Inés! He was big, I grant you, and loomed black out of the darkness, but I saw no horns, either before or after he died! They were men, Inés—bad men with evil intent, but men! Sir Thomas killed the one you saw."

Inés crossed herself again. "The Saints be praised!"

"Pour water to bathe Juan's wounds," ordered Margot briskly. "Then I must wash myself and find something clean to wear. Jump to it, girl!"

She helped Juan into the tent and retrieved her dagger from the ground where it had fallen. Much good it had done her! she thought angrily as she thrust it back in its sheath. How helpless she'd felt! Submitting to that beast would have been humiliation and torture far exceeding anything she'd endured with Roberto, however much she had hated and feared her husband. At least he'd kept himself clean! Another time… Please God there would be no other time! But, if there were, she would acquit herself better, that she vowed.

After traces of battle were removed, burial rites for the two guards and the three bandits killed performed and mass said, they moved off, later than normal.

Margot shuddered as she took one last look at the place where her attacker had fallen. Smelling blood, the vultures were already gathering, but all the bodies should have been safe enough in the graves hastily scraped in the rocky soil.

Lancaster was right. His men's lack of vigilance could have cost all their lives. As it was, they were short of food and she had lost a couple of her coffers, containing mostly clothes. She would need to replenish her wardrobe when she reached England. Thanks be to God her jewels were safe, hung in leather pouches around her waist under her surcoat by day, and making a pillow for her head at night.

England! It lay on the far side of a stormy sea. A small, secret smile curved her lips, and Thomas, watching, wondered what thought could bring such an expression to transform her face.

Margot had discovered that she did not mind being forced to cross the sea. In fact she was suddenly looking forward with keen anticipation. For the first time since she could remember, she was thoroughly enjoying herself! A taste for adventure, long repressed by the dictates of obedience and convention, had finally been released.

The remainder of the journey passed without serious mishap. Once into the comparative safety of Gascony, the Duke decided to press on, leaving Thomas, with half his retainers, to escort her more slowly.

Thomas was not pleased. Since joining John of Gaunt's royal household as a squire some ten years since, he had shared in his young master's romantic escapades, seen him marry and promptly fall in love with his bride, a young maid whom Thomas himself worshipped from afar.

The Lady Blanche, a younger, paler replica of his beloved Eleanor, represented Thomas's beau-ideal; but she was unattainable, so he contented himself with the favours of one of her ladies-in-waiting. An attractive, well-endowed woman married to an elderly knight, Beth was glad of the attentions of a young and virile man, and would vow any child to be her husband's. So far she had borne only one baby to term, and would not swear to the identity of its father. Thomas privately thought the boy his, and watched with some amusement when the old man proudly presented the infant as his heir.

Sometimes the tug of affection he felt for the child took Thomas by surprise, and for a time his spirits would drag. Being unable to show a father's love was harder than he'd anticipated. But he would lay no claim to young Robert. Beth was his chosen mistress precisely because he had no wish to bring an unwanted bastard into the world, to suffer as he had done. As things were, his child would be reared in a royal court and one day be the lord of several rich manors. How could he deny his son that prospect out of sheer maudlin sentiment?

He brought his thoughts back to his present problem with a snort of disgust. John had knighted him and given him the trusted position of commander of his personal guard. Was he now to be shut off from the presence and confidences of his lord because some Spanish widow needed a keeper?

Margot seemed in a particularly buoyant mood, which irked him further. She had emerged from the mountain pass to sniff the air of Aquitaine and smile so broadly that he half suspected she might attempt to escape to her father's castle. On the other hand, all her previous signs of discontent had disappeared, and she behaved as though she were travelling of her own choice, as though she were actually looking forward to seeing England!

He frowned. Could Cedric be the reason for her change of mood? They were much in each other's company, and had become quite intimate. Cedric needed a wife, every member of the family agreed on that. But Margot?

The idea was distasteful to him. She was too young

for Cedric. He had personal knowledge of what happened when a man married a woman much younger than himself.

How old was Margot? Married at sixteen eight summers since, she must be about four or five and twenty, though sometimes she looked much younger.

God's teeth! Thomas's thoughts suddenly pulled up with a jerk. Cedric was no more than fifteen years her senior!

His bad mood deepened.

Vineyards lined the banks of the Garonne almost to the gates of Bordeaux, a bustling, noisome town through which they needs must pass to reach the royal palace, where they were welcomed with all the respect due to those carrying papers from the Sovereign Prince of Aquitaine. Margot was glad she'd had the chance to freshen up the previous evening in a merchant's house in the bastide town of Bazas, for here in Bordeaux she was surrounded by great splendour.

"The Duke of Lancaster sailed two days since," the steward told Thomas in answer to his question. "The weather was fine, with a fair wind. He should be in England ere the week is out."

"God willing, we will follow on the morrow." Thomas turned to the outriders he had sent in advance to make enquiries. "Are there vessels? Are the tides favourable?"

"Aye, sir," answered the elder of the two men. "The *Lady Anne* and the *Queen of the Seas* will be ready to sail an hour after Tierce. They should be well down the estuary by nightfall, an the wind holds."

"How long will the voyage take?" enquired Margot.

"Depends on the winds, my lady. One week or two.

It has been known to take a month, if there are storms in the Bay, but the weather seems set fair for the moment.''

Margot turned to Thomas. "What is the sea like? Is it very frightening? I've never seen it."

She appeared eager as a child. Thomas grinned, his depression of the last days lifting suddenly. Mayhap it was the prospect of the sea voyage, of the shifting deck under his feet, of the salt air in his lungs. He had ever loved the sea, and would be happy to show it to her.

"Wait and see, *doña*. It will surprise you, that I'll warrant!"

"You do not hold it in fear," observed Margot with a small smile. "Then neither shall I!"

The steward bowed. "The Princess of Wales requests that you join her at the high table for supper, my lady. Pierre will show you to your chamber."

He bowed again and bustled away, leaving Margot to follow the small Gascon. Thomas inclined his head, taking her hand. An unusual gesture which sent a small tremor along her arm.

"I shall be seated with other knights, *doña*. Mayhap we shall not meet again until morning. I trust you will have a restful night."

"Thank you, Sir Thomas." Margot hesitated, dying of curiosity, but dubious of his reaction if she voiced it. However, her thirst for knowledge was not easy to deny. "What is the Princess like?" she asked breathlessly.

"She is still very beautiful. In her youth she was known as the Fair Maid of Kent, and Prince Edward waited years until she was free. I well remember the furore when he insisted on marrying a woman of thirty-two with four children by former husbands! The King had long wanted him to make a political alliance, but the Prince would have none of it!''

"How I envy anyone who is able to marry for love! And now she has given him two sons."

Those strange eyes held a wistful gleam. Thomas lifted the hand he held to his lips.

"Aye," he acknowledged, "Edward is a fair and charming child. Let us hope little Richard proves as robust." He pressed the hand to his lips again. "Look to the future, lady," he advised softly. "Mayhap you will find happiness in marriage yet."

If she loved Cedric and he her, why should the idea of their union cause him such disquiet? She was far above Cedric in rank, just as she was above himself. Yet stranger alliances had been made in the name of love. He could do no less than wish them well.

Margot gently disengaged her fingers from his warm clasp. She said nothing to contradict his hope. He could not be expected to understand the fear of physical intimacy which precluded any such thing.

Chapter Five

Bordeaux, curving along the great arc of the Garonne, faded inexorably into the distance.

Standing in the shelter of the embattled fighting aftercastle of the *Lady Anne*, Margot let her eyes linger on the dominating spires of the cathedral, on the formidable castle and stalwart wall, before returning to the ant-like men swarming between busy quay and moored ships.

Cursing, shouting, heaving, they unloaded tin, wool and linen from England, bales of costly, exotic stuffs from the Orient, spices and strange timbers from other far-off lands. Cask after cask was rolled aboard to fill the empty holds and decks, each one filled with fine Bordeaux wine to tempt the palates of the rich throughout the world.

Carrying above the general bustle, she could hear the shrill neighing of terrified horses as they were unwillingly embarked.

Poor Fleurette! The palfrey had been frightened out of her wits, and all Margot's soothing had been in vain. The lesser animals had been sold to a merchant, but some horse-flesh was too valuable, too well-loved to abandon.

"She'll do herself harm!" Margot had almost wept, seeing her beloved mount rearing against a cradle of supporting-straps and snorting in fear as four men attempted to fix a blindfold and force her across the gangplank. "She'll lame herself beyond remedy!"

"Once the blindfold is on she'll quieten down. Rasmus made the voyage over," Thomas told her soothingly. "He survived. The horses will be stalled and firmly tethered in the shelter of the forecastle. They are unlikely to do themselves or others harm."

Only partially reassured, Margot had followed Fleurette aboard, petting and soothing, leaving her to Juan's care only when the mare had quietened.

As the ship left the Garonne and turned into the wider waters of the Gironde, Bordeaux finally disappeared from view. Along the banks, the chime of village and monastery bells echoed across the water, marking the hour of Sext. The noonday sun cast a glaring white light over the lush vegetation, the vineyards, the yellowish waters of the river. Margot was no stranger to the brilliance of a cloudless sky, and her narrowed eyes devoured everything in sight. Like the *Lady Anne* and the *Queen of the Seas,* which carried the remainder of the retinue and horses, many ships were sailing with the tide, their great painted sails billowing in a fresh south-westerly breeze.

A step behind her, the jingle of a spur, brought her head round.

"Sir Thomas!" She smiled a greeting, slightly shy because of a sudden she remembered the moment the previous evening when their eyes had met over the heads of the throng of men and women supping in the Great Hall of the Royal Palace.

Thomas—how long had she been thinking of him simply as Thomas?—had been at a side-table among others of his rank. After her presentation she had been seated near the Princess of Wales.

The court at Bordeaux glittered despite the Prince's absence and that of many of his leading courtiers. The rich brocades and velvets, the silks and furs of the costumes, the costly sparkle of the precious metals and gems worn by both men and women brought awed wonder to Margot's eyes, eyes which narrowed as she took in the colourful wall-paintings and exquisite tapestries, the silver and gold platters and goblets gracing the tables, the food presented with elaborate ceremony to deafening flourishes of the heralds' trumpets. The opulence, the extravagance on every side, explained the Prince's need to tax his vassals so severely that they were showing signs of open rebellion!

As the daughter of one of the leading counts of Aquitaine, despite her position as hostage, she was accorded all the deference due her rank. Margot found the grandeur unwelcome, the ceremonial astonishing and her own position amusing. It had been while smothering a chuckle at the deference and courtesy offered to a hostage that her eyes had strayed down the Hall to find Thomas's fixed upon her.

Hers must have revealed her secret amusement, for Thomas suddenly grinned and, for an instant, they had seemed to laugh together over the absurdity of their respective positions.

Margot had never allowed rank—her own or that of others—to impress or intimidate her.

Thomas had certainly never allowed it to affect his attitude to her! She recalled the leading-rein and other small indignities with a flash of annoyance, but her lips had already curved into an answering smile.

Now, remembering, she wondered what Thomas had thought of her, sitting at the high table in her outmoded Spanish fashions, her hair loose almost to her waist, her high, tubular head-dress, jewel-encrusted though it was. The ladies all around had worn their hair in coiled braids, some covered in gem-spattered frets of silver or gold, some by veils, and most had worn circlets set with gleaming cabochons of ruby and sapphire, topaz and emerald. The Princess, dazzling in cloth of gold, had set upon her fair head a regal golden coronet studded with huge diamonds, sapphires and rubies.

"You are taking leave of your homeland?" queried Thomas as he joined her. "Do not despair, *doña*. I have no doubt that you will return ere long."

She shifted slightly, making room for him to stand beside her. "Leaving Aquitaine does not sadden me, sir. In truth, I am looking forward to seeing the land of my mother's birth. Mayhap I can visit the manor which now belongs to me."

"You have a manor in England?" Thomas did not seek to hide his astonishment. "Where does it lie?"

"In Kent, near the port of Rye beside the River Rother, though it is known as Idenford. 'Twas my mother's dowry, then mine, but yields little profit."

"I do not know that part of the land, but I believe much of it is marsh. No doubt revenues will be due from it. When we land I will send a messenger to discover its condition."

"Any income would be welcome. I have little money, and I shall need new clothes, since most of mine were stolen."

"The Duke's purse will provide your needs while you are his guest."

"*Guest?*" Margot laughed, not harshly.

In fact, thought Thomas, she sounded highly amused, just as she'd looked last evening. Since leaving Castile she appeared to have cast off all care, behaving as though the journey was one long adventure. Even the attack in the mountains had not dimmed her evident pleasure for long. He found her attitude refreshingly different, and had begun treating her as a companion, as someone who could share his own delight in new experiences. Almost as another man.

Unfortunately he was inclined to forget his responsibilities. To forget that he would be in trouble if anything untoward happened to her. To forget that she was a hostage of the heir to the Realm of England.

Almost as another man, but never quite. The disturbing thing he found it increasingly difficult to forget was that she was very much a woman. He moved away slightly, leaning his shoulder against the higher merlon.

"You will be treated with all honour and courtesy," he said stiffly, covering his uncomfortable thoughts with a show of coolness. "As long as you remain in my care you will have no cause to complain of your treatment."

"I have no complaint, Sir Thomas." Margot turned swiftly to face him. Why had he suddenly withdrawn? She felt an unaccountable sense of disappointment. They'd been exchanging pleasant conversation, or so she'd thought. Surely he hadn't been offended by her laugh? She hadn't meant it unkindly. She desperately wanted to restore the warm feeling that had existed between them for days now. It seemed necessary, somehow.

"I know you but do your duty. I could not resist mocking my situation," she assured him gently. "But tell me about yourself. You have manors, Sir Thomas?"

He eyed her warily, but her interest seemed genuine.

"Aye," he told her, "two by the generosity of the Earl of Wenstaple, my half-brother. They provide income enough to allow me the honour of wearing cloth of gold and miniver." He grinned wryly, referring to the recently passed sumptuary laws, and added, "I rarely visit them, being in the Duke of Lancaster's service."

"You are with him constantly?"

"Not entirely. I make periodic visits to Wenfrith, which I still regard as my home. 'Tis where I was born, and I bear its arms."

"The castle and the lilies?" Margot drew a deep breath and risked the question she'd been longing to ask for almost as long as she'd known him. "Who was your father, Sir Thomas?"

He was in no way ashamed to admit the identity of his sire, but watched her expressive face intently, his eyes veiled, needing to see her reaction. "William d'Evreux," he told her, "a baron of Norman lineage, the Lord of Wenfrith."

Margot's brows lifted. "But not Earl of Wenstaple?" she asked.

"No. My brother was granted that honour after Crécy."

She nodded with swift understanding. "And your mother?" she persisted softly.

The sardonic smile this question brought to his face ill-suited his open features. "A villein's daughter," he supplied tersely.

Margot met his suddenly challenging gaze without flinching. "But a good woman?"

"I believe so. She loved my father. But I scarce remember her. She died before I was five."

She was stirred to ask quickly, "Who brought you up?"

Thomas saw the emotion clearly mirrored in her eyes, and revolted against her pity. His brows flew up. "That is more than enough about me!" he snapped.

Too late Margot realised that she had trodden on delicate ground. She cocked her head, meeting his eyes with a swift smile. "Tell me about your brother's wife," she invited lightly.

Thomas's expression cleared. A soft glow lit the depths of his grey eyes, stirring something deep in Margot, a kind of longing she could not understand.

"Eleanor? She is of Saxon stock, the daughter of a Colchester wool merchant. Beautiful, loving, courageous, everything any man could possibly desire in a wife. Like Lady Blanche."

"I shall meet her?" asked Margot softly, discovering a need to see a woman whose mere name could inspire such emotion in Thomas.

"Mayhap. We land at Wenstaple, but the Earl and Countess are unlikely to be in residence there. They spend most of their time at Wenfrith, a half-day's journey thence, though they may still be at Court if Richard went to Windsor for St George's Day. If they are at Wenfrith I shall visit while I am so near. Cedric will be journeying there, to stay awhile."

"I long to see Wenfrith."

Because Cedric would be there? "I will arrange it that you do," he promised gruffly.

The breeze stiffened suddenly, heeling the ship to starboard, swelling the great sail, painted with lilies and leopards and a huge red rose, so that it strained at the rigging. The banner of St George fluttered over the forecastle, another red rose on a long pennant streamed from the masthead above the top. The retinue formed a carpet of red roses and crosses to cover most of the main deck.

The chequered flag of the master, who was directing operations from behind them, cracked and slapped above their heads.

Margot gripped the rail and threw back her head in exhilaration. Her hair streamed from under her coif, the flowing skirt of her silken kirtle flapped around her legs, moulding her form.

"Sir Thomas!" she exclaimed exultantly, "I have seldom known such a joyous feeling! Why should this be so?"

"You have never sailed before," laughed Thomas, forgetting his pique, admiring her slender grace. "I always find a sense of peace and freedom on board a ship—until a tempest rages! In weather like this there can be nothing to match the swell of the wind in the sail, the chuckle of the water running under the hull. But we are not yet at sea. Wait until the morrow! Meanwhile, would you not prefer to sit under the canopy on deck? The shade will be kinder to your complexion. I came to tell you that, since we missed dinner, a meal is being served."

Reluctantly, Margot left her post at the stern and climbed down to the main deck. She would sleep in the master's cabin under the after-deck, sharing with Inés half its panelled and brocaded comfort, while Cedric and Thomas used a section screened off by a curtain. But while the weather held she intended to spend every possible moment in the fresh air, enjoying the wind and the sun and the tang of salt on her lips.

Cedric was reclining on a pallet under the azure and white striped canopy when Margot stepped under its shade. One look at his face filled her with concern.

"You are ill again, sir?" she asked anxiously.

"A little seasick, I believe." He smiled wanly. "My

stomach was never strong when crossing the Channel, and I fear it will be worse this time. We have not yet reached the open sea, and already I am turning green! Mayhap I should have remained in Bordeaux,'' he grimaced.

''But then you would not have seen your sister,'' Margot encouraged with a smile.

''Pray God we get no storms,'' muttered Thomas. ''Biscay can be a devilish place when the wind and tides rage. I wish I could offer you some comfort, brother.''

''We are in God's hands. Just pray that we make good speed! I am not sure how long my vitals can survive another assault.''

''This is different,'' soothed Margot. ''Sip your wine, Sir Cedric. And then try to sleep.''

She knew nothing of seasickness, but hoped the same remedy would prove effective.

For the remainder of the day Margot either sat on her folding stool under the canopy or wandered around the decks, her complexion protected by a mantilla pulled forward to cast a shadow over her face.

Just before she retired to her cabin for the night she visited Fleurette. Rasmus, in the neighbouring stall, whickered softly and Fleurette seemed well content. Reassured, Margot stroked the mare's soft muzzle and murmured soothing words.

''They are quiet enough,'' observed Thomas, joining her and giving his Great Horse a fond pat. ''You're getting quite used to the sea, aren't you, Rasmus, old boy?''

The huge chestnut shook his golden mane, acknowledging his master with another soft whicker.

''I trust you will sleep well, *doña*. On the morrow, you will see the ocean.''

''I am looking forward to it, Sir Thomas.''

Margot repaired to her cabin with a sense of loss. Foolish woman, she derided herself, as Inés used a carved ivory comb to remove the tangles put in her hair by the breeze. How stupid to feel rejected because Thomas had forgone his place in the cabin, professing a preference for sleeping on deck.

Not until the ship came to round the jagged coasts of Finistère did the tricky winds of Biscay cause trouble. Then, of a sudden, a giant hand seemed to take hold of the ship, threatening to lift it from the sea and hurl it on the rocky shore. The bottom smashed down on the water again with a sound like a clap of thunder. The timbers shook, the ship reeled, and Margot was shot out of her bunk.

She picked herself from a tangle of demolished curtain in an uncomprehending daze. The ship twisted and heaved and slapped down again, throwing her back towards her bunk. Inés screamed, vomited all over her pallet and dissolved into pathetic moans. Cedric woke, but held himself together, giving her a wan, reassuring smile which she could barely see in the flickering light of the one swinging horn lantern left burning.

A great commotion outside indicated that the crew had been prodded into furious activity.

She pulled her scattered wits together enough to find Inés a cloth, thank the Saints she was already fully clothed, and cover her head with the mantilla. Fastening the latchets of her shoes, she heard the master's voice, slurred with drink, raised in urgent supplication to the Blessed Virgin of the Sea.

The chaos outside seemed preferable to remaining in the cabin, not knowing what was going on and having her stomach turned by the stink of vomit. She opened the door to be met by a blast of rain and spray-filled wind which threatened to squeeze the breath from her lungs.

"Margot!" Thomas was immediately beside her, his arm around her shoulders, spreading his cloak to encompass her, sheltering her from the worst of the storm. "You should not be out here! You must return to the cabin, where you will be safe!"

"Do not say so! If I return I shall be ill! I must breathe fresh air!"

"I sympathise with your desire, *doña*, but I—"

"Do not banish me inside, Sir Thomas! I promise I will not stir from here, or cause you any greater concern."

Against his better judgement, "Then stay, *doña*," agreed Thomas reluctantly. The men of the Duke's retinue were lashing themselves to the deck. "We should do the same," he told her.

She made no demur as he passed a length of rope first around her waist, then his own, before securing it to a ring set in the timbers of the deck. Only the seamen were moving freely, defying the danger in order to save their ship.

How comforting his arm was. She let her head rest against his shoulder, accepting his support without question as they huddled in the shelter of the projecting afterdeck, watching the helmsmen struggle with the long, heavy tiller. The dark beard he had allowed to grow since leaving Burgos brushed fleetingly against her forehead.

"Poor Inés," murmured Margot. "She has been queasy since we entered Biscay; the very sight of so much water frightened her half to death! But now she is being as sick as a gluttonous child!"

"How is Cedric faring? Guy could go to him."

"He seemed to be all right. There's naught Guy could do to help."

She sounded regretful rather than concerned.

Thomas's hand tightened on her shoulder. "I looked forward to showing you the ocean in all its vast glory, but not in a fury such as this! Are you much afeared?"

"Not over-much." She laughed lightly. "I imagine the master and crew have survived worse storms than this!"

Thomas bent in the dim light to scan her features. "The master is drunk!" he informed her drily.

"So I had imagined!"

She saw the sudden amusement light the grey eyes peering into hers. "I believe you are enjoying yourself!" he accused in wonder.

"Why should you be surprised?" She gasped as a wave curled high over the bow and broke, swamping the deck in water and wetting them to their knees. His arm had tightened around her as the deck swung dizzily and the surging water threatened to drag her off her feet. His other arm was locked around a steadying timber, although the rope anchored them both to the deck.

"Thank you!" She laughed again, a trifle breathlessly this time. "I find a little danger exhilarating, and a battle with the elements somehow satisfying. Don't you?"

"Aye, but I'm a man! Women are normally timid creatures."

"Perhaps just the ones you have met. Would the Countess of Wenstaple be frightened?"

"I think she would," Thomas admitted judiciously, "but she would put herself in God's hands and do her duty, whatever that might be. She would overcome her fear."

"So she is not a timid woman."

"No."

"And the Duchess of Lancaster?"

Thomas laughed ruefully. "She is no timid woman, either. You are tying me in knots, *doña.*"

His admiration was not won by piteous, clinging females. The thought brought a smile of quiet satisfaction to curve Margot's lips. She had given him credit for more spirit, more generosity than that, and she had been right.

Though, to be fair, she was clinging with all her might at that moment! As the ship lurched and the deck again became awash with water, she threw both her arms around Thomas's waist.

Obeying the master's hoarse commands, urged on by his curses, the crew swarmed over the deck and up the rigging in an attempt to lower the great sail. An unearthly, piercing wail brought Margot's heart leaping to her throat. She lifted her head from the shelter of Thomas's shoulder.

"Man overboard!"

Margot clutched fiercely at Thomas as the cry went up and a dark shadow fell from the rigging. Strain to hear as she might, the splash as the man hit the water was swallowed up in the fury of the lashing wind and waves. Thomas bellowed an order to his men. She felt his tension as he battled with an urgent desire for action, realised his frustration, lashed to her as he was.

Some of his men threw off their tethers and helped to throw a line, sloshing about in the swamping water in fearful danger of being swept overboard themselves, but their efforts proved futile. A last, despairing shriek, all but lost in the howling wind, rose to harrow their ears as the doomed sailor was swept away by the relentless sea.

Automatically, Margot crossed herself. "God save his soul!" she murmured.

"Amen."

"Get ye to your cabin, noble lady!" bellowed the master, scandalised, leaning from the fighting after-castle above their heads. "I didna realise ye were ootside! T'open deck is no place for ye the nicht!"

"I wish to remain here!" Margot shrieked back. "I shall be ill if I return to the cabin!"

"Then I'll not be responsible! And ye're washed overboard, 'twill be no fault o'mine! Ye'll answer, noble sir!"

Margot met considering grey eyes close to her own. "Well, Sir Thomas?"

"We will remain here." The eyes began to dance. "If one of us is swept overboard, both of us will die. I shall not be alive to answer for your safety, *doña!*"

Her laugh was a delighted chuckle. "But you do not believe we are in too much danger, Sir Thomas? I must confess I feel safe enough here."

"Aye. We are safe provided we remain where we are, and my muscles do not tire!" The arm around her tightened. "Are you warm enough?"

"Quite warm enough, I thank you."

His solid body gave both warmth and support, but Margot had little time to appreciate either as her gaze followed the mariners in their efforts to save their ship.

Once the crew succeeded in lowering the great sail, the motion of the ship eased, and with it the noise. She saw a couple of large baskets thrown overboard to trail behind the ship.

"As a sea-anchor," murmured Thomas in her ear. "To reduce our speed."

Now Margot could hear the pumps at work, emptying the hold of the water seeping in through creaking timbers. Could hear the terrified cries of the animals tethered in their stalls.

"Fleurette!" she exclaimed.

"There's naught we can do."

"I know."

The ship was heaving and wallowing as though tossed by some horned monster of the deep, and to throw off their rope to make an unnecessary journey across its wind-lashed deck would invite disaster.

"Juan is probably with Fleurette," murmured Thomas, reading her thoughts accurately as the sound of equine shrieks and trampling hoofs smote their ears.

"And Edwin with Rasmus?"

"Aye. He's devoted to the horses."

"What are those lights?" asked Margot suddenly, as the ship hovered on the crest of a wave.

"Where?"

"They've gone now. Wait!" As the ship spun on the top of another roller, "Yonder!"

Thomas followed the direction of Margot's pointing finger. She felt his muscles bunch. Her own tightened in response.

"What are they, Thomas?" she whispered. "Hobgoblin's lights?"

"Wreckers' fires," he told her grimly. "On the Point du Raz most likely." He raised his voice. "Ho! Captain! See those flares? D'you know where we are?"

"Off Finistère, noble sir."

"That I know, dolt! Can you not place us more nearly than that?"

The master's previous uncertain confidence had deserted him at sight of the wreckers' lights. He stared fretfully into the night. "How should I know, in this darkness?" he demanded sullenly. "We've been drifting for upwards o' an hour. Ye must pray, all o'ye, that the wind do blow us to sh-shea. Elsh we'll be sh-shwept into the arms of those murthering wretches waiting on the shore!''

"Drunken sot!" muttered Thomas angrily.

"He couldn't prevent the storm," Margot pointed out. "The wind is blowing us back towards Bordeaux, is it not? Not towards the land?"

"Aye, pray it remains so! I had not counted on falling foul of wreckers!"

"Nor I!" For the first time a trickle of fear slid icily down Margot's spine. "I have heard they show no mercy."

"Nor do they. But we shall not fall into their hands, *doña*. We will drown first. But it will not come to that!"

Thomas's ebullient spirits lifted and he laughed into the teeth of the gale. "God's bones! But we are weaklings to be speaking of death!"

"I have yet to live! I cannot die before I have seen England! We must pray!"

Margot pulled her beads from the girdle at her waist and held them clasped against her breast while she recited a paternoster. Thomas's low murmur joined hers and followed it into an ave.

So, pressed together, they watched the twinkling lights which appeared whenever the ship crested a towering wave. At first they appeared to grow nearer. The ship swung and they were on its beam. Swung again and they disappeared to stern. By the time they reappeared on the starboard beam they had diminished, and before long had become pricks of light all but overwhelmed by the sun creeping up over the horizon, shining crimson beneath the louring storm-clouds.

Dawn brought a change. The clouds scurried away, the wind abated, and the seas became less high.

"Give thanks to the Virgin of the Sea!" cried the master with profound relief as the fear of shipwreck receded. "Caulk the leaks, yes worthless wights! Get ready to make sail!"

"Well." murmured Thomas, glancing down at the serene face so close to his own, "It seems our prayers are answered and we are not destined to end our days at the hands of savage wreckers." He bent his head to kiss the soft lips so invitingly near his own. They tasted of salt and the indefinable essence that was Marguerite Sedano. "Let us see how Cedric does," he suggested gruffly, untying the knots which bound them together.

Confused by that unexpected kiss and her own chaotic response, Margot hurriedly released herself from his hold.

Pushing trembling fingers through hair tousled by wind and drenched by sticky salt-spray, she looked down at her sodden gown, knew she looked a disreputable mess, and wondered why Thomas had kissed her.

Perhaps from reaction after shared danger? That made sense. The first time he had saluted her in that way she had just narrowly escaped capture and he had fought a bloody battle. So there was no need for her to get upset about it.

"And poor Inés," she murmured, in a voice rather less than steady. "Perhaps one of the hands will clean the cabin once we are under sail."

Thomas walked to the rail and sniffed the morning air. "The wind is freshening from the south," he told her cheerfully. "The storm is behind us. Methinks all is now set fair to take us quickly to England's shores."

Chapter Six

The weather, having done its best to sink the ship, turned benevolent. Over the next few days the vessel scudded along before a brisk south-westerly under a blue sky scattered with high-flying, feathery white clouds.

But the reassuring presence of another sail close by had gone. The *Queen of the Seas* had disappeared. Both ships had been blown off-course by the storm, and anxious eyes scanned the horizon for any sign of the vessel which carried so many of their comrades.

Due to the huge, rolling swell in the Channel, the ship continued to heave and rock, climbed one mountainous wave and hovered on its crest before swooping down to wallow in the trough, gathering its forces to scale the next wall of water. Margot gave up expecting Inés to carry out her duties, and resigned herself to tending her own needs until they landed.

During the day both Inés and Cedric lay on the deck under the striped canopy while Margot sat by, keeping her hands occupied with embroidery.

Life in the open air must suit her, she thought wryly. She had never felt more physically fit in her life. Yet the same could not be said of her mental state. Thomas was avoiding her.

Puzzled, hurt and depressed, she watched him from a distance while he immersed himself in honing the fighting skills of his men—a difficult enough task on the tiny, heaving decks. Since the night of the storm he had withdrawn the tentative, delicate friendship she had sensed forming between them.

Margot stirred uneasily whenever she thought of that night, and red flags of embarrassment burned in her cheeks. How could she have allowed herself to spend so many hours wrapped in Thomas's cloak, so close that she could feel his heartbeat through his tunic? Or allowed him to kiss her the way he had without protest? Perhaps he thought her forward, wanton. Now the danger had passed he wanted to make it clear that his impulsive kiss had meant nothing.

Irritatingly, she found Thomas's attitude hurtful, difficult to shrug off. Sweet Jesu! She had realised at once that it meant nothing, without his rubbing it in so pointedly! And, in any case, what did the opinion of a rather obscure knight matter? She would soon pass out of his ken.

She glanced up to encounter Thomas's regard across the width of the vessel. His eyes held nothing, no laughter, no warmth—no censure either. Disconcerted, she dropped her head lest he see the tell-tale colour rising to her cheeks.

Foolish woman! To let his opinion upset her! She breathed deeply, eyeing the tossing seas thoughtfully. Certainly, she felt more alive than ever before! So why was her heart gripped by pain? Surely not because one man rejected and distrusted her!

She could but live each day as it came, and ignore a future she could do nothing to shape.

And ignore, too, the author of her discontent.

"Land ho!"

The cry from the look-out in the top at the masthead brought answering shouts from below, and the master from his cabin.

Four days after the storm, the coast of England swam hazily into Margot's eager view. She hung over the ship's side as it drew nearer, seeing the high cliffs, the rocky coves which, like those on the coast of Finistère, could spell doom to a ship in bad weather.

"There are wreckers here, too."

The familiar voice behind brought her head round. Her eyes sparkling with excitement, for the moment she forgot Thomas's strange withdrawal and her determination to ignore him. He was close to her now, a solid, comforting, relaxed figure with a rakish grin on his face, his eyes laughing, once again reading her thoughts with uncanny skill.

"I'm glad the weather is fine! Those rocks look dangerous!"

"Aye. We'll reach the Wen estuary before nightfall, but the master says we'll have to wait for the morning tide before we can cross the bar and sail into port. One more night aboard, *doña*."

"I have enjoyed the voyage"

"As have I. I shall be sorry to step ashore. We will lie at Wenstaple Castle for at least one night."

He gave her a last, brief smile and turned away. To say that he would be sorry to go ashore was true in one sense. He always enjoyed being at sea. But on this occasion he would be glad to escape the confines of the ship.

Margot's presence was disturbing. Holding her in his arms during the storm had been a mistake, kissing her a disaster, but he had acted instinctively, driven by that cursed need to protect. So warm, so vital, so courageous she had been! Marguerite Sedano was not the type of woman who normally attracted him; yet from the first he had felt invisible ties drawing them together. Her subtle allure threatened to lead him into behaviour at odds with his duty.

He had a mistress, he wanted no other, though God knew when he would see Beth again. And honour prevented his taking advantage of his position as Marguerite Sedano's protector to impose himself upon her. So he had made a strategic withdrawal. His duty was to guard her and see to her needs, nothing more.

By George! But he hoped soon to be relieved of that duty!

The last dying rays of the sun lit the granite walls and towers of a castle standing high on the red cliffs guarding the entrance to the Wen Estuary. The ship rocked gently, waiting for the moment when the great sail could be hoisted again.

"Wenfrith," Thomas told her, lowering his defences further as the moment of release drew near. "The chief manor of the fiefdom granted to the Baron Jean d'Evreux after the Conquest, and passed on through his issue since then. Where William, my father, lived, where I was born, and where my brother Richard prefers to reside."

"And where I was knighted," said Cedric, who had joined them at the rail despite the tinge of green still colouring his complexion.

Thomas wandered off, his gaze fixed intently upon the castle above. When he strolled back from the fore-castle, his eyes were still strained towards the buildings.

"They are in residence!" he exclaimed. "See, Richard's arms fly from the tower!"

"Mayhap he did not travel to Windsor this St George's Day. I hope everyone is well," said Cedric in concern.

"I was there in the autumn. Everyone was bursting with health. Perhaps the master would lower the boat, and put you ashore at Lower Wenfrith," suggested Thomas.

"I will ask him! Tonight would suit me well. Could we not all go ashore, and let our baggage follow?"

"I must see to the men and horses when we arrive at Wenstaple. And Doña Sedano remains with me."

"You would not trust her to my care?"

"She is my responsibility," Thomas reminded him heavily.

"I am sorry to be such a burden," shot Margot angrily. "An you would trust me, Sir Thomas, your duty would be less irksome!"

She spun on her heel and stalked off to the cabin. With Inés incapacitated she had packing to do, and another moment of Thomas's company would bring the tears, already pricking her lids, to her eyes. Tears of frustration and anger, she told herself grimly, ignoring the strange ache in her heart.

Cedric and Guy came into the cabin to collect a few things, and minutes later she went out to watch them climb down the rope ladder hanging from the stern. The rowboat, occupied by four sturdy oarsmen waiting to make the long pull ashore, rocked gently beside the huge rudder.

"I will look forward to seeing you in a few days, lady," he murmured as he took her hand and lightly kissed her fingers. "The Earl and Countess will be expecting you."

"I look forward to the visit, sir."

Watching Cedric descend the ladder with unexpected agility, "He will recover more quickly ashore," she murmured.

"Aye." Thomas stood beside her to monitor his brother-in-law's progress. "You will not be parted for long."

Margot moved away abruptly. Thomas annoyed her with his innuendoes. What did he mean? Did he imagine she would pine for Cedric? Stupid man!

With Cedric gone there would be more room within the confines of the small cabin. No doubt Thomas would choose to lay his pallet on deck, as usual. Not that she blamed him for preferring the open deck. She would welcome the chance to sleep there herself.

And she had to admit that his presence inside would have badly affected her slumbers. His nearness evoked a mixture of excitement, irritation and security she found it difficult to explain or ignore.

She heard the boat return and the crew clamber aboard. Although the ship was in sheltered waters, the constant rocking motion as it rode at anchor had intensified rather than helped Inés's sickness. Poor child! Margot thanked the Blessed Saints for her own strong stomach and fell asleep with a smile of anticipation on her lips.

Tomorrow she would stand on English soil for the first time, and see Thomas in his own surroundings. Not as a soldier fighting in a foreign land, but as an English knight on familiar territory. In a couple of days he would be among his kin. A man was most himself when he was at home. With a stab of alarm she realised just how much she desired to see him truly himself, and pushed the knowledge to the far corner of her mind.

During the night, the *Queen of the Seas* dropped anchor near by. The relief aboard when she was sighted at dawn brought Margot early to the deck, to join her delight with that of all the others.

Thomas's pennoncel streamed from the masthead as the ship crossed the bar, leading the way up the Wen. His herald blew a fanfare from the forecastle, and the plaintive note of an answering horn drifted down from the castle watch-tower.

Margot craned her neck to glimpse the fortress, whose walls, built so close to the edge, seemed to descend into the waves breaking against the sharp granite rocks at the foot of the cliff.

On they sailed, passing the small fishing village where Cedric must have landed the previous evening. The sun had risen not long since, neither so fierce nor so bright as it was in Spain. It cast a softness over the landscape, restful to eyes used to the harsh glare of Castile.

In places the trees came down almost to the water's edge. In others, open, sloping fields held grazing cattle and sheep, or men toiling on their strips. Wooded or open, the land bordering the estuary was beautiful, green and fertile. Isolated hamlets, marked by church towers, hove into view and passed out of sight in their wake.

As the ships neared Wenstaple, their companies raised rough voices in a ragged yet touchingly solemn chant, a hymn of praise to the Virgin of the Seas, who had brought them safely to port.

"You must rejoice to be almost home!" she exclaimed.

When Thomas turned to answer her his eyes shone with a glad light he did not attempt to disguise.

"Aye, home," he murmured, with so much feeling that Margot's breath caught. She had realised he loved Wenfrith, but not quite how much. Or was it the shadowy Countess of Wenstaple he loved?

Something of the brightness of the morning seemed to dim.

By noon the ships had tied up. Thomas supervised the disembarkation while Margot sat on the after-castle deck, out of the way of the noise and bustle, awaiting her turn, the last to step ashore.

At last Thomas was ready, and came to fetch her. Inés followed at their heels, staggering across the gangplank to stand dizzily on the quay.

"The ground is moving!" exclaimed Margot with a grimace, swaying slightly herself. "I feel more strange now than ever I did on board!"

Thomas moved to help her, taking her arm in a firm but gentle grip. The first time he'd touched her since the storm. The effect on Margot was like a thrust from a dagger. She flinched, and Thomas instantly released her.

"'Twill pass," he told her expressionlessly. "Your horse is saddled. Let me help you to mount."

"We are to ride?"

"Aye, those of us still with mounts. We will enter by the main gate, which is outside the borough's walls."

Edwin reached down to Inés and lifted her into the saddle behind him with the ease of long practice. She moaned and rested her swimming head against his broad back, clasping the lean young man tightly about his waist.

Margot smiled slightly to herself. It occurred to her that Inés had long ago forgotten Domingo.

She placed her daintily shod foot into Thomas's cupped hands, and he threw her into Fleurette's saddle. The mare was restless, eager for the exercise denied her for so long. Margot soothed with words and hands, hoping that her head would stop swimming, that she wouldn't fall from her seat. How she would have valued Thomas's steadying hand now! But she had offended him with her stupid reaction to his touch.

All the horses were equally restless, eager to be off now they were freed from the stalls which had imprisoned them for so long. Even Rasmus was excited, and Thomas's hands were fully occupied as he brought the great destrier under control. He quietened him quickly, though most of the other animals continued rearing and stamping. They snorted, their shoes rang on the cobbled surface, their harnesses jangled, the men shouted and cursed.

Thomas raised his arm and his voice. "Advance!"

Out of the town gate they streamed, a furl of banners followed by a tramping phalanx of halberds and bows. Then through the barbican, over the drawbridge and under the raised portcullis, their arrival heralded by a blast from Jack's trumpet.

They dismounted before the main steps.

"Come," said Thomas, "let us find our quarters. No doubt you will relish a bath."

There he spoke the truth! "I long for one!" she admitted with a quick smile. "The salt has stiffened my gown and seems caked over my entire body!"

Then she blushed, realising that her enthusiasm had led her into an embarrassing statement.

Thomas did not seem to notice her confusion.

"The constable and his lady will be ready to make us

welcome. Come, *doña*. Let me put you in the capable hands of Lady Appleby.''

They climbed the steps and entered the Great Hall, where they were greeted by a stout, breathless lady of advanced years. Clad all in black, she wore a widow's barbe and veil.

''Lady Appleby?'' Thomas bowed, his voice anxious and uncertain as his clear grey eyes took in the woman's garb. ''You...Sir Hugo?'' he finished helplessly.

''God's greetings, Sir Thomas.'' The woman curtsied, summoning a smile to her round face. ''You have not heard. Sir Hugo died a month since.''

Thomas took her hand. ''How?''

''Struck down in his sleep. When morning came we could not wake him. God gave him fifty-three years of life,'' she added quietly.

''A good age, and he did not suffer,'' said Thomas gently. ''But you remain here?''

''For the time being. The Earl, God bless him, has given me time to rearrange my life. I shall go to my daughter in Hampshire. Earl Richard was in no hurry to replace Sir Hugo immediately, and left the castle in my charge, with Sir Robert Asham to organise its defence. He intends to offer the office of constable to Sir Cedric de Clare.''

''To Cedric? That could be a timely appointment! Sir Cedric travelled from Castile with us and is already at Wenfrith. Your husband's death must be the reason for my brother's not being at Windsor.''

''Aye. He and the Countess were at Acklane when the news reached them. They returned immediately. But we keep the lady waiting, Sir Thomas!''

A burn of red coloured Thomas's cheekbones. ''My apologies, *doña*.''

Margot gave a dismissive shake of her head. "No apology is necessary. Introduce us, sir, that I may offer my condolences."

He did so, and Margot smiled at her hostess with sympathy.

"I, too, am recently widowed, though I believe I grieve less than you, my lady. Mine was not a happy union. I had no opportunity to purchase mourning before I was ordered to accompany Sir Thomas to England, and now I see no point in wearing it. I wish to make a new life, and resume my old style as daughter of the Comte de Limousin, that of Lady Marguerite de Bellac. Do you think me unfeeling?"

"I would not presume to judge, my lady." Lady Appleby's plump features beamed a kindly smile. "But you must be fatigued. Will you not follow me? I will show you to a guest chamber. Sir Thomas, your usual chamber is prepared, as ever. Come!" she ordered briskly.

Margot glanced instinctively to Thomas for permission. He nodded imperceptibly before bowing with courtly grace.

"No doubt we shall meet at supper, *doña*."

"That young man looks uncommonly serious," wheezed Lady Appleby as she puffed up the twisting stone stairs ahead of Marguerite. "Perhaps 'twas the battle that changed him. 'Twas his first really bloody encounter."

Margot doubted that, remembering the confident, smiling, teasing man who had accompanied the Duke of Lancaster to Sedano. No, that serious, repressive mantle had not descended upon him until the encounter with Domingo and his cronies. It was the responsibility of guarding her that had taken his light-heartedness, and she regretted the change. But neither that incident nor

his consequent distrust had been caused by any fault in
her. To feel guilt was irrational.

"You know him well, lady?" she asked.

"Aye, tolerably. My husband had been constable here
for ten years. Sir Thomas was a mere stripling when first
I met him, just about to enter Prince John's service he
was, and proud as a peacock."

The widow spoke affectionately, and Margot wondered if anyone disliked Thomas. Especially women.
She recognised instinctively that he could charm any
member of the opposite sex, whatever her age. If he
wanted to.

But other women were not his prisoner; for, however
carefully her position was wrapped about with words,
that was what she was. Perhaps only she had seen the
stern side of Thomas. His ambition, his lack of trust, had
made him overly harsh in his attitude towards her. Yet
through it all his charm had surfaced from time to time,
and she was no more immune than the rest of woman-
kind, she realised ruefully.

"He has done well, the Duke trusts him implicitly,"
she responded pleasantly.

"Aye, he's a good lad. Will this suit Your Ladyship?"

Her escort flung open a heavy oak door hung on long
iron hinges, and stood aside for Margot to pass.

The room was not spacious nor the window large, but
the latter overlooked the river and was filled with little
panes of glass fitted into strips of lead. The big bed was
draped with dark blue damask, dominating a chamber
whose walls were hung with red and azure cloth. A heap
of kindling lay ready in the hearth, but the fire was not
alight.

"I shall be comfortable here."

Rushes stirred, releasing a sweet smell as she walked across to an arched opening on the other side of the room, to find a small pallet-chamber.

"Your maid can sleep in there if you wish. I will have a pallet brought up, and your coffers, of course."

"Thank you." Inés had followed the ladies up, and Margot motioned her into the small room. "You will sleep here," she explained in Spanish.

Lady Appleby prattled on. "The privy is along the gallery, to your left."

Here Margot nodded. Her nose had already located that necessary convenience.

"An you need aught else, send your maid to me."

"She speaks but a few words of English," admitted Margot ruefully.

"Then I will send you one of my maids. Make what use of her you like. She will ensure that your wishes are met."

"Thank you." Margot smiled warmly. "You are most kind. I so look forward to discovering my English heritage! I was never happy in Castile."

"It must be difficult for you, being brought here against your will. Sir Thomas did not fully explain your situation. He calls you *doña* still?"

"Aye." Unless he forgot. Margot thought wistfully of the couple of occasions when he had called her not even Lady Marguerite, but Margot. She shrugged, annoyed with herself for caring, and explained her position to her interested hostess. "I am in his charge, and I believe he uses my Castilian title as a reminder of my position."

The stout little woman suddenly grinned, her shining red face sceptical in its frame of white. "As a defence, I'd say! He is afraid of becoming too attached to a lady ranked so high above him! Your father is a *comte*, my lady. He is but a knight, and a bastard.''

Such an idea had never occurred to Margot. One of their rare moments of rapport had been when they'd exchanged distant humour over their different stations. No, that could not be worrying him. And as for his fearing to form an attachment, that idea was quite simply ridiculous. He had made it unflatteringly plain that she was not the kind of woman to arouse his admiration.

She laughed lightly, though the sound rang forced in her own ears. "I think you are mistaken, lady. He merely wants to keep me aware that my freedom is extremely limited!''

Lady Appleby shrugged, unconvinced, but said no more on the subject, promising as she left to send up a tub and kettles of hot water so that Margot could soak the salt and grime from her weary body.

Thomas might be a bastard, thought Margot later, but in this castle he was treated as though he were the Earl himself. At Sedano he had usurped the lord's seat, here it was accorded him as of right. And, since Lady Appleby relinquished her normal place to one who outranked her, once more Margot and Thomas sat side by side, presiding over the meal.

This Hall was larger than Sedano's, and would have been dark without the multitude of candles and torches used to illuminate it. The walls were hung with rich tapestries, banners, shields and weapons.

Linen clothes covered all the trestles, and gold and silver graced the high table. The many courses all tasted delicious after the meagre rations available on board the *Lady Anne*.

Inés appeared to have recovered her spirits and even

her appetite. Edwin was flirting outrageously with her, and Inés, flashing her dark eyes, was positively encouraging him. Margot pursed her lips, deciding she'd have to have another word with her maid.

Thomas had followed her gaze. "Your serving-wench appears to have recovered quickly. You are feeling refreshed, *doña?*" he asked.

"Aye, sir."

With a contented smile on her face, Margot remembered the sheer heaven of immersing her dirty, weary body in hot, scented water, and having it scrubbed by Inés and Jane—the little maid Lady Appleby had sent to help her—and then dried with a large, soft cloth.

"You have braided your hair. Very fashionable."

Margot felt the embarrassment rise in her cheeks. He had noticed, and not been afraid to remark!

"The maid Lady Appleby sent me is skilled in such things. Inés must be taught. I have little reason to dress fashionably, but nevertheless I do not wish to be branded a dowd. I must preserve some self-respect, Sir Thomas."

"Why so defensive, *doña?*" he grinned. "The braids suit you, and your circlet is beautiful. Such exquisite workmanship, and the gems shine with a brilliance to match your eyes. Did it come from the Orient?"

Margot swallowed down acute discomfort. Compliments from Sir Thomas? What next?

"Possibly," she answered stiffly. "It has been in my family for years. Mayhap some ancestor brought it back from the Crusades."

She returned to her meat with determination, though her appetite had gone. She ate in silence for a while, struggling with herself. She did not wish to ask Sir Thomas for a favour, but needs must.

"My coffers were stolen in the Pyrénées," she reminded him abruptly, breaking a silence which he had not sought to fill. "I must replace the apparel I lost. May I visit the town? Lady Appleby can probably advise me."

Thomas chewed for a moment, swallowed the mouthful of venison, and threw the bone to be fought over by growling dogs.

"Of course, *doña*. If we delay our journey to Wenfrith for a couple of days, no doubt at least some of your new garments can be completed before we leave. The remainder can follow."

He smiled, a warm, friendly smile which sent an unexpected quiver to knock at Margot's heart. "We can exercise early on the morrow, if you will, after which I will escort you into the town. 'Tis a long while since I visited the mercer and tailor myself."

Despite all his sweet talk, thought Margot, her spirits sagging, he still didn't trust her to visit the town without him to guard her. Where did he think she could go in a strange land?

Then she remembered the ships tied up along the quay.

Perhaps he thought she'd attempt to buy a passage across the Channel.

It was an idea. But not one to be contemplated with any seriousness.

She had, after all, given her word, and, however worthless Sir Thomas might think it to be, to her it was sacred. And, besides, she had no desire to leave the English shores as yet.

Chapter Seven

Three days later they set out for Wenfrith. Margot sat straight in her saddle, pleased with her new travelling attire—a green sendal kirtle, the tight sleeves buttoned down to her knuckles, and over it a short scarlet cotehardie trimmed with gold braid and fastened by gilt buttons down the front. Because the spring day had a chill in it, she also wore a silver-grey velvet riding cloak lined with scarlet and green striped Alexander and trimmed with white miniver fur. A chaplet of twisted matching fabrics sat fashionably atop the veil, protecting her braided and coiled hair.

As promised, Thomas had purchased all her new garments from the Duke's purse. Margot accepted the help with reserved dignity and hidden relief. Her slender funds might have to last a long time.

The expedition into the bustling town came after a restless night she had been glad to abandon as dawn streaked the sky. How could she sleep when the bed appeared to heave and heel under her the moment she laid her head on the silken pillow? When the silence had seemed almost threatening after so many nights rocked to sleep to the sound of creaks and slaps and hissing waves? When her thoughts sent confused pictures to tease her mind with new impressions and old memories in which Thomas figured all too prominently?

With the sun sending its first rays to tint the greyness of the dawn with gold, she had met him at the stables, as arranged the previous evening. Fleurette greeted her with a soft snuffle, dancing her dainty hoofs in her eagerness to be off. Rasmus tossed his head and snorted as Thomas leapt into his saddle, and then they were galloping through green English countryside along a track leading westwards towards the distant, mist-shrouded moors. Being a heavily built charger, Rasmus was less fleet of foot than Fleurette, and Margot delighted in teasing Thomas with her speed.

His beard had gone. She preferred it that way. Her breath caught on a laugh.

"Knowing I was embarking for Castile, I left my lighter horse at Wenfrith when last I was there," Thomas informed her gaily. "He will give Fleurette a good race!"

"What is he called?" asked Margot.

"Pegasus! He flies like the wind! A dappled grey, bred by my brother from a line begun when his stallion was mated with Eleanor's mare twenty years ago." He wheeled Rasmus to face the way they had come. "We had better turn back an we want to break our fast before setting out to visit the town."

"I do not know what I want most," confessed Margot as she reluctantly turned Fleurette's head. "A longer ride or new clothes!"

"You can ride on many another day!"

Margot soon realised that she had misjudged Thomas. He had not escorted her into town as her warder. He truly did wish to buy cloth for himself and visit the tailor on his own behalf.

For the journey to Wenfrith he had shed his armour in favour of his new apparel—saffron tights which clung to his horseman's thighs revealing every movement of his strong muscles, and an azure cote-hardie trimmed with cloth of gold. A deep-blue velvet mantelet, fastened on his right shoulder with an ornate gold brooch studded with precious gems, swung gracefully from his shoulders to brush his horse's back, its white silken lining gleaming as he moved. The same materials swathed his felt hat and draped in swinging folds over his left ear. His golden spurs of knighthood were attached to a pair of cordwain buskins reaching almost to his knees.

His lean fingers held the reins lightly as they rode the ridge overlooking the Wen Estuary. Margot glanced his way and a sudden, disconcerting tension in her nerves gripped her yet again. Armour carried with it the glamour of honour and chivalry, but in this outfit Thomas was the picture of a perfect, gentle knight, fit to turn the head of any maiden.

Or widow, she thought ruefully. Were she not immune, she could fancy herself attracted by her custodian. Under the fashionable hat his brown hair waved carelessly on his forehead and at his nape. The cleft in his chin emphasised the lean squareness of his bronzed, clean-shaven face, a face full of inherent command which attracted attention and respect without any help from those lively grey eyes—eyes from which she sometimes found it impossible to tear her own once their gazes locked.

Undoubtedly he stirred feelings in her she found strange and unwelcome yet pleasurably compelling. When she thought of where they could lead, her mind balked and her body shrank. Thomas was red-blooded, strong, all man. He would not be content for long with languishing looks and love songs, poetry and sighs. He might admire an unattainable woman like the Lady Blanche, but he would not waste much time brooding because he could not have her. He would need to express his feelings in a physical way, to possess the woman he loved.

Feminine instinct told her he was not entirely indifferent, despite the fact that she wasn't fair, she wasn't beautiful, had little physically to recommend her. Perhaps that was what Lady Appleby had noticed. Lust. Hadn't she seen the blaze of desire in his eyes in the pavilion at Burgos? Felt the promise implicit in the touch of his lips? And, like other men, he would probably take any woman who showed herself willing.

It was at this point in her musings that the memory of Roberto's possession intruded. Revulsion sent a shiver through her body. Her thoughts shied away. At all costs, she must not let Thomas guess…he might interpret it as an invitation… A nervous tremor skittered along her nerves, and she tore her eyes from his erect figure to stare energetically at the track ahead.

Her hands moved spasmodically, jerking at Fleurette's rein, and the horse snorted in protest. Margot smoothed the mare's neck in apology, straightened her shoulders and forced herself to concentrate on the ride.

They were a small party—just Thomas's groom, archer and man-at-arms, her Juan and Inés, with six additional men-at-arms to protect them and their possessions on the safer English roads, where the fear was of attack by footpads or bands of outlaws rather than either enemy or rebellious forces. The remainder of the Duke's retinue had been dismissed at Wenstaple to scatter to their own homes until called back into service.

Their way was soon joined by another track, which Thomas informed her led to the London road, and shortly afterwards he reined in by a gap in the trees.

"Wenfrith," he told her, nodding towards the pile of buildings glowing golden in the noonday sun. They were too far away for her to see clearly, but Margot felt a surge of excitement not unmixed with apprehension as she glimpsed their destination.

"How long before we arrive?" she asked.

"A couple of hours. We should be in good time for supper."

His muscles rippled as he pressed his thighs against Rasmus's sides. The great beast moved forward, and Fleurette needed no urging to follow.

They breasted a rise to see Wenfrith spread out before them—the great turreted keep surrounded by outbuildings and fortifications, with newer buildings, which must be the manor house, nestled in its lee with an extension to the protective curtain wall.

A church lay between the huddle of cottages and the castle; red fields and green pastures spread over a sweep of land right down to the waters of the estuary.

"There is Lower Wenfrith, where Cedric landed," Thomas told her, pointing. "See? Those dwellings and the jetty by the water's edge."

"I see it. The land looks well cultivated, I love the red soil. Is it fertile?"

"Tolerably, I believe. You must ask Lord Richard. He has become an enthusiastic farmer over the years. I once had dreams of cultivating our strips here, helping my brother Stephen." He paused, and his lips twisted in a spasm that looked remarkably like pain. Then he laughed lightly, his vibrant eyes alight with self-mockery. "But, as you can see, my way has taken another course."

"Yet you have lands you could cultivate, if you so desired. The dream could not have been too enticing."

"Perhaps not." He glanced at her quickly. "Sedano was well husbanded, yet Don Roberto was much abroad. Was that your doing?"

"Partly," she admitted. "At first I did it from necessity, since our steward had become lazy without supervision, but my interest deepened over the years. There is great pleasure in making the soil yield one's needs. And our soil there, despite the proximity of the stream, was arid. Not as unproductive as the plain, but poor enough. Vines grew well."

"Hence your excellent vintage! Vines grown here often produce sour wine. Perhaps that is why most people content themselves with brewing ale or fermenting honey for mead."

She laughed happily. "I shall look forward to sampling your brews!"

Her moment of unease had passed. She had her emotions well in hand again. Thomas was once more just a pleasant, informative companion who might turn into a stern, accusing warder at the drop of a kerchief. Just as it should be.

As they approached the castle and passed through the scattering of cob cottages in the village, Margot noticed that all the roofs were newly thatched. Those children and adults who stood bowing and greeting Thomas as he passed were not ragged. The little community exuded an air of modest prosperity.

"'Tis different from when I lived here," murmured Thomas, reading her face as though it were a parchment-scroll. "My brother has done much to improve his people's lot. For one thing, there are no serfs left. All are free men, paying rent or tithes for the land they hold. His own demesne is worked by hired labourers.''

''And this has brought prosperity?''

''It seems so, in some degree. He maintains that men work better when they are free, though many of his peers dispute his claim. Come!'' he cried in a ringing voice. ''Herald, sound the horn! Welcome to Wenfrith!''

The little procession clattered across the drawbridge, under the portcullis in the gatehouse, and on across the castle bailey to a new gate in the old curtain wall which led to a bridge across the moat and so to the private ward. Here, Margot could see for the first time the graceful proportions, the decorated arches, the stained glass in the windows of the buildings which lined it on three sides. The home the Lord of Wenfrith had built for his bride.

Grooms rushed forward to help them dismount. The first person to emerge from the great oak door was none other than Sir Cedric, though he was not alone. Two boys of about twelve and eight dashed out behind him, surrounded by a barking pack of dogs.

''Uncle Tamkin! Uncle Tamkin!'' chorused the boys, pausing only to execute sketchy bows before making a bee-line for Thomas, whose grin widened until it threatened to split his face.

''Nicholas! Philip! How are you? How are your parents?''

''All right,'' Nicholas told him offhandedly as Thomas laid an arm round each small shoulder, ''but how was the battle? Did you kill anyone?''

''Bloodthirsty youth!'' grinned Thomas affectionately as the two lads, Nicholas dark, Philip fair, began emulating the leaping dogs in their boisterous welcome.

"I've had a hard time persuading them that I am not a wounded hero, like their father, but a poor soldier with a weak stomach," grinned Cedric cheerfully. "Welcome, brother. Welcome, Lady Margot."

Thomas turned the boys to face Margot, who stood quietly by.

"Nicholas, Philip, make your bows to the Doña Sedano." His laughing eyes met her more sombre gaze, brooding, unfathomable as the sea, he thought. "I am sure she would prefer to be addressed as Lady Margot. Lady Margot," he continued softly, "meet my brother's younger sons."

Her eyes lit up at his words and tone. She smiled fondly at the children.

"Nicholas, Philip, I have heard much of you," she told them a trifle untruthfully. "I met your brother Richard in Castile. I am honoured to meet you both." She dropped them a small curtsy, which they returned with well-schooled bows.

"You saw Dickon? Uncle Cedric says he was knighted!" exclaimed Nicholas excitedly. "He must have killed lots of the enemy!"

"Not necessarily, Nick," chided Thomas, dampening his nephew's blood-lust with a scowl. "But you can be sure he fought with bravery and skill. As did Sir Cedric."

"As did we all, to the best of our abilities," said Cedric quietly. "And, God be thanked, we all came through unscathed. Now come inside and meet the remainder of the family!"

Margot gathered up her skirts to step across the cobbles to the door. Behind her, the ward had been grassed or paved and planted with bushes and herbs. A peaceful haven, so different from the bustle of the bailey left behind on the other side of the moat.

She was led past the screens and into the Great Hall. A chamber seemingly full of light, since the side next to the court consisted almost entirely of high, mullioned windows with trefoil tracery decorating the arches. The coloured glass threw strange patterns on the linen cloths already laid on boards set ready for the evening meal. Servants bustled about, the steward of the hall directing operations from the dais. A fire blazed in a hearth built into the massive side wall. The sound of minstrels tuning their instruments drew her gaze to the gallery above.

As Margot hovered, waiting for Sir Thomas or Sir Cedric to lead her forward, she became aware that both men were watching the rapid approach of a slender woman dressed in pale blue, who greeted Thomas with outstretched arms.

"Tamkin! How good it is to see you!"

"My lady!"

Thomas dropped to one knee and took the outstretched hands, kissing the cool fingers clasped in his. Then he jumped to his feet and wrapped the lady in a bear-hug. She threaded her arms around his waist and rested her golden head, the colour only slightly dimmed by streaks of grey, on his broad chest.

"Thank God you are safe!"

"Aye, that *all* our loved ones are safe, and that He gave the Prince of Wales victory at Nájera. Welcome home, Thomas."

"Brother! I did not see you coming!"

"Nay," laughed Richard, "you were too busy embracing my wife!"

Margot had noticed the tall imposing figure limping towards them with a young girl at his heels, although

most of her attention had been focused on Sir Thomas
and the Lady Eleanor. The affection between those two
was evident, yet she knew it had nothing to do with the
carnal love found between men and women. 'Twas more
like that between mother and son. And, although
Thomas had called the other man brother, the greying
Earl regarded the young knight from eyes not only filled
with fatherly affection, but so like Thomas's own that
Margot felt a jolt of shock.

The Lady Eleanor gave Thomas's chest a gentle pat
and he let her go to greet his half-brother. The two men
clasped arms and then the girl was lifted in a bear-hug
and swung inelegantly off her feet.

"Uncle Thomas!" she protested, her pretty, flushed
face full of indignation. "You must not treat me so! I
am no longer a child!"

"Nay, Thomas," laughed her father as Thomas obediently put her down and she straightened her red silk
skirts, tossing her dark head in reproach. "Isobel is of
marriageable age now, and goes to join her betrothed's
family in just a few weeks!"

"I am sorry, Lady Isobel," said Thomas with a deep
bow, his serious expression belied by the laughter in his
eyes.

Margot thought she had been forgotten until Thomas
turned to take her hand and lead her forward. The
warmth of his hold seeped up her arm, making her heart
jump.

"My lord, my lady. Sir Cedric will have told you that
I was bringing the Doña Sedano with me. I am sure she
will find a welcome here. *Doña*, this is my half-brother,
Richard d'Evreux, Earl of Wenstaple, and his Countess,
the Lady Eleanor."

Greetings were exchanged, and this time it was Sir

Cedric who said, "Call her Lady Margot, 'tis what she prefers!"

Margot smiled quietly, and nodded. "Now I am widowed, I shall revert to my family name, de Bellac."

Eleanor smiled, taking her hand in a comforting clasp. "We will abide by your wish," she promised.

Inés was volubly appreciative of the guest chamber into which they were shown, admiring the window overlooking the sea, the azure damask drapes embroidered with the Wenfrith emblems Margot had come to know so well. Straw matting covered the rough-hewn planks of the floor, and a fire already blazed in the hearth, warming water for washing.

The quiet days passed so fast that Margot's new wardrobe arrived before she had much chance to miss it. She was made to feel so welcome, so much at home. Her appreciation of the Earl and Countess brimmed over into affection.

"Richard is often away for months at a time," lamented Eleanor sadly as they sat one sunny noon in the shady court, enjoying the fresh air.

Her ladies sat some distance away, and all were occupied on some necessary task to do with spinning, sewing or embroidery. The baby toddled about the grass under the strict eye of a woman called Kate, whose looks were marred by a split upper lip, and Eleanor's old nurse, Joan, who had recovered from an illness of the winter, though she looked frail. The two women between them had run the nursery since Dickon's birth, and all the children regarded them with affection.

"But I would not prevent his going if I could," Eleanor went on with a smile. "Richard needs to feel that he is serving his Sovereign. He has a sound head on his shoulders, and his advice is valued."

Margot nodded her agreement. "Sir Thomas always speaks of you both with great respect and affection. Of course, he feels he owes his present good fortune to your intervention in his life."

She was fishing for information, and if Eleanor recognised this she chose to gratify her guest's curiosity.

"When I first came here he was working as a scullion in the kitchen." She smiled reminiscently. "Poor little lad! He was only seven, and so thin! Of course, I had no idea who he was when I decided to make him my page."

"Did Lord Richard know?"

"Nay! He was as surprised as I to find that he had two half-brothers living on the manor!"

"Many men would have turned them off."

Eleanor smiled. "Richard is basically too fair and generous for that—though he does have his prejudices," she admitted with a fond, rueful smile. "He brought them into the family immediately."

Margot smiled back. "I'm sure he is! But the other brother—where is he?"

"Stephen? He was much older." Eleanor paused, sighing slightly before she continued. "Richard made him seneschal of all the manors within the Wenfrith fiefdom, but I am afraid he abused his position."

"How dreadful." Margot could feel the other woman's anguish, a palpable thing hanging between them. "What did he do?" she whispered.

Eleanor concentrated on twisting thread on the spindle before pulling more wool from her distaff, her normally soft lips set in a grim line. "His ambition brought about his downfall," she told Margot at last. "He tried to murder Richard—and me, for I was carrying Dickon at the time—in order to claim Wenfrith and all that went with it. Richard locked him away while he decided what to do with him, but he escaped.''

Margot gasped. ''Do you know what became of him?''

''We believe he died in the great pestilence. Despite widespread enquiries, he has not been hard of since.''

''Poor Thomas!''

''Aye. He was not knowingly involved, but he was young and trusting. He did what his brother told him.'' Eleanor concentrated on her spinning again before she looked up. Her clear blue eyes met Margot's with an intent, searching gaze. ''When he discovered that he'd been administering his lord—he did not then know who his father was—poison instead of the healing herbs Stephen had said, he was distraught.''

Margot stared, speechless. Her whole person seemed to freeze as she imagined the emotions which must have racked Thomas when he'd found out. ''So I should imagine!'' she whispered at last. ''Poor, poor child!''

''His brother's dishonesty affected him badly,'' said Eleanor quietly. ''Tamkin finds it difficult to put his trust in anyone now.'' Her lips curled in a rueful smile, but her eyes were watchful. ''I notice he seems to take his custodial duties very seriously. He will not allow you to ride out without him, even here, where you could scarcely hope to escape your unfortunate bonds, and it irks you.''

The directness of her gaze brought colour to Margot's cheeks. The Lady Eleanor knew her questions were far from disinterested! Margot lowered her lids, evading that penetrating blue gaze. ''I am sorry I make it so plain. But I have given my word of honour and, even if I wished to escape, I would not do so.''

Eleanor seemed to relax, and smiled mischievously.

"His reason for accompanying you may not be quite what you think. But even if it is," she went on quickly, seeing Margot frown, "try not to resent his distrust of you, Lady Margot. He cannot help himself. Try to understand that he was taught an early lesson in betrayal. In his heart, I am sure he knows his attitude is wrong. One day he will acknowledge it."

Margot shrugged, assuming a carelessness she did not feel. "His attitude makes little difference to me."

"Does it not?" Eleanor allowed a small smile to touch her lips before she spoke again.

"Thomas was not the only one to suffer at Stephen's hands. He stole my brother's affianced bride."

"Sir Cedric's?"

"Aye. Anne Radcliffe helped Stephen to escape, and probably perished with him. It soured poor Cedric, who was such a merry, carefree lad."

"He seems happy and light-hearted enough to me. When he is not ill, at least," added Margot with a smile.

"Mayhap, but he has never married, and has devoted his life to soldiering." Eleanor sighed, and shook her head sadly. "He always wanted to be a knight, but he need not have spent his entire life abroad fighting. I do not believe I have thanked you adequately for your care of him."

"I did no more than I would have done for anyone in his condition."

"Nevertheless, I thank you. You have won his gratitude and admiration." Eleanor shot her another look, then lowered her lids to shield the expression in her blue eyes. "I wish he could find himself a wife. He will need one when he takes up his duties as Constable of Wenstaple."

Margot recognised the probe, and hid her embarrassment behind another smile. "He has accepted the appointment? Perhaps that is why he spends so much time with one of your ladies—the pretty dark one—the Lady Matilda, I think she is called."

"Matilda!" Eleanor showed surprise, though Margot thought she was not displeased. "She is also a widow," she murmured, "and of the right age. I wonder…"

"As you say, he will need a wife." Margot had seen the blossoming romance and silently applauded. Sir Cedric needed a woman's loving ministrations if he was to completely recover from his illness.

"Perhaps he realises it is time to forget the past and to settle down. He has fortune enough. And such a marriage would cause you no distress?" asked Eleanor, with a return to her normal directness.

"Me, my lady? No, why should it? I have a friendly interest in your brother. I like him, I enjoy his company, but no more." She had better get things straight once and for all. "I have no desire to remarry, I intend to remain single."

"You are still very young, my dear—"

"I know, but marriage does not attract me."

"Do not allow one unfortunate experience to prevent your enjoying the blessings of a true and loving union. I speak as one who has found great joy in my husband's love."

"You cannot imagine what I had to suffer."

"Perhaps not, but all men are not brutes like your late husband. Do you imagine that Cedric, or Thomas, or Dickon would treat any woman so? Most men are capable of care and tenderness in their loving."

A delicate flush rose to Margot's cheeks and she applied herself to carding the fluffy wool in her hand. "No. Yet I have no desire to experiment."

"Then what will you do with your life, Lady Margot? You do not strike me as one suited to the cloister."

Margot chuckled. "Nay, I am not! I believe I would die of boredom! As you know, I have a manor in Kent. Once I am free I shall go there and bring it back to profitability. I could offer a home to widows not so fortunate as myself."

Eleanor eyed her consideringly. "And will you be content?"

"I shall make myself so," replied Margot firmly, crushing down the doubts crowding her mind.

The prospect of such an existence appealed now even less than it had earlier. But what else could she do? Returning to her father's castle held no allure. She would lose her freedom if she lived under his roof.

"Here come the men!"

Margot looked up to find Thomas's gaze resting on her. He shifted it quickly. Cedric's, she noted with secret amusement, was bent towards Matilda. Richard, as usual, had eyes for no one but his beautiful wife.

Nicholas and Philip bounded at their heels still waving their blunted swords, which they immediately threw down in order to begin wrestling on the lawn like puppies. Philip would miss his brother when Nick went off as squire, thought Margot affectionately. The older boy was leaving at the same time as his sister, entering the service of Isobel's future father-in-law, to Eleanor's sorrow.

"But I have the comfort of knowing that they will be together," she had confided to Margot. "Unlike Dickon. He went alone to the Prince of Wales in Aquitaine. I was so anxious for him."

"But he came to no harm, my lady. And you will

have the baby Elizabeth at home for many a year yet,"
Margot had consoled.

Her eyes, unconsciously longing, strayed to the plump
child crowing with delight at the sight of a pretty but-
terfly flitting among the flowers.

While the ladies sat quietly at their tasks, the men had
been indulging in more strenuous pursuits, and Thomas
was the only one of the three whose feet did not drag.

"I am getting too old for this game," grinned Richard, ruefully rubbing protesting shoulder muscles and
easing the heavy chain-mail of his hauberk into a more
comfortable position as he sank down on a nearby
bench.

"You are fit as you ever were!" protested his wife
severely.

"And I have only now realised how much strength I
have yet to regain!" cried Cedric mock-tragically.
"Your fitness is disgusting, Thomas!"

"'Tis youth you need to regain," chaffed Thomas,
slapping Cedric's back so hard that the older man almost
choked. "Fighting is a young man's game!"

"Yet we old greybeards can teach you striplings a
thing or two when it comes to skill," rejoined Cedric
pointedly. "Richard disarmed you!"

"Aye, Richard can do so on occasion, but no other
man, save only John of Gaunt!"

"Remember Eltham?" laughed Eleanor. "The Prince
disarmed you even then, though you were both but children."

"And told me to go to him when I was ready, that he
would need good men if he were to serve the King his
father well! Aye, I remember, sweet lady. You were, I
believe, taking me to feed the ducks in the pond!"

"While my dear lord caroused with other Knights of

the Garter! John kept his promise, Tamkin. You have done well in his service, become one of his closest confidants and companions.''

"Aye. Until now."

Margot reddened again and shifted uncomfortably. Why could not Thomas stop resenting the order making him her guardian?

Eleanor heard the bitterness Thomas could not quite conceal, saw Margot's distress, and hastened to pour soothing balm on their hurts.

"He had entrusted you with a task of great importance both to himself and his brother of Wales. He knew he could rely on you to treat Lady Marguerite with the utmost chivalry, and to keep her safe. Is that not honour enough?"

"Aye." Thomas had the grace to look sheepish. "'Tis just that I am used to ensuring his safety, to being at his side whenever he needs me!" He turned suddenly to Margot, a winning smile giving him an irresistible, boyish charm. "Forgive me, Lady Margot. I fear I have been taking out my bad temper on you. My dear sister is right to chide me."

As Margot met those vibrant grey eyes something clutched at her heart, making breathing difficult. Thomas contrite and charming was too much for her composure.

"I know I am a trial to you, Sir Thomas," she managed to say, keeping her voice even with an effort. "Mayhap my situation is a burden to both of us."

"I have not forgotten that you are not with me from choice. Yet I do not think you are finding your stay at Wenfrith unpleasant." His smile deepened as he dropped to one knee and picked her hand from where it rested idly in her lap. "Let us resolve to be friends."

His lips were warm on her skin. A shimmer of awareness ran along her nerves. Margot's eyes dropped to her fingers, still clasped in his.

"Aye," she murmured.

Friendship was so easy with Cedric. Her eyes strayed to where he had moved to lounge at Matilda's feet. But with Thomas?

Her gaze returned to find Thomas's eyes already clouded with doubt. No, friendship with Thomas would be no simple thing, no easier to cultivate in the future than it had been in the past. Not when he could be so prickly, and while she must strive to keep her emotions from straying down frightening paths.

Chapter Eight

"Will you ride with me after dinner, Lady Margot? 'Tis a beautiful day. You have not yet explored Wenfrith to the full. There is much for you still to see."

Margot looked up from her needlework with a welcome smile. Thomas was doing his best to cement the new relationship between them, and she could not deny that an outing would be welcome.

"Thank you!" Her voice held genuine pleasure. "'Tis indeed a lovely day, and Fleurette will benefit from the extra exercise."

Margot rode alongside as Thomas walked his horse towards the village, stopping eventually by the ruins of a small cob hut with a crumbling doorway and no roof.

"This is where I was born," he told her sombrely. "My grandfather held twenty acres in villeinage from the Lord of Wenfrith. When his daughter was dishonoured he allowed her to remain in his cottage and work for him. She could not, in any case, have left the manor, since she, too, was tied to the land."

"Poor woman! How she must have hated her lord!"

Thomas shook his head. "By all accounts she loved

my father. He was the only man who had ever treated her kindly. I believe she was fair to look upon.''

"Yet he allowed her to remain with a father who despised her?"

"Aye. His wife was alive, he could not cause *her* grief.'' He shrugged his broad shoulders. "Why my father refused to acknowledge his children and left her to fend largely for herself, I do not know.'' He looked down, staring sightlessly at the reins gripped in tense fingers. "'Twas something between them alone,'' he went on gruffly. "When she died my brother Stephen took over the land and, although he could have claimed his freedom, seeing who his father was, he did not.'' He looked up again, his eyes bleak. "Since he went, those acres have become part of the lord's demesne.''

"You did not try to inherit them?"

Thomas laughed, his mood suddenly lightening. "At eight years old? Richard has given me far more land since.''

"Which you do not value," she accused.

"Oh, I value it right enough!'' He grinned straight into her serious eyes. "One day I shall give up my soldiering and become a typical lord of the manor interested only in corn and cows and sheep! Meanwhile,'' he added more seriously, "I see that my stewards keep the manors in order. Richard helps, he still visits Acklane most winters and makes sure all is well.''

Silence fell for a while as they viewed the remains of Thomas's birthplace, until he roused himself from his reverie and stirred Pegasus into life.

"So now you have seen my humble origins,'' he smiled, not looking at her directly, but throwing a sideways glance which told her more than he knew.

He wanted her assurance that such an inauspicious beginning didn't matter. She chose her words with care.

"Although you blazon your base birth for all the world to see, I believe it bothers you, Sir Thomas," she observed softly. "It need not. Already your position in society is assured." She gave him a teasing, warning smile, at the same time pulling on the reins to quash Fleurette's skittish desire to gallop away. "Do not let your origins sour you or make you too eager to assert your rights. People do not like *upstart* bastards!" She laughed, to take the sting from her words. "But, Sir Thomas," she went on earnestly, "if you continue to behave honourably and expect to be treated as other men are, you will be—as you are even now!"

"Except in inheritance or marriage," grunted Thomas. "You must be aware of the limitations there! Look at Trastamara! You say he made a better king, the Pope has excommunicated Pedro, which seems to justify your claim, yet the law of God and man says Don Enrico may not inherit the throne of Castile. *We* fought to uphold the principle of legitimacy, which I do not dispute. I have seen where such unlawful aspirations can lead a man," he added grimly.

"Stephen has paid for his evil deeds."

"Aye." He was silent for a moment before he gave a short laugh. "As for marriage—what responsible father would wed his daughter to a bastard who can inherit nothing?"

"Plenty! It depends upon the father and the man! Were he a king's son, he would be acceptable enough! And remember William of Normandy? A bastard who founded a dynasty of English kings!"

"Aye, the exceptions. For the rest of us—life is frustrating!"

"Not for you, Sir Thomas! You have lands and a position of responsibility! And there must be many fathers who would be happy to consider an alliance with a—" she hesitated over her adjective "—a personable young man of considerable wealth with the benefit of both the Duke of Lancaster's and the Earl of Wenstaple's patronage!"

"Aye, perhaps," he said thoughtfully. "A younger, less well-endowed daughter. Even so, I would not despise such an alliance an I loved the maid, and she me. But—" he laughed wryly "—having seen a union such as that of my brother, I cannot contemplate the thought of marriage as a convenient means of securing an ally or extending my fortune. I will not settle for a loveless match," he finished emphatically.

Margot nodded vigorously. "I have every sympathy with those sentiments! Yet the Lady Eleanor says *they* did not love before their marriage. Lord Richard needed a wife, and was not averse to securing her dower, despite his prejudice against her Saxon origins, while she was merely conforming to her father's wishes for her to marry a Norman noble. Attraction was there, but love grew."

Thomas raised his brows, his lips quirking into an impudent smile. The veneer of careless self-assurance was back in place, his vulnerability hidden. "So, you've been exchanging confidences, have you?" he said, and adroitly changed the subject. "What think you of the Lady Eleanor?"

Margot fought down a sense of disappointment. That glimpse of the inner man had awoken a hunger to discover more.

"She is beautiful, kind—as you have said, everything a woman should be," she told him quietly.

"Come," grinned Thomas, pleased, "let us give the horses their heads! I need to feel the wind in my face!"

Margot pressed her heels into Fleurette's flanks but the mare needed no urging to speed after Pegasus. The big grey covered the ground with long strides, leaving them struggling to keep up. When Thomas stopped on the cliff-edge, Margot eased Fleurette to a canter, then reined in beside him.

Thomas's expression held more than a hint of triumph. "I told you Pegasus would outstrip your mare!" He patted the sweating neck as Edwin and Juan cantered up. "We'd better walk awhile, to let the horses cool off."

"I love these cliffs," Margot told him as they idled along the well-worn track. She'd been out riding most mornings with Richard and Eleanor—and Thomas, of course. But never with him alone. The grooms did not count.

"Aye, so do I. I have something special I want to show you." He nodded towards the sea below. "You do not mind a climb?"

"Down to the beach? No, I should love it!"

Shortly afterwards Thomas swung from his saddle and stood courteously ready to help Margot down. He was careful not to hold her too close, though even so the warmth of his hands on her waist penetrated the layers of clothing as though they were not there, adding considerably to the healthy flush already colouring her cheeks.

"Edwin, wait here with the horses."

"Aye, Sir Thomas."

"Wait with him, Juan."

"Aye, my lady."

"This is the path."

Thomas went first, leading the way and helping her over the steepest, narrowest stretches. The loose stones shifted under her feet, hard but not too painful through the soles of her riding shoes. Thomas's buskins also had thick, hard leather sewn underneath, and he didn't appear to feel any discomfort. Margot held the voluminous skirts of her kirtle in one hand while using the other to find her balance. Thomas's firm grip on her elbow saved her from any nasty slip.

At the bottom the path suddenly died some four feet from the sand. Thomas leapt lightly down and turned, his arms held out to catch her.

"Jump!"

Margot hesitated only a second. If she didn't jump, she would not see whatever it was Thomas had in mind to show her.

Thomas's arms broke her fall, and for a moment she was held hard against his chest. She could feel the beat of his heart, strong and steady. Then he released her and took her hand.

"Follow me!"

"Where are we going?"

"To a cave. My retreat when I was young. When I could escape from the kitchen, this is where I came."

Margot's gown was soon saturated around the hem as she followed her guide across damp sand and over low rocks covered with slippery seaweed and sharp barnacles, which were interlaced with deep pools of trapped water where tiny fish and crabs scuttled for cover at their approach. She did not care that her shoes and hose were soaked, that her carefully coiled hair had begun to come loose.

The blood was singing in her veins. This was adventure! Discovery! Never having been to the seashore before, she had not known such fascination existed!

She was panting slightly by the time Thomas led her into the mouth of a cavern formed by countless tides wearing away soft rock at the base of the cliff.

"Is it safe?" she asked breathlessly, staring in wonder at the jagged sandstone above their heads.

"Aye, quite safe, and the tide is yet on its way out. We could remain here for hours without its troubling us."

"Were you ever caught?"

"By the tide? Once. I learned my lesson that night! I slept up there!" Thomas pointed to a ledge high above the tide mark. "I was dreadfully cold and so hungry by the time I returned the next morning, and all I got was a beating for my pains!"

"How old were you, Thomas?"

"Six, I think."

"And working in the kitchen?"

"Aye. I'd not been there long, and was not finding the company to my liking."

Margot swallowed the sudden lump in her throat and, without thinking, put her hand up to touch his cheek.

"Poor little boy!"

"Nay!"

His head went up in proud denial. Margot realised he did not want her sympathy, and shrank inwardly as he quickly captured her hand and led her to a lower shelf, just inside the cave, where he sat, drawing her down beside him.

"I soon got used to their rough ways," he went on with a shrug. "I became tolerant and independent, able to fend for myself. Not unworthy assets, I believe. But what did you learn as a child?" he challenged. "You, the privileged, pampered daughter of a French noble? To be sweet and kind and generous?''

''Or autocratic, selfish, intolerant!'' she shot back, recovering her poise. ''I don't know that I learned anything much,'' she went on more calmly. ''And pampered? Perhaps, when I was very young, but I was often beaten for disobedience, and at sixteen I was wedded to a man I loathed. That was no privilege, and hardly pampering.''

''Yet such is the fate of many of your class,'' he observed, his tone devoid of sympathy. ''Could you not accept it?''

''I did.'' Her lips compressed, her eyes became dark and stormy. She would never be able to speak of the brutality she had suffered, the small pains which had pricked and pinched and buffeted her until she'd cried out for mercy. ''Oh, yes, I accepted it. What I found less easy to accept was the discovery that I was barren. Have you not wondered why I have no children, Sir Thomas?''

His confused eyes avoided hers. ''Aye,'' he muttered.

''So now you know.''

''Aye.'' Compassion overcame the last remnants of his own resentment. ''But you are nevertheless a woman,'' he assured her warmly. ''A woman capable of love, of being loved!''

He spoke to reassure her, but somewhere deep down amidst the pity, the tenderness, the admiration, burned a flame which set his loins on fire, proving beyond doubt that his words were but the truth.

He reached out to turn her face to his. His touch seemed to scorch her skin.

''Believe me, Margot,'' he said deeply, ''you are a most desirable woman. Any man would be privileged to find his pleasure with you.''

Mesmerised, Margot drowned in the shimmering silver depths of the eyes so close to her own. When his face moved closer her mouth opened instinctively to utter a protest, but before she could speak his lips touched hers. Her eyes closed and she forgot all about protesting as she gave herself up to the pleasure of the gentle, softly sensuous movement of his firm, warm lips on hers.

"Margot!" he murmured hoarsely.

Missing his touch, she opened her eyes and looked in wonder at the taut face, at the sudden darkening of those vivid grey eyes. Slowly, gently, he stood up and eased her to her feet. His arms closed round her and somehow her hands crept to his shoulders, then tangled in the curling hair at his nape.

Again his mouth found hers. Teasing, gentle kisses plucked at her lips. Her legs lost their strength, she clung to his neck, her body melting into his. Thought fled. She only felt.

Thomas held the pliant body closer. With the sweet knowledge of victory came a new surge of desire, a desire which thrust itself against her abdomen, tightened his arms, firmed his lips, demanded what he had been fighting against seeking since the night of the storm.

Margot sensed the change, felt the hardening of his body, the rapid beat of his heart, recognised the threat of sudden urgency. Alarm bells sounded in her head, unknown fires raged in her body sending panic signals of danger. Her hands pushed against Thomas's shoulders with sudden strength, pounded in desperate protest.

"No!" she gasped. "No, Sir Thomas! Stop! You must stop!"

Slowly, Thomas's arms dropped to his sides. His breathing became harsh, uneven. His face was suddenly grim and haggard.

"Why?" he demanded with fierce, angry pride. "Why, my lady? Is it my birth?" His jaw clenched. "Is it Cedric?"

"No! No. Just…just leave me alone," she pleaded piteously.

Her whole body shook. He could see the tremor in her hands, the agitated flutter of her lips. What ailed her? She must know he would not treat her as her cursed husband had! She was no inexperienced maid to be upset by a man's natural desire!

A desire which had become a hard stone of frustration in his gut.

Because her legs would no longer sustain her, she sank back on the ledge, her head bowed. He gave her a few moments to compose herself, then strode to the cave's mouth.

"It is time we returned, *doña*. Are you ready?"

Margot struggled to her feet. All the magic of the afternoon had gone. She felt chilled, despondent, unaccountably guilty.

Thomas had done no more than kiss her. Her response had hurt him, driven him back into that formal manner he adopted when he found her an irritation.

Yet she had not been able to help herself. He had not hurt her, had come nowhere near it, and at first she'd known an undreamed of pleasure in his kisses. Had he not become more insistent… But any man would become insistent, it was in their nature. And, because of what Roberto's insistence had meant, she had panicked.

Possibly she always would. Which condemned her to a lonely, arid life just when she had glimpsed a shining alternative.

Her feet dragged on the way back. Her soaked shoes rubbed uncomfortably, her skirt flapped wetly around her ankles. She had to accept Thomas's help to regain the path, and use the grip of his strong hand to hoist herself up the steeper inclines.

The ascent was made in silence, and Edwin's cheerful smile died on his face when he saw their grim expressions.

A sombre party made its way back to the stables at Wenfrith.

"Margot, my dear, what ails you? You have been so pensive these last days."

Margot met the troubled gaze of the Lady Eleanor and felt the tears prick her eyes.

The two women were alone for once, apart from the baby Elizabeth, sleeping in a crib in the corner of the solar. It was the quiet hour after dinner, that same hour when she and Thomas…

"'Tis nothing, lady."

Margot found she could barely control her voice, and the threatened tears overflowed to trickle warmly down her cheek.

"My dear, it is certainly not 'nothing' to cause those tears! Come, child, cannot you tell me what is amiss?"

Kind and understanding as she was, how could Margot tell the Lady Eleanor that her despondency was due to Thomas's kisses? It would be like telling a mother that her son was in some way at fault. When in fact his only crime had been to assume she was a normal woman!

As she hesitated, Eleanor laid down her tapestry and held out her hand.

"Come here, Margot."

Reluctantly, Margot left the window-seat and came to kneel on the rush mat at Eleanor's feet. Eleanor took her hands in one of hers, and with the other smoothed away the betraying tear.

"Is it Tamkin?" she asked softly.

"T—Thomas?"

"Aye, my dear, Thomas. He has been like a bear with a sore head, quite unlike his usual self, and you have been moping. It does not take a soothsayer to see that something is amiss between you."

"Oh, my lady! I feel such a fool! So inadequate! What can I do?"

"Tell me, child."

Eleanor's quiet voice inspired confidence. To her own amazement Margot found herself pouring out the sorry tale of her marriage, all the indignities and hurts of those dreadful years.

When it was done she felt cleansed, at peace. She looked up into Eleanor's compassionate face and a tiny, wavering smile touched her lips.

"I did not mind his kissing me, you must not think that. Truly, I enjoyed it at first; he was so tender, so gentle, I could not believe such pleasure was possible. But then, when he began... I could not respond," she finished desperately. "I just wanted him to stop!"

"Before he turned into the demon your late husband seems to have been? I cannot blame you, my dear. But you must forget the past! Take each man as he is. You have nothing to fear from Thomas. He would not use you ill. Perhaps through him you could find your true womanhood."

"That will never be possible. I am barren, remember. True womanhood is not open to me."

"But still. Think on it, my dear."

"I offended him. He will not wish to repeat so disastrous an experiment."

Eleanor gave her quiet smile. "You will spend much time together over the next months. Relax, my dear. Let things happen as they will."

Was Eleanor hoping to wed her beloved Tamkin to a title, offspring or no? For a moment the suspicion burned in her brain, but then she saw the honesty in Eleanor's eyes and knew she had misjudged her. Eleanor wanted only Tamkin's happiness.

But the Countess's dream was too far from reality to have any chance of coming true. Thomas would never consider taking a barren woman to wife. Or one he did not love. Because he had kissed her it did not mean he loved her. Had he not intimated beforehand that he was only trying to prove to her that she was a desirable woman? One who could give a man pleasure?

On both counts she was unsuitable marriage material. But, Margot realised, the pious Eleanor had not mentioned marriage.

Her nerves tightened. A strange kind of excitement took her by surprise. She thrust it down.

Did Eleanor think her suited to the role of bastard's mistress? If so, she had another think coming!

"Thank you for listening, my lady." Margot's voice was quiet and cold as she rose to her feet. "I was glad of someone to tell of my troubles. Unburdening myself has given me new hope for my future, but please treat what I have told you as confidential."

"Of course, my dear. I am honoured that you should have felt able to confide."

Eleanor's eyes held a question as Margot turned away. She did not understand her young companion's sudden change of mood.

But then, Margot hardly understood it herself.

* * *

"Thomas tells me he must make ready, that you depart on the morrow. We shall be sad to see you leave."

"As I shall be sorry to go."

Margot suddenly smiled at the older woman, contrite over her unaccountable descent into pique. On the surface the two women had continued friendly, but Margot knew that her coolness had hurt and puzzled the Countess.

Eleanor had meant nothing sinister by her remark! She had been too sensitive. As for Thomas, she had barely seen him.

He had come to her earlier in the day, warning her that the time had come for them to continue their journey to Leicester.

"I have dallied here too long already," he had stated abruptly. "It seems I am like to forget my lord Duke's orders."

Her heart had begun to thump uncomfortably. Here, she was insulated from Thomas's presence by that of his family. Once they left the shelter of Wenfrith she would be entirely at his mercy once again, thrown into his company for endless days of travel. She resorted to dignity to hide her sudden apprehension.

"I shall be ready, sir."

"We shall leave after hearing morning mass, at Prime. I have ordered victuals to be packed so that we may break our fast along our way."

Margot nodded. "How many days will the journey take?"

"Six or seven, mayhap. Unless we rest at Acklane for a day or two. 'Twould be well for me to inspect the manor in passing."

"It will be as you wish, sir."

"Don't be so damned accommodating!"

Margot blinked and stared at Thomas's thunderous face.

"I beg your pardon?"

"I said don't be so damned submissive! The role suits you ill, *doña!*"

"Then do not call me *doña!* I had thought you sensitive enough to realise how I hate that form of address! 'Tis a constant reminder of Castile, of all I wish to leave behind! Even Inés and Juan have learned to call me 'lady' since we have been in England."

"I apologise." Thomas bowed in instant contrition, lowering his eyes lest they show the thoughts whirling around in his brain. He had *not* realised quite how much she had hated her existence with Roberto del Sedano. She had not been happy, that he had known. And Eleanor had hinted… Nay, more than hinted. She had told him quite clearly, though without going into detail, that Margot had suffered, that she was therefore nervous of men.

He remembered the tapestries in Roberto's chamber at Sedano and it was though a shaft of light entered his brain, illuminating certain things with painful clarity.

Insensitive fool! he berated himself. Of course, that was it! She was afraid of the things a man did to a woman in the act of mating.

He forgave her rejection on the instant. But he had been warned. He would not give her reason to repeat a slight which he had found as painful as it had been unexpected. Although he did not indulge his fancies often, women were normally only too happy to succumb to his virile charms. At Court he had to fight off the attentions of bored ladies. It really did not matter one whit that this one woman—a woman he had come to like and respect—did not welcome his amorous attentions with open arms.

He lifted his eyes again to meet hers, still dark and stormy. "I apologise," he repeated softly. "Believe me, Lady Margot, I did not realise you disliked your Spanish title so heartily. I cannot, of course, alter your status as hostage, but while you are in my care I will endeavour to make your confinement as pleasant as possible."

Once again he sent up a fervent prayer for release from his responsibility. Perhaps he should not dally long at Acklane. The Duke would not linger in England, despite his joy in his new heir. Until the reward Pedro had promised was paid and ransom terms settled, his duty lay in Castile with his brother and, if Thomas wanted to be by John's side when he returned, he knew he should make haste.

"Thank you, Sir Thomas!" Relief brought warmth to Margot's voice and a smile to her lips. "I am sure," she added warily, "that we shall deal well together in the future, as we have done in the past."

Forget that incident! she prayed silently. Let things be as they were!

And it seemed God was disposed to answer her plea. Thomas had smiled, kissed her fingers and departed whistling under his breath.

So she felt able to make amends to Eleanor, who had shown her nothing but kindness. The regret would remain with her always were she to depart Wenfrith leaving constraint and ill-feeling behind.

"My lady," she said quietly. "Forgive my behaviour the other day. I was—somewhat disturbed by old memories, but I had no right to treat you with coldness—you, who have welcomed me here as a daughter!"

"I wish you were my daughter," said Eleanor. "Then

you could remain here to cheer me when Isobel departs! But please take an old woman's advice.''

''Old woman? My lady, whatever are you saying? Why, you are still of child-bearing age!''

Eleanor smiled serenely. ''Older woman, then, if you prefer, but old nevertheless in experience. Do not close your heart, my dear. Or your mind. Accept life as it comes. You confess to enjoying the adventure of travel, of crossing the sea and coming to England. Accept adventures of the heart, too, of the spirit, of the mind, anything Our Gracious Lord sends.''

''You speak wise words, lady.'' Margot bowed her head to hide the sheen of tears blurring her eyes. ''I will try.''

Chapter Nine

Leicester Castle finally loomed into view at a time when Margot was too damp and chilly to take much interest in the mist-shrouded towers or the graceful spire of a church rising ethereally above the embattled bailey walls. Everything appeared insubstantial seen through the shifting vapour which rose from the river and the common fields lining its banks. Of Leicester town she could see almost nothing.

Behind her, Inés, swathed in an enormous frieze cope, coughed to clear lungs congested by the continual damp.

"Por Dios!" she complained to Edwin, whose face was all but hidden by the hood of his chaperon and the liripipe wound around his throat. "Is summer?"

The groom responded with a good-natured chuckle. "You'll get used to it, my little Spanish flower. 'Twill pass! Tomorrow you'll be scorching in sunshine!"

Margot suppressed an involuntary smile. Inés now communicated quite satisfactorily with Edwin, though her accent was atrocious. But Margot doubted whether the Englishman's idea of scorching would impress the girl clinging to his wet mantle, used as she was to the heat of the Burgos plain. But any sun would be welcome! Since leaving Acklane the weather had steadily deteriorated, souring all their tempers.

She had spoken little with Thomas since their departure, though before setting out she had sought to consolidate the tentative peace between them.

"Sir Thomas." She had stopped to clear her throat. "Can you not accept my word that I will not attempt to escape? As for so-called 'friends' mounting a rescue, that is surely unlikely, here in England?"

Thomas, with charming cool friendliness, had smilingly agreed.

"I had not intended a return to the leading-rein, if that is your concern. I dispensed with it the moment we stepped on English soil, as you must have noticed."

Margot nodded, relieved by his less formal tone. "I had, and I thank you."

"The escort is with us purely as a precaution against the normal hazards of the road. We shall be leading a number of pack-animals carrying precious cargos, remember."

"I had not forgot." She had glanced down at the shimmering bronze brocade threaded with gold dropping gracefully from her hips to the rushes, and smoothed the material absently. "The replacement coffers containing my new gowns and those holding furnishings from Sedano would make a rich haul for rogues."

"My own possessions are not inconsiderable," he'd commented drily. "Ned has his armour, and the other men own things they would be loath to lose. We need good protection."

Having been firmly put in her place, Margot had lifted flaming cheeks and glared at the cool young man who held her comfort and safety in his lean, strong hands. "I am grateful we are to have it," she had snapped, jerked her mind back to the point at issue, and compressed her lips. Thomas could be so *charmingly* evasive! "But 'tis your attitude which concerns me, sir! You will be better able to arrange the journey without harbouring unwarranted fears of my possible attempt to escape!"

"My lady." He had taken her fingers to his lips, his eyes suddenly smiling, though with amusement at her vehemence rather than with the warmth she had come to value. "After our stay here, your friendship with my noble brother and sister, how can I doubt your word?"

The taut muscles around her soft lips had relaxed and her eyes taken on a softened gleam at his words, sending a guilty pang through Thomas. He'd wished he were entirely sure that he believed what he had said. But he would behave as though he did. He knew his doubts were irrational, Eleanor had told him so.

Margot could glimpse Thomas's Lincoln green cloak at the head of the column, where he had chosen to ride for most of the journey, chatting with Ned yet ever on his guard against attack. Occasionally he had fallen back to see how she did and exchange a few words, ordering a short halt if he thought she was weary. His consideration had never failed, but Margot was dismayed to find how much she missed his company. His presence at her side, however reluctant and resented, had relieved the tedium of the long journey from Castile.

There was little to add interest to this hurried trek, though it took them along highways lined with leafy bushes, their roots buried in banks of fragrant wild flowers, their branches interlaced with dog roses and bindweed. On they travelled, through stretches of beautiful, rolling English countryside, through strip cultivations, woodland, and meadows already rich with colour. So anxious had Thomas been to press on that they remained only one night at Acklane, to Margot's disappointment.

He had glanced around the Hall regretfully before saying on a sigh, "'Tis a pity I can afford to spend so little time here."

"Why can you not linger a short while?"

His eyes had left hers and he'd fiddled with the knife at his hip. "I must rejoin His Grace before he departs again for Castile."

"You would return with him?"

"Aye."

Instead of the relief she had expected to feel at news of his imminent departure from her life, Margot's heart had seemed to contract.

"You will find the Burgos plain an inhospitable place," she'd murmured huskily as the pain in her breast receded, "and sickness runs through your camps—"

"Is that reason to neglect my duty? I have no wish to choose the soft life, my lady."

Margot had made no reply. What was there to say? Thomas was a soldier. He would go where his duty led.

Her foreseeable future lay in fortresses such as the stone pile they were approaching now. And after that, if fate was kind, the unknown Idenford.

The horses plodded across an arched stone bridge spanning the river.

"This is the Soar," Thomas informed her, making one of his infrequent forays to her side, "and ahead is another bridge, over the new course cut many generations ago. The castle is no longer heavily defended, though my lord Duke keeps a small retinue here. There is no need to maintain a large garrison, for the land is quiet under our gracious King Edward. The old tower up there on the motte is almost derelict now."

The new castle stood elevated on a bank rising steeply from the water's edge, though the old tower on its man-made mound stood even higher.

The flourish of trumpets announcing their arrival echoed eerily around the mist-shrouded walls. The cavalcade made its way through a turreted gateway and across the bailey, where Thomas dismounted before a large building and turned politely to assist Margot from her saddle. Across the yard she noted the shadowy outline of the church whose spire she had seen earlier.

The steward and his timid wife appeared, to bow them into the chambers used by the Duke and his family.

"The constable is not here?" asked Thomas, a frown of annoyance crossing his face. "I had thought he would be here to greet our honoured guest."

"He was ordered to Pickering, Sir Thomas. I was instructed to greet you in his stead." The rotund figure made a deep bow of obeisance, his voluminous blue houppelande scattering rushes as he did so. "His Grace came here on his way from Bolingbroke to the Savoy, from whence he will travel to Castile, and left sealed orders for you, lord."

"His Grace has left already?" snapped Thomas, annoyed. "Where are his orders?"

"In my chamber." The pink face glistened with sweat above the high collar of a garment better suited to deep winter than a chilly day in summer. The twisted folds of the capuchon wound round his head looked ready to flop down and cover his anxious eyes. "I will fetch them directly. The Great Chamber has been made ready for you, Sir Thomas."

Thomas's brows lifted, but he made no comment and the steward continued with his anxious explanations. "Lady Marguerite is to use the Hainault Chamber." He

bowed to Margot, who resisted an impulse to reach out
and tuck back a loose fold of his headgear. "I trust you
will be comfortable there, my lady." He paused, turning
with evident relief as another person hurried up, and
Margot heard Thomas give a gasp of surprise. "Ah, My
lady," went on the steward eagerly, "may I present
Lady Horsley? His Grace has appointed her your chief
lady-in-waiting. Should she not suit, or should you require others…"

"His Grace is kind. For the moment his arrangements
will suffice. I have my own tiring-maid with me."

As Margot acknowledged the introduction and scrutinised the small woman sinking into a curtsy with a
rustle of green satin, Thomas spoke.

"Beth! What do you here? Should you not be at Bolingbroke?"

"My lady! Sir Thomas!" The woman's curtsy em-
braced them both, but her pale blue eyes swiftly found
Thomas's and her provocative smile was for him alone.
"His Grace desired Lady Marguerite to have a lady to
keep her company, as befits the daughter of Monsieur le
Comte de Limousin. I volunteered."

Thomas's chuckle brought a cold heaviness lurching
to the pit of Margot's stomach. Her eyes went unbidden
to his face, and what she saw there did nothing to dispel
her unease.

"I had not thought to see you for many a day, Beth.
This is indeed a pleasure!"

"I thought to advance our reunion!" Her arch manner
was nicely done, not too brash but infinitely inviting and
more than a little possessive. "But I am neglecting my
duty!"

Thomas laughed, his expression still amused, yet Margot thought she detected a trace of uneasiness, even an-

noyance, enter his manner, which was confirmed by his next words.

"Aye, Beth, Lady Marguerite has been kept standing here quite long enough! See that she lacks nothing for her comfort."

"My apologies, my lady! If you will follow me, I will show you to your chamber."

Since she had no choice, Margot lifted her chin and marched after the woman who it was plain to see was more to Thomas than an acquaintance. How well did he know her? The hussy's bold looks suggested they were lovers, and the initial warmth of Thomas's greeting had served to confirm the impression.

Trying to ignore the pain which seemed to have lodged permanently in the pit of her stomach, Margot trailed after the small figure sweeping gracefully before her, lifting her own damp, mud-spattered skirts to mount the wooden spiral to the upper storey. When she entered the chamber she was to use, her gasp of surprise made her companion smile, if a trifle sourly.

Just because this plain, dowdy woman was the daughter of some count in Aquitaine she had been given the chief guest chamber. Beth, though a knight's daughter and wife, was unlikely ever to be treated with so much deference. She clenched her fists at her sides, where they were hidden by the folds of her gown. Much she cared! At least she'd share some of the luxury here, just as she did wherever she travelled as one of the Duchess's ladies, and then, of course, there was Thomas...

The smile turned into a scowl as she remembered the expression in Thomas's eyes when he'd looked at this dull creature. A kind of concern he had never shown for *her* welfare. Thomas was normally an eager lover despite—or perhaps because of—his long absences. But he had changed. She could sense it. And she had a feeling this woman was to blame.

Cavorting all over Europe in her company—was it any wonder? Beth decided she had best consolidate her position as soon as possible. Her nerves tightened in anticipation and a flush rose to her already rosy cheeks. Night could not come swiftly enough for her.

She hid her resentment and uneasiness behind a new, forced smile, and said cheerfully, "The tapestry was worked in Hainault, hence the name of this room. 'Tis beautiful, is it not?"

"Exquisite!" Margot had seen nothing of the emotions passing over her companion's face. Her eyes had been busy taking in the luxury of the furnishings, the huge soft bed, before focusing on the enormous wall-hanging, an idyllic scene depicting lords and ladies in rich, colourful dress at play in a sylvan setting. Animals and birds peeped from every thicket and branch, and wild flowers bloomed in profusion. "This will give me great pleasure while I am here!"

"His Grace wishes you to be comfortable. My orders are to ensure your pleasure. Perhaps your tiring-woman will find something more suitable for you to wear while I order water to fill the bath tub?"

"Thank you, Lady Horsley."

Beth produced her most friendly smile, showing her uneven teeth. "Please call me Beth. Almost everyone else does."

Including Thomas, thought Margot sourly. However, she acquiesced.

Inés flung off her damp cope, and supervised the disposal of their coffers in the adjoining wardrobe, as Beth sent a waiting page for a supply of hot water.

Margot wished Beth Horsley would go while she

bathed, but on so short an acquaintance did not like to dismiss her out of hand. The woman had been sent to serve her and provide companionship and, really, her intimacy with Thomas was no good reason for Margot to be rude to her. So she curbed her growing dislike and tried to be affable.

"His Grace, the Duke, thought you might like several ladies to keep you company, Lady Marguerite. You have only to speak," Beth informed her.

"Perhaps, when I have had time to settle. I have no idea of how long I am likely to be here."

"How unfortunate for you! I should hate to be in your position, my lady. Believe me, anything I can do to relieve your detention..."

Margot lifted her chin. "Monsieur le Comte, my father, will doubtless see that I am speedily released." If only she could believe that! "Meanwhile, I am grateful to His Grace for his thoughtfulness in sending you to me." She paused a moment before undeniable curiosity made her ask, "Were you not sorry to leave Bolingbroke?"

"Oh, yes, my lady. I enjoy serving Duchess Blanche, and the new baby is a bonny little fellow, we all dote on him. And I left my own son, Robert, in the care of his nurse. Mayhap, later, I can send for him."

"How old is he?"

"Three, my lady."

Although Margot guessed the woman's true reason for being at Leicester, she could not stop herself from further probing.

"I wonder at your volunteering to attend me."

"There were—other attractions here."

She was kneeling at Margot's feet, drying between her slender toes with a soft linen cloth. She glanced up from under colourless lashes, and Margot knew she was assessing her reaction to this statement.

So she schooled her face and voice as she asked, "What could they be?"

"Bolingbroke is isolated, with only a village near by. Leicester is a busy borough, with merchants, shops and weekly fairs..."

"And that is reason enough to leave your child and the service you enjoy?"

"Nay, lady." If the stupid woman wanted the truth, let her have it. Beth suddenly smiled, a little self-satisfied smirk which set Margot's nerves jumping. "I knew Sir Thomas d'Evreux was escorting you here, and was to remain as constable and castellan."

Margot couldn't help her gasp of surprise. "He is?"

"Aye, my lady. We have a—an acquaintance which goes a long way back."

"Indeed!"

"Aye, my lady."

Beth concentrated on her task, a secret smile pinching the corners of her small, ripe mouth. Suddenly she raised wide, apparently guileless eyes to meet Margot's.

"We are lovers," she announced without a blink. "He is a handsome man, do you not think?"

Margot found herself short of breath. "Some may think so," she returned stiffly, when she was able. "Are you not married, Lady Horsley?"

"Oh, yes."

"And does your husband know of your adultery?"

Beth laughed lightly. "He would kill me! But—" she shrugged "—he is old, my lady. And we are much apart. I take my pleasure where I can."

Margot breathed in deeply, steadying her racing heart. "Then Sir Thomas is not your only lover?"

"I did not say that, my lady."

But you meant it, thought Margot grimly. How stupid men were! Or didn't Thomas care who else made love to this woman? A deep sense of inexplicable disappointment added to her outrage. Most men went with whores, they didn't seem to object to sharing their women, and many boasted of their infidelities and conquests. How should she know how Thomas thought? She realised miserably that, despite her stay at Wenfrith, her pleasure in watching him in the bosom of his family, in reality she knew very little about Sir Thomas d'Evreux.

And she didn't want to, she told herself grimly. If only the Duke *would* take him back to Castile! But it seemed, if what Beth said was true, that he was to remain her custodian. And that would please neither of them.

His new duties and responsibilities would keep him busy, she need see little of him, she assured herself firmly. Though quite how she would occupy her own time she was not at all certain. Endless needlework would bore her. She was used to a busy life. And the last weeks had revealed in her a need for challenge, for stimulation.

She realised with sinking despondency that a trying time lay ahead.

But she would not allow Beth Horsley to guess at her depression. She gave a light laugh.

"Your affairs are no concern of mine, Lady Horsley."

Inés was busy rubbing dried lavender and rose petals over her skin. "That's enough," she told the girl in Spanish. "Hand me that clean smock, then find my amber sarcenet kirtle and the green velvet cote-hardie. And I'll have jewels threaded through my hair tonight."

As Inés disappeared into the wardrobe, Beth stood up,

her own task completed, a calculating expression in her pale eyes.

"Your maid does not speak English?"

"Very little," said Margot.

"Excellent. Then we may speak freely."

Margot stood, too, slipping the thin chaisel undergarment over her head. She headed Beth by at least a hand's breadth. "Have we aught to say that my maid may not hear?" she asked coldly.

Beth shrugged. "Probably not. But it is pleasant to know that any indiscretion cannot be repeated."

"Like your admitting to being a whore?"

Beth's face turned the colour of the cliffs at Wenfrith. Fury, Margot realised, and wished her dislike had not led her into such a confrontation.

"And if I am, my lady, and I do not admit the charge, what is it to you?"

"Nothing," said Margot vehemently. "I have already said that your affairs are of no concern of mine! We will not speak of this again!"

"Of course not, my lady, if that is your desire."

Inés had returned. Beth snatched from her arm a silken garment glowing with heavy embroidery. "May I help you on with your kirtle?" she asked with insultingly mock deference.

"Thank you."

Hateful woman! Why, oh, why had the Duke not provided someone from outside his wife's household?

Above all, how could Thomas like Beth? She was fair, but her hair was like straw, dusty straw at that, thought Margot bitingly. Eleanor's had been golden in its prime, like ripe corn. And by all accounts the Lady Blanche's tresses were the colour of the sun's pale golden rays as they glanced through the clouds after rain. Although

Beth was small and graceful, her trim figure showed
every sign of being voluptuous under its satin covering.
Perhaps that was what attracted him. Not, surely, the
witch's face. Comely enough, but hard. Like her eyes.

The memory of the sweetness which had swept over
her during those first moments in Thomas's arms sent
an ache of longing through her body. Oh that the sensation could be repeated! Was it possible for such delight
to continue? Was that why a woman like Eleanor—even
like Beth—sought the arms of their lovers with such joy?
If only...

Margot cut her thoughts off short, unwilling to admit
to a growing urge to know. To contemplate giving herself to a man she had just realised she scarcely knew,
who could amuse himself with a woman like Beth Horsley...

Unwilling to acknowledge jealousy. Yet unable to
bear the thought of Thomas holding Beth in his arms.

Doux Jésu! What had come over her?

She had nothing to offer a man like Thomas d'Evreux.
For a delightful moment he had wanted her, only she'd
panicked and hurt him. And now he had nothing but
contempt for a woman who was no woman at all.

"Inés!" she called abruptly. "Bring the hairbrush.
Comb out these tangles!" Turning to Beth, she forced a
smile to her lips. "No doubt you will wish to make your
own toilet. You have a body-servant?"

"Aye, she will see to my needs. My chamber is beyond that door, my lady. I shall be within call day and
night."

Margot's fingers were trembling as she laced them in
her lap. The motion of the bristles through her hair
soothed, lulling her back to serenity.

If she wanted Beth Horsley gone she had only to say

the word. Thomas would not go against her wishes in
that. Yet she knew she would not dismiss the woman.
Would not give anyone the chance to suspect the jealousy raging in her breast.

She would not give Beth Horsley the satisfaction.

Thomas must never guess.

She was placed in the Duchess's canopied seat on the
dais in the Great Hall that evening. A Hall magnificent
enough for a King, its massive roof timbers supported
by rows of wooden columns forming aisles down which
an army of varlets hurried from the service-rooms beyond, carrying platters of roast goose and duck, dishes
of tongues and elders, wild fowl and fish, platters of
mince pies and venison pasties, custards, tarts, flagons
of wine, mead and ale.

The few trestles were set at their feet, leaving most of
the Hall empty. Without the Duke's or the Duchess's
courts, or their armies of retainers, the numbers at
Leicester were small. The round-headed windows, tiny
compared to those of the new building at Wenfrith, gave
little light. Torches flared from bronze sconces on the
walls, and candles in silver or pewter sticks flickered
along the length of the tables, lighting warm sandstone
walls enhanced but not covered by a brilliant assortment
of tapestries, banners, shields and armaments. The whole
place had been recently cleansed for the Duke's visit, so
the marsh on the floor was comparatively sweet. Before
she sat, Margot kicked a mouldy hunk of bread and a
gnawed bone to one side.

Thomas, in his new capacity of constable, was entitled
to take his lord's place in every way, using the Duke's
Great Chamber and sitting in his state chair at the high
table. Because no one of greater rank was present, the

knight in command of the garrison joined them with his lady, and so did Beth. The anxious steward and his wife were too busy supervising the serving of the meal to add their presence, so the large table seemed empty.

Beth was not sitting next to Thomas, but constantly leaned across her neighbour, the knight, to speak to him.

Margot ate in silence. She had dressed with care for this occasion, knowing that all eyes in the Hall would be upon her. The amber silk warmed her skin, the green of the cote-hardie reflected its colour in her eyes. Strings of jewels sparkled in the coils of brown hair framing her face. The transformation from weary, drab traveller was complete, and Margot was quietly exultant in the fact.

Thomas had noticed. A gleam of approval had entered his eyes at sight of her. She in turn had noted his purple cote-hardie, richly embroidered with gold thread, the jewelled knightly belt holding his knife at his hips, the creamy-white perfection of his hose and the pointed toes of shoes which were fashionable without being ridiculously extreme, like the poulaines worn by the steward, who should have had more sense.

This was an important occasion for them both. Thomas had to impress his position of authority, she had by no means subject status. Only Thomas could gainsay her wishes here. And he had been ordered to keep her happy.

Her reverie was interrupted by Beth's high voice calling to Thomas.

"Sir Thomas, you have no chatelaine to order the household! An you would wish me—"

"Nay, I thank you, lady." His response was swift and definite. "The steward and his lady will manage quite well without other than my supervision. 'Tis what they are paid for, after all!"

Beth dimpled, a feat which Margot eyed with cynical contempt. "You know you have only to ask—for whatever you want."

Her meaning was all too plain. Margot flinched inside, awaiting Thomas's answering sally. To her relief he ignored the innuendo, simply saying, "I thank you," in a chilly voice.

He turned immediately to her.

"What think you of this place?"

Pleased, Margot smiled and answered him with enthusiasm. "Magnificent!"

"Parliament met here in the eighteenth year of Edward's reign. The King was always a welcome guest, even before his son became Earl of Leicester. This Hall has seen some lavish entertainments in its time."

Because the Duke was not present, and his minstrels service the Duchess at Bolingbroke, entertainment that day was simple. A travelling band of jongleurs performed for their food, causing the company to gasp at their skill and split their sides at their antics. Margot joined in a lively round of applause before answering.

"I can imagine. But, Sir Thomas, I do not think I wish to eat here every day. A quiet meal in my chamber would suit me better."

"If you desert me, with whom shall I share this board?"

Margot froze. Of course, if she ate in her chamber, so would Beth.

"Your captain and his lady," she told him tartly. "And if you cannot do without the company of Lady Horsley, I will release her to eat with you here."

"Beth? Oh, I think I can manage without her presence," he said softly. "But yours... It would appear as though you disdained the company of all those here ordered to serve you.''

"Your noble brother and his wife do not always eat in their Hall," she pointed out.

"True, but they already know every man, woman and child on their manor. If you retire to your chamber you will remain a stranger to everyone here.''

"I cannot see that it matters. I am here against my will, and shall be leaving as soon as I am able.''

"Margot," he whispered, "I had thought you reconciled to your sojourn here. Had even begun to suspect that you were enjoying the adventure. You cannot be uncomfortable in the Hainault Chamber? What ails you, lady?''

"Ails me? Why, nothing! Nothing at all!''

His smile held warmth and a hint of mischief. "Mayhap 'tis the knowledge that you have arrived at your final destination and that I am to remain as your guardian?''

"You do not appear as disappointed by your new orders as I would have supposed!" she retorted sharply.

He considered her from under lowered lids. "Mayhap I am not. His Grace appears to have greater need of my services here.''

"And the appointment is a preferment, a great honour and responsibility," she commented drily.

"Aye, 'tis so.''

"Then I congratulate you. Mayhap my misfortune has been to your advantage.''

"I would it were not so. Believe me, lady, I shall not attempt to keep you confined here. You have given me your word, which I accept." And, strangely, that was now the truth. "But you will take an escort whenever you venture beyond the castle walls.''

"Your escort, sir?''

He grinned. "Sometimes." His voice suddenly softened and deepened. "Would it amuse you to know, my lady, that I missed our sparring on the way hither? I wished I had not set myself to free you of my company."

"Oh!" The unruly colour surged into Margot's cheeks. She dared not meet those glinting eyes, and doubted whether her voice would obey her command. She lifted the mazer she shared with Thomas and took a deep draught of the sweet, spiced mead while she took time to recover from the shock of his confession.

"I missed it, too," she confessed at last, and looked away quickly lest the sudden blaze of delight she saw in his eyes wrecked her composure completely.

102   *As You Fro My Dream*

Chapter Ten

Slipping under a fine lawn sheet and a thick, exquisitely woven rug, Margot nestled in the downy softness of the great curtained bed.

Thankfully, she dismissed her new attendant. "That will be all, Beth, until the morning."

"God give you a good night, my lady."

"And you. Inés, you may retire to your pallet."

"*A Dios, doña.*"

Inés flounced through to the wardrobe. The Spanish girl had been difficult all evening. Margot knew she resented Beth, whom she considered a usurper, and had insisted on talking volubly in her native tongue to cut Beth out and show her displeasure. And, Margot thought with a tinge of guilt, I did nothing to stop her.

Pretending to settle down to sleep, Margot watched Beth glide through the connecting door to the small chamber she would perforce share with any other ladies Margot decided she needed—though needed would not be quite the right word. She could see herself forced to summon other women to attend her simply to avoid being thrown too much into Beth Horsley's company.

But for the time being Beth had the small chamber to

herself. The moment she disappeared Margot sat up, pulling her soft woollen chamber-gown around her shoulders. She would not sleep until she knew. Knew whether Thomas would be visiting Beth that night.

Part of her wanted to remain ignorant, to believe that what Beth had told her was a lie. But the pragmatic part of her knew that such clandestine affairs were normal in the world to which they all belonged. The King's court was notoriously licentious. Didn't the ageing King Edward allow Alice Perrers to twist him around her dainty little finger? To sit by him in public? While poor Queen Philippa lay on her sick-bed, her suffering body swollen with dropsy.

The King was in his dotage, everyone said so. She had heard the talk wherever she went. For such a great and glorious monarch to come to this! Yet they loved him still for what he had been. And, although they thought his excesses scandalous and bad for the realm, all except the priests and the most devout or self-righteous were ready to excuse and condone, because many were no better themselves.

Men were men, they had their needs; 'twas women like Beth, who had taken the Holy Church's vows to cleave only to their husbands, or who were promised as virgin brides, who suffered the full condemnation by society if they strayed from the path of virtue—and were discovered.

Thomas could hardly be blamed for his part in the affair. Beth was the adulterer, the deceiver, the breaker of God's Holy Laws.

This train of thought did little to comfort Margot. Thomas's conscience was hardly her affair. 'Twas not the rights and wrongs of the liaison which so disturbed her, but the fact that Thomas might actually desire to lie with Beth Horsley.

And why should he not? taunted her inner voice. He is nothing to you, you are nothing to him.

Inés was already deeply asleep in the adjoining closet, judging by the sound of the soft snuffles, the regular breathing emanating from behind the arras separating it from the bedchamber. Margot slid from the bed to the creaking step and thence to the floor.

From beyond the closed door of Beth's chamber the small sounds of preparations for retirement ceased. Straining her ears against the wood, Margot heard her dismiss her tiring-maid, heard hinges squeak and the latch fall as the girl left for the dorter she shared with others of her kind.

After a period of near silence the unseen hinges protested again and Margot's heart began a heavy thudding as she strained to hear Thomas's voice.

Silence. Absolute silence.

Was anyone there? How could she know? To open the heavy communicating door to peep was impossible, the great iron hinges or cumbersome latch were certain to make a noise. But—she could open it confidently to demand Beth's services!

What for? Inés could do anything necessary... No! Inés did not speak enough English to ask in the kitchens for a hot drink!

But what if Thomas was there?

Then he would know she knew, she thought grimly. And perhaps that would be for the best.

Her thoughts carried her no further. She rapped on the wooden planks, lifted the latch, and flung the door open.

Margot's aching gaze searched the shadows, but

Beth's chamber was empty. A single candle flickered by the untouched bed.

Closing the door quickly, Margot stood with her back against it, breathing heavily, feeling stupid, weak, mildly hysterical. Having gathered herself for a confrontation, the anti-climax was somehow ludicrous. She crossed to the bed and climbed in on shaking legs, half laughing, half crying.

It was quite some time before she remembered to wonder where Beth had gone.

The soft tap, the immediate opening of the Great Chamber's door, came as no surprise to Thomas. Enjoying the luxury of the Duke's apartments, stripped to shirt and hose, he was playing a last, desultory game of chequers with Ned before sending the lad to his pallet.

Although he was not surprised, he felt none of his usual pleasure in her appearance. He smiled a reserved welcome. "Beth! Come in!"

As though she ever waited for an invitation, he mused cynically, watching her slip quickly inside and close the door behind her. From the first she had sought him out, stealing into his room at night to offer him the delights of her body. He'd not been loath. She made a buxom armful, and he'd soon discovered that bed-sport with Beth was highly enjoyable.

Tonight he was weary. The long journey, the new responsibilities, had tired him. He was not really in the mood for Beth. However, he dismissed Ned with a nod and held out his hand.

Beth needed no urging to move to where he sat by the hearth. She flung off her mantle and sat on Thomas's knees, offering her lips for a kiss which did not materialise.

"How is Robert?" he asked quietly.

"Robert?" muttered Beth, her mind on other things.

"You remember. Our son," said Thomas drily.

"Oh, Robin. He may not *be* your son," she told him impatiently. "He's well, thriving in fact. Amy is a good nurse."

"Better than you are a mother, 'twould seem. But I'm glad you didn't bring him here."

"Why so?" she demanded irritably.

"He is too like me, whatever you protest about his parentage."

"Your guilt makes you too sensitive, Tom; no one else has remarked! Having him around has never bothered you before, so why now?" She peered at him from slitted eyes in which suspicion was growing. "Is it because of your precious Lady Marguerite?" she demanded jealously.

She watched his face, saw the clenching of a muscle in his jaw. She was right! Hadn't she felt a difference in Thomas, right from the first moment of greeting? "She knows we are lovers," she told him tartly.

"What?" he barked. "How?"

"I thought she should know," smirked Beth. "So, you see, there is naught to hide."

Thomas stood suddenly, tumbling Beth unceremoniously from his lap.

"You bitch!" he snarled. His face was bone-white, his eyes blazing with such anger that Beth quailed.

"I...I didn't think it could matter," she protested. "Really, Tom, such a fuss..."

Through clenched teeth, "I am her custodian, her guardian, her protector," Thomas snarled. "These duties have been laid upon me by His Grace the Duke of Lancaster, on behalf of his brother the Prince of Wales. I therefore take them extremely seriously.'' He stopped to draw a deep, painful breath, and gazed down on her with that natural authority and arrogance she had always found attractive—until now. ''You are supposed to be attendant and companion to the Lady Marguerite. What of her feelings? How will she view such an association? She is a virtuous woman. Such knowledge can only offend her!''

''You're in love with the Spanish whore!'' spat Beth incautiously.

Thomas's nostrils flared. ''I am in love with no one, least of all you, my lady! But I do care about Lady Marguerite's happiness. She is a woman in unfortunate circumstances and, incidentally, is neither a Spaniard nor a whore. That epithet more correctly describes you, my dear. Lady Marguerite de Bellac was born of an English mother into the French nobility. It would be well if you remember that, if you wish to remain here.''

Beth was really frightened by the fury still latent in Thomas's eyes, and dismayed by his brutal words. She swallowed as she shifted to kneel at his feet. She bowed her head.

''I am sorry, Tom. I will,'' she promised through tight lips, while fury to match his burned in her breast. ''You—you will not send me away?''

Thomas shrugged wearily. ''Not unless she requests it.''

So the bitch's wishes came first! Hiding her chagrin, Beth gazed up at him invitingly, attempting to recover lost ground. ''And now?'' she asked throatily, ''Shall we lie together?''

''Nay, woman! Get yourself out of my sight! I am in no mood for dalliance this night!'' He flung her mantle at her. ''Go, Beth, before I lose my temper!''

Beth jumped to her feet and fled. But he hadn't said to stay away forever. Only that night.

Margot heard the door of Beth's room open and close again. She glanced at her candle. It had barely burnt down at all. The woman hadn't been gone long. Surely not long enough for...

With a small sigh of relief, Margot settled down to sleep. Her dreams were jumbled and when she woke she could remember nothing except an impression of Thomas smiling at her in a way that set her pulses pounding and left her body throbbing in a new and uncomfortable way. She got out of bed and padded restlessly about the room. 'Twas a long time since she'd had such a vivid dream, and in brilliant colour, too. Such dreams came when she was emotionally disturbed.

For the first time fear clutched at her nerves. She hadn't realised before quite how deeply everything about Thomas affected her. Yet look at her behaviour tonight! She put cold hands to burning cheeks at the memory of her compulsive, stupid actions. Could she really be suffering from jealousy?

And these strange physical manifestations, dying away now and leaving her feeling curiously empty. Thoughts of Thomas were the cause of those.

Thomas. 'Twas no use evading the truth any longer.

She dropped to her knees at the prie-dieu, gazing up desperately at the gilded effigy of the Blessed Virgin Mary.

"Sweet Lady, help me," she whispered.

She loved him. Loved his strength, his honour, his pride, his loyalty. Loved the way he moved, the way he talked, the way he laughed, the way his eyes shone with irrepressible mischief. She wanted to be with him always.

She had thought herself incapable of love. Yet she wanted to touch him, to have him touch her. This one man might be able to overcome her fears, to lead her into undreamt of realms of delight.

Yet still part of her shrank from the acts necessary to know that joy, and what use to dream, anyway? Thomas would consider her so far above him in rank and birth that he'd surely not even attempt… Yet he had done, once.

But never again. She knew that with an inner certainty that left her feeling chilled.

If she wanted Thomas to wipe out Roberto's legacy of dread and disgust, hers would have to be the first move.

And she could not imagine herself ever making it.

She bent her head and whispered an ave and a paternoster, and followed these with formless, wordless prayers of yearning, of supplication.

The cock crew before she was able to return to her bed in some kind of peace to sleep uneasily until morning, only to rise feeling limp as a wet rag.

As soon as she could find him available, Margot quelled her nervousness, hid her newly awakened awareness behind a determined mask, and asked Thomas to find two more ladies to attend her. Somehow, she must insulate herself from Beth Horsley's animosity and undivided attention.

If he found her request strange after her previous reluctance to increase her following, he made no remark.

"I'll see to it immediately," he promised, asking with a quizzical smile, "Would you prefer them young or old?"

"Whatever you think, Sir Thomas." Margot lowered her eyes to avoid that smile. Her emotions were singularly difficult to control in the face of his charm. Her fingers itched to stroke the creases which slashed his lean cheeks when he smiled, to thread through the tumbled mass of curls crowning his shapely head. "You will know their family circumstances, I do not. I would not wish to call a lady from her household duties unless she could easily be spared."

"I'll consult the stewards, they visit the manors, though any lady would be honoured to obey His Grace's command to attend you, Lady Marguerite." He eyed her with an anxious frown she did not see. "Beth Horsley is proving satisfactory?"

"Aye, thank you," said Margot shortly, looking up at last and catching the relief on his face as the frown lifted.

So, she thought dully, he is glad Beth is staying.

Over the next days Beth kept her animosity well hidden. As far as Margot could tell, she did not leave her chamber at night.

Margot began to suspect that Thomas had sent her away. Her heart rejoiced. Jealousy was an uncomfortable emotion to live with.

She filled her days with determined activity, exploring the castle, inspecting the buttery, the still-room, the cellar, the kitchen. Although there were apothecaries and physicians in the adjoining hospital and in the town, Margot found her niche in treating the minor ailments of the castle officials, her squires, the pages, the varlets, churls and even the soldiers of the garrison.

Before long she was spending long hours in the still-room brewing, infusing and decocting her herbal remedies, mixing electuaries, balms and ointments. She made

several forays into Leicester for supplies of ingredients
not to be found in the herb garden, which adjoined the
colourful, leafy pleasance situated at the foot of the
grassy eminence on which the castle stood.

Lady Blanche's grandfather, Henry of Lancaster, had
built a hospital as an act of charity and dedicated it to
the Holy Trinity. The defensive walls of the castle had
been extended to enclose it. Margot, therefore, needed
no escort to go there, other than a reluctant Inés.

As her mistress passed among the old and infirm people lying on straw mats in the bays of the aisled hall,
Inés trailed behind holding a bunch of herbs to her nose
to sweeten the fetid, evil-smelling air. Margot barely noticed the stench in her concern for the unfortunates with
their palsies and sores, their cankers and swollen, knot-
ted joints.

Visits to the town, however, were necessarily more
formal. Beth, only too glad to be excluded from visits
to the sick, was not so willing to forgo such an expedition, and the ladies were always escorted by at least
two armed retainers.

About a month after her arrival, riding sedately towards the Wednesday market to inspect the merchandise
on display, Margot's attention was drawn to a tall man
staring intently at their party. A sense of *déjà vu* brought
a gasp to her lips.

Where had she seen him before? While her mind grap-
pled the problem, he turned and disappeared down a
narrow lane.

Cudgel her brain as she might, memory of a past
meeting eluded her. But she was totally aware of the
menace implicit in the narrowed gaze, the set of thin lips
above a straggly, greying beard.

A shiver sped through her body and Fleurette, ever

sensitive to her mistress's moods, tossed her head, skittering nervously and scattering Inés and the escort, who were on foot.

Margot recovered quickly, brought the mare under control, and peered down the mean alley as they passed. Several dogs and children scratched among the refuse, a man with one leg swung awkwardly along on a rough crutch, but of the tall stranger there was no sign.

The sun cast deep shadows between the huddled dwellings. He could be hidden in a pool of darkness, or he could have entered one of the squalid cottages. She shook her head impatiently. 'Twas no use wondering or worrying! But the sight of him had given credibility to Thomas's warnings! The man was probably covetous of her finery, her purse and her horse. There would be plenty of others like him.

"Is aught amiss, my lady?"

Beth was following behind, and her horse had caught Fleurette's nervousness.

"Nay, she shied at some shadow, no doubt. Or mayhap she has caught wind of a stallion in the horse-fair yonder!"

Beth laughed. "Mayhap. The market will be busy this day."

Her voice throbbed with suppressed excitement. The nice weather, the stimulation of the bustling town, had dispelled her recent sombre mood. Margot prayed this was the cause of Lady Horsley's improved temper, refusing to contemplate any reason which involved Thomas.

Apart from medicinal herbs and spices, which were charged to the Lancaster purse, Margot was tempted by braids to decorate her gowns and a silver caul to net her hair. She had a few nobles of her own since Thomas's messenger had returned from her manor of Idenford. Not many, for his news had been distressing.

The poor man had been almost afraid to speak.

"Come, varlet," Thomas had urged impatiently. "No one here will flog you for bringing bad news! Tell Her Ladyship what you found!"

"My lady!" The man fell to his knees at her feet, his head lowered. "Most of your lands lie fallow. Many of the tenants died in the great pestilence, I was told, and others have fled to the towns seeking their freedom. Few remain, but the steward collects what rents he can. He gave me this."

He had held out a small pouch. Margot had taken it and tipped the gold and silver coins into her palm.

"So few nobles?" interjected Thomas incredulously. "How long is it since dues were last paid?"

"I do not know, Sir Thomas. I could not check his records, for I cannot read. But this is all the steward had to give."

"He's filled his own coffers, I'll take my oath! 'Tis time your serfs paid their rents, Lady Marguerite. Shall I send a dozen men to enforce the payments?"

"Nay, gently, Sir Thomas, I'll not have them bullied, nor their homes laid waste. My husband neglected the manor for long enough; 'tis not their fault there are too few labourers to work the land."

"No men of mine would lay waste homes, my lady, except when ordered to do so in war."

Thomas spoke with frigid dignity, offended.

Margot glanced at him quickly, regretful of her ill-considered words. Of course Thomas would not be so cruel! She hastened to appease. "Nay, but away from your control they might be tempted, if they could do your bidding no other way. Perhaps someone of learning could be sent, who could check the accounts... God grant, 'twill not be long ere I can travel there myself!''

Thomas had bowed and said stiffly, ''I do not wonder that you are anxious to depart, my lady, though I have tried to make your sojourn here as pleasant as possible.''

''Nay, sir,'' protested Margot quickly, anxious to re-establish the ease which had lately grown between them, ''I am not unhappy here, 'tis just that I cannot please myself! An I could travel to Idenford to tend my manor I would gladly return here, where I have been made to feel an honoured guest.''

''I am glad you are content, for I fear I cannot give permission for such a journey, for the moment at least. I still await the Duke's final orders.''

''He has not yet returned to Castile?''

''I do not know, Lady Margot.'' Thomas's tone indicated a return to the frustrations which had plagued him earlier. ''I am no longer close enough to John of Gaunt to know where he is or what his intentions are.''

That had been a couple of days earlier. Now she was rashly spending some of the meagre gold on finery she hardly needed... But for the first time in her life she wanted to enhance what small charms she possessed, to compete with the other ladies who graced Leicester Castle with their presence.

When they returned to the castle Margot discovered the reason for Beth's suppressed excitement. As they crossed the bailey a page ran up to her and bowed.

''My lady, your son has arrived. I am to tell you that he is in the pleasance with Amy, his nurse—''

''I know who Amy is, you stupid child!''

The boy cowered from the unwarranted sharpness of Beth's tone and, as she swung from her saddle in a flurry of silken skirts, stepped back to be out of reach of her stinging hand.

"Off with you," she ordered imperiously. "Tell Amy to bring him to me at once!"

"W-where will you be, my lady?"

"With Lady Marguerite, of course!" Suddenly remembering her position, she turned to Margot, a smile breaking the impatient lines of her face, though it was the feverish excitement in the woman's eyes which impressed Margot. "With Your Ladyship's permission?"

Herself dismounted, Margot lifted the hem of her fine, gold-embroidered kirtle and began to pick her way over the cobbles towards the door. Was Beth really so fond of the child, or was it something else causing such edgy, taut anticipation?

"Naturally, Beth," she replied coolly. "You will wish to see your son as soon as possible. Why was I not told of his coming?"

Mother of God, she prayed silently, give me patience! Send the other ladies soon!

"I did not know myself, my lady," explained Beth smoothly. "Only that I had asked for him to be sent at the first opportunity…"

Margot spoke over her shoulder. "I see. You could have told me that much, at least."

"I apologise, my lady," said Beth humbly.

Margot, unimpressed by her attendant's apparent humility, distrusted the faint smirk touching the woman's lips. However, her impulse was to make the child welcome. She said, "I shall look forward to meeting him."

The page scooted off in search of the child and his nurse, and Beth followed Margot up to her chamber. Inés was still tidying Margot's hair when a rap on the door announced the new arrivals.

A small boy walked in on sturdy legs, his fair hair flopping forwards over apprehensive grey eyes as he bowed reverently to greet his mother. One day, thought Margot, he would have a cleft in his chin and the ladies would love the gentle curve of his shapely lips. She glanced from the boy to his dam, noting the similar colouring, though the child's hair was finer, more golden than Beth's.

"Robert! Come here, child. Kneel to the Lady Marguerite!"

Without lifting his eyes, the boy shuffled forward and dropped to his knees. He wore tiny tunic and hose of azure and gold with the Lancaster rose embroidered on his chest. He had barely looked at his mother, and Beth had little of softness in her eyes as she ordered the boy to make his obeisance. She had made no move to take him in her arms, to greet him with a kiss.

On impulse, Margot reached forward and drew the child to his feet, pulling him to her knee.

"So you are Robert," she said kindly. "I expect you are glad to be with your mother again."

Robert said nothing. His mother clucked impatiently. "Have you lost your tongue, Robin? Answer the lady!"

"Aye, lady," muttered Robert uneasily.

"I expect he is missing his playmates at Bolingbroke," went on Beth, aware that her son was not showing the joy at seeing her that others would expect. "He keeps company with the Duchess's children there," she explained with satisfaction.

"There are children here," Margot reminded her. "The steward and other officials have their families with them. He will soon make new friends, no doubt." She smiled at the woman still standing in the doorway, whose kindly, weathered face with its deep-set, soft brown eyes and generous mouth was framed by a wimple kept in position by a barbette of stiffened linen, a fashion long abandoned by all but the elderly or lower orders. "You are Amy?"

The woman dropped to her knees. "Aye, my lady."

"Take your charge through to the next chamber, Amy. He may remain with his mother until the steward has had time to arrange nursery accommodation."

She smoothed the child's golden hair before giving him a gentle push in the direction of his nurse. He trotted obediently to Amy's side as the woman scrambled from her knees. His small hand nestled confidingly in her large, worn one as she led him through to Beth's bedchamber.

"Have you spoken to the steward, Beth?"

"Not yet, my lady."

"Then I suggest you do so at once—unless you wish the child to remain with you until the other ladies arrive?"

"Nay, Lady Marguerite." Beth smiled rather grimly. "I want no puking infant in my bed at night!"

No, thought Margot, suddenly sickened. You want a man, preferably Thomas!

"What of your husband?" she asked abruptly. "Does he wish to visit you here?"

"Not at present. He is in London, on business."

Beth had no wish to endure the fumbling advances of her elderly spouse, unless she managed to lie with Thomas and her womb quickened. Then she would perforce have to send for Sir Robert or travel to him in haste, as she had before, or face ruin, probably banishment to some dreary nunnery.

A place was soon found for little Robert and his nurse and, since the child was not old enough to sit at table in the Hall, and Thomas was busily engaged at other times, it was a day or so before he became aware of his son's presence.

A summons to the pleasance one afternoon, brought by a page who did not seem sure exactly which lady had asked for his presence, sent him striding down the steps built into the grassy slope in some annoyance.

He saw Margot sitting on a bench in the shade of an apple tree, embroidering what looked like blue harebells on the bodice of a cream kirtle, while Beth sat near by, chatting with a newly arrived lady—a stout woman with bright, bird-like black eyes and a ready tongue.

Margot appeared lost in her own thoughts, allowing the sound of the vivacious voice to drift over her head with the notes of the pipe being played by a squire lounging artistically in red and saffron against the dark green background of a yew. At a short distance a couple of nurses and a group of officials' wives and children made a pleasing sight on a sunny afternoon, and much of Thomas's annoyance at the mysterious summons dissipated.

At the crunch of his feet on the grit path, Margot looked up. Caught unawares she looked like a startled doe, he thought indulgently, surprised by the sudden pleasure in her expressive eyes, the slight heightening of becoming colour in her creamy cheeks.

He bowed. "You sent for me, Lady Margot?"

"I?"

Margot looked puzzled, and Thomas felt a momentary disappointment that it was not she who had sent the page. It must have been Beth, he thought, all his irritation returning. She had waylaid him time without number over the last weeks, and he was tired of her attempt to rekindle a passion which, for him, was dead. He called across, his tone curt.

"Was it you, then, Beth?"

"Aye, Tom. There is someone here I thought you would like to see."

Before she finished speaking a childish cry rang out.

"Sir! Sir!"

Robert raced across the grass on flying legs to pull up short a yard from where Thomas stood. Remembering his manners, the boy executed a low bow before throwing himself at Thomas, who lifted him up and held him close.

The soft, tender expression on his face was one Margot would rather not have seen. And Beth's triumphant little smile, her sidelong glance to assess her reaction to the reunion, confirmed what she had already guessed.

Thomas was bound to Beth by more than a passing fancy. She was the mother of his child.

Chapter Eleven

Roberto's cruelties had hurt Margot, had perhaps maimed her emotionally, but had never touched the innermost core of her womanhood.

She had wanted to have a child by him for all kinds of reasons which had nothing to do with the simple desire to hold in her arms the baby of the man she loved, to see him gaze with tender affection on the result of their union.

Margot looked away abruptly. If she had been jealous of Beth before, it was nothing to the blanket of consuming envy which threatened to smother her at sight of Thomas holding their son.

And Robert. The exuberant joy with which the child had greeted the man was so at odds with his stolid, deferential attitude to his mother.

"You remember me, you young puppy!"

"Course I do!"

Thomas's delighted chuckle as he held the child in the crook of his arm and inspected the rosy, baby face gave Margot a sharp pain deep in her belly. She felt sick, dizzy, but she knew she must control herself, not let Beth guess how acute was her suffering.

Beth was using Robert as a weapon, to hurt her and to try to regain Thomas's attention. Margot knew it as surely as if she could see into the woman's mind. Yet Margot also knew that in her own careless, selfish way Beth was fond of the boy. She had chosen a loving, faithful nurse for him, and when he grew to manhood she would be immensely proud of his achievements. To enjoy cuddling a sometimes messy baby was not in her nature.

But it *was* in her nature to scheme and manipulate to get her own way. In a moment, Margot's resolve hardened. Beth should not win this time! But how was she to stop her? Seduce Thomas herself? Only a jester would think that a possibility.

She was shaking all over. The sound of children playing, the sweet notes of the flute floated above her head as though from some distant place as she raised her face, a smile on her quivering lips.

"Is he not a bonny child? He has been here some two days now, and we have already become good friends, I think," she said.

Willing her hand not to tremble, she lifted it to capture the small fist clinging to Thomas's arm. Robert did not snatch it away, but smiled confidingly.

"Sir Tom p'omised to buy me a pony!" he announced excitedly, his free hand curled coaxingly around Thomas's neck. "You did, didn't you, sir? When can I have it?"

"Soon, Robin, soon. As soon as you have learned to ride one of the stable ponies."

"But I have already!" He appealed to his nurse, who had come to retrieve her charge. "I have, Amy, haven't I? Tell him!"

"Almost," the woman confirmed with a smile.

"Mayhap Sir Thomas will watch you one day. He must be the judge."

"Soon! Watch me soon!"

"All right, you young cub! On the morrow, when the bells toll for Tierce. I'll be in the stables with a pony." He turned to Amy. "You'll bring him?"

"Of course, Sir Thomas."

Thomas put the boy down, patting his head in dismissal. No doubt Thomas could afford to indulge a child for whom he held such obvious affection, yet towards whom he bore no responsibility for discipline. Yet, were the circumstances more normal, Margot believed he would behave no differently. Though he would always insist on obedience and manners, he would be a loving father. That he could not openly acknowledge his son must give him immense pain. Margot's compassionate heart bled for him.

Robert immediately made for Margot, holding out his arms to be lifted to her lap. She helped him up and let him play with the cross and keys hanging from the jewelled belt at her hips.

The smile had not deceived Thomas. Her eyes had given her away, so full of hurt, so soft with longing. What a cursed waste, he thought furiously, for a woman like Margot to be condemned to sterility while a hard burd like Beth could conceive and flaunt the product of her infidelities in her face. Trying to hurt Margot because he, Thomas, had not been interested in having Beth in his bed since their reunion.

For a moment he weakened. If he indulged Beth's desire... His blood stirred at the memory of past pleasures. Beth had given him passion and a strong, healthy son, even if he wasn't able to recognise him as his.

But the almost instinctive stab of desire lasted no

more than an instant, replaced at once by distaste amounting to revulsion. Beth would just flaunt her victory as she was flaunting her son. His eyes hardened as he glimpsed the trembling of Margot's hand when she bent to pick up a bauble the child had dropped.

"Did you know Robert was coming, lady?" he demanded.

"Nay. Beth thought to surprise us all, I think."

"She has certainly done that," he retorted grimly, startled that Margot's hurt should affect him so deeply.

He strode to Beth's side and imperiously waved her companion away.

"I am governor of this establishment," he reminded her abruptly, though his voice was pitched low enough to be inaudible to anyone else. "You did not ask my permission to bring Robin here. Why not?"

"I did not think it necessary," answered Beth with a shrug. "Robin is normally with me. I thought *you* would be pleased to have him near," she added archly.

"After what I said when you came to me that first night?" rasped Thomas angrily. "You knew my objections. You went against my express wishes quite deliberately!"

"But you said that before you knew I had told Lady Marguerite—"

"Be quiet!" hissed Thomas. "Do not add to your indiscretions, Beth!"

"Let me come to you tonight," she wheedled. "Would you not like another son, my Tom? Think of the pleasure—"

"You disgust me," said Thomas brutally, astonished at the depth of his revulsion. He'd tried to let the woman down gently, and what had she done? Embarrassed him and caused Margot pain. "Behave yourself, Beth, or you will find yourself banished to your husband's estates!"

Beth tossed her head angrily, all signs of pleading gone. "*She* won't have you," she hissed venomously, "and even if she would, she couldn't give you sons!"

"Lady Marguerite has nothing to do with my changed feelings for you," growled Thomas, almost believing it. "Perhaps 'twas Nájera, perhaps the separation, but I can no longer appreciate your charms as I did."

"Then do not think to come creeping back when she turns you down," snarled Beth. "And do not imagine you have any right to see Robert, either. I shall send him back to his father!"

"Now he is here, he will remain." Thomas's face hardened, his cheekbones stood out stark and white beneath suddenly icy eyes. "Do not think to blackmail me through the child, Beth. I love him, but not enough for that threat to work. I can get other children."

"But not by her!" spat Beth viciously.

Thomas's hands bunched into fists. He longed to thrust them into that malicious face. Instead, he swung on his heel and strode from the pleasance.

Margot knew they'd quarrelled, could see the way keeping control of himself made Thomas's carriage stiff, his facial muscles taut. He walked past her and Robert without a glance.

Her heart yearned for him, for his unhappiness, though she wasn't sure what was causing it. Did he still love Beth? The only words she'd caught of their low-spoken argument had been "Now he's here, he will remain", said loudly and violently before he'd dropped his voice again. Something to do with Robert?

Her arms tightened around the child just as Beth's

voice, pitched several tones higher than normal, called him.

"Robin! Come here, child! Come to your mother!"

Emphasising her possession, thought Margot wryly as she let the small body slide from her lap. She dropped a kiss on the shining golden locks.

"Your lady mother wants you, darling," she whispered, giving the reluctant child a slight push to speed him on his way.

No further message arrived from the Duke of Lancaster, though from time to time an Earl, Baron or Knight would arrive with his retinue, seeking a night's lodgings. On such occasions all was bustle. These comings and goings were the only happenings to ruffle the surface of Margot's quiet routine.

Both her new ladies were pleasant enough, though the older woman's incessant chatter was inclined to get on Margot's nerves. But Beth lapped up the gossip. Mistress Margaret Throstle could be no threat to Beth where looks were concerned, with her gap-toothed smile and the heavy folds of flesh hanging beneath her almost invisible chin. From the first the two spent many hours together, which relieved Margot of Beth's unwelcome company.

The other woman, a knight's wife of little more than Margot's own age, had been delighted to leave her husband to join Margot's court.

"Do not think me lacking in maternal love, my lady," pleaded Lady Fairfield when Margot had shown surprise at her willingness to leave her family. "My children are in good hands, they have three nurses with my mother-in-law to supervise. But I needed a respite. I am too fertile." Her pale, drawn face flushed slightly as she pleated the cloth of her kirtle with a fragile white hand. "I know it is my duty to bear my husband sons, but I have borne him seven children in the past seven years; two have died and the last was still-born. Even he could see that my health was suffering. I must regain my strength before we add to our brood."

"'Tis kind in your knight to allow you the freedom, Kate," observed Margot sincerely. "He must love you."

"Aye, I think he is fond of me." Katherine sighed fretfully, closing her fine blue eyes and drawing a sighing breath before going on. "As I am of him. But I fear he will seek his pleasure elsewhere while I am absent from his bed. 'Tis a man's right, no doubt. I do not want to leave him, I want to bear his children," she protested fiercely. "Dear Mother of Heaven, why am I brought to child-bed so often? Other women go for years before bearing again!"

"And others do not conceive at all," remarked Margot quietly. "Your condition is sad, but not so sad as that of the woman who can never bear a child. Be grateful, Kate, that you have such a sturdy family."

Kate lifted her fair head on the thin stem of her neck to gaze at Margot in consternation. "Lady Margot! You mean you...? I am sorry! Forgive my thoughtlessness!"

Margot smiled sadly. "It seems few are completely satisfied with their lot in this world. We can only accept God's will."

In the month she'd been at Leicester Kate had regained much of her strength. Margot watched her recovery with satisfaction, seeing the flesh return to cover those fragile bones. Soon Kate would want to go back to her husband and children, and she would certainly not stop her. Meanwhile, she had a congenial companion, one who was not afraid to accompany her on her visits to the hospital, and whose compassion for the poor souls' suffering matched her own.

They saw little of Thomas, except at meals and on the occasions when they rode out together. Margot caught glimpses of him as he went about his duties, and then her pulse would quicken and she'd have to steady the beat of her heart.

What a fool she was! Behaving like some inexperienced, lovesick maiden, when the object of her adoration barely knew she existed! Thomas was always polite, invariably concerned for her welfare, even, on occasion, relaxed and friendly, but never by word or gesture did he show any sign of wanting to deepen their fragile relationship.

And she? She was careful to guard her feelings, to show nothing of the tumult of emotion his presence brought to tease her senses.

A merry hunting party left the castle one breathless July day, crossed the Soar, and headed for the forest, passing like a colourful swarm of exotic birds through the open fields. In some, corn was already beginning to ripen. In others, serfs paused in their labours to watch their progress before bending again to scythe the hay, their women and children to raking the cut grass into heaps.

Released from cadge or wrist, sparrow-hawks, goshawks and merlins soared high into the cloudless sky before stooping on to a variety of small animals and birds, all of which would add variety to the dinner and supper tables.

Although the grace and beauty of the birds in flight never ceased to fascinate Margot, she preferred the more energetic chase, when the horns sounded, the hounds bayed, and the horsemen raced in full cry after a prey which would provide a rich supply of venison or pork.

The dappled shade of the tracks and glades of the forest welcomed her after the heat of the open country. Margot rode joyously, inhaling the sweet scents of moss and bracken, leaf mould and damp earth, enjoying the song of the birds, safe here from winged menace, the chatter of the men and women around her, the snuffles and short, excited barks of the hounds.

Suddenly, the dogs caught the scent of a group of bucks drowsing in a hawthorn thicket. Led by a whooping Thomas, the men were off, singling out a startled buck with a large spread of antlers, not the largest of the group, for the best must be left to breed.

Led deeper among the thickets by the bounding, majestic, spotted buck, the huntsmen parted company with the ladies and their male attendants. Margot led the following chase along the easier, wider tracks, the more open spaces.

Kerchief flying, bent low over Fleurette's neck to avoid overhanging branches, she did not at first realise that they had been joined by a new group of riders. She heard shouts behind, followed by the din of conflict. Before she could rein in to discover the cause of the confusion, she became aware of thudding hoofs near by, of Fleurette's wild eyes and laid-back ears as a strange horse thundered alongside.

She glanced sideways to see a blur of russet, a groping hand, and gasped as steely fingers grasped her upper arms and began to drag her from her saddle.

She tangled her fingers in Fleurette's mane, holding on with desperate strength, screaming for help. For one dizzy moment she thought it had arrived as another horse drew level on her other side, but her relief was premature.

This was yet another grim-faced opponent, who reached out with a knife. Margot's throat closed on a scream as she waited for the blade to strike, but the man aimed low, cutting her stirrup leather. Then he brought the flat of his short sword down on her clutching fingers and thrust her forcefully towards the man who still held her arm.

There was naught she could do. Her fingers opened convulsively, the skin of her knuckles broken. For a moment her foot caught in the remaining stirrup, but came free with a sickening wrench of her ankle. The man hauled her across his horse's withers, throwing her face down like a sack of grain. The breath was knocked from her body by the impact of his pommel.

The rider's hand held her firmly on the horse, whose flying hoofs seemed to be just under her drooping head. She gasped as a huge clod of earth hit her face, and squirmed wildly, but her captor simply tightened his grip.

He didn't want her dead, she thought, as her first panic subsided, or she'd be lying in a pool of blood by now. So what did he want? Did he know who she was? Or was it a random abduction of a lady who looked worth ransom?

Panic rose again to choke her. The hot, steaming smell of horse, the constant pounding of the hard leather in her midriff threatened to make her spew up the contents of her stomach. She swallowed down the bile, closed her eyes to shut out the sight of thudding hoofs and flying turf, and clutched at the horse's girth, remembering that other time when Thomas had killed the man who had attempted to abduct her. Where was Thomas now?

All other sounds had died away. She was alone with the man and his sweating horse, which was slowing now the first urgency of flight was over.

"Let me up!" gasped Margot. "Please—let me up..."

"Be still!"

The hard voice held not an ounce of compassion for her discomfort.

He bent over her body, presumably to avoid a low-hanging branch, and Margot caught a waft of sweat, hot leather and metal. She felt brambles or twigs clutch at her skirt, while something whipped away her chaplet and then her veil.

He had left the main trail and was following a narrow, winding deer-run. Trying to throw off any possible pursuit?

Above the throb of blood pounding in her ears she heard the thud of distant hoofs. A soft curse told her her captor had heard it, too.

The following horse faltered for a moment, then began a steady advance. She tried to cry out, but her hoarse shout carried but a few yards. The man's hand tightened cruelly on her back. He cursed roundly under his breath as he twisted in his saddle, then uttered another oath, fierce, lewd and blasphemous. His legs moved urgently to spur his tired mount into a faster gait.

They joined a wider track, and the animal's pace picked up to a full gallop. But still the sound of hoofs drew nearer, and Margot now could hear their pursuer bellowing for them to stop.

Just a single horse, she thought, and her heart sank again. Could one man prevail against an armed bandit? She could see the man's great sword, feel as well as smell the chain-mail under the russet surcoat, though his legs and arms were not protected—nor his head, for she remembered he wore only a cap.

The men in the hunting party carried swords and crossbows, some bore spears, but they wore no armour.

What could she do? If only she could reach her knife she'd put it to good use this time! Reminded of its presence, she realised that her belt had become hitched up, that the things suspended from it were sticking into her ribs. She let go of the horse's girth with one hand and searched frantically among the folds of her gown. Her captor was too engaged in trying to outrun his pursuer to do more than utter another stream of curses and tighten his grip. He could not prevent her desperate squirming.

At last! Her fingers found the sheath. She eased it free, plucked the knife out, shut her eyes and lunged it into her captor's thigh.

He let out a yell of anger and pain, followed it with a vicious oath, and pounded his clenched fist down on her defenceless back. Margot winced and cried out, but before he could do her serious injury his horse gave a shriek of pain, stumbled drunkenly and fell, tumbling them both from its back.

Margot lay winded for a moment, a mass of hurt. She cowered from the hoofs of the struggling, screaming horse, seeing through dazed eyes the crossbow bolt in its rump.

Then, a throb of hope and joy rising irresistibly within, Margot saw Thomas throw himself from Pegasus's back to stand over the wounded man, his sword drawn.

"Get up," he snarled.

Hand on his own sword, the man gingerly did as bidden, hampered by the weight of his chain-mail and the deep wound dripping blood down his leg. Of Margot's dagger there was no sign.

"With pleasure, little brother," he drawled.

Thomas took a step backwards, as though he'd been struck in the face. He peered keenly at the thin, hard face with its straggling, greying beard, at the lank hair, fully exposed now the cap had fallen off, and, finally, reluctantly, it seemed to Margot, met grey eyes not unlike his own, except that they were smaller, harder, and any amusement they held was malicious.

"*Stephen?*"

Thomas's whisper held complete incredulity.

"Aye, brother. Not dead, as you'd no doubt hoped."

Thomas winced. "And Anne?" he demanded hoarsely.

"Oh, she died of the plague in Bristol," Stephen told him with a shrug. "Just as well. I couldn't have kept her with me."

"Devil's spawn!"

Time seemed to spin backwards and he became again the child who had rushed into the Solar at Wenfrith to see his brother stretched out unconscious on the floor. How bewildered he had been! How unwilling to believe it when Eleanor had gently explained that Richard had prevented Stephen from knifing them both to death. And the feeling of ultimate betrayal when he had realised how his brother had used his childish trust to introduce poison into their father's wine.

Thomas drew a deep breath and collected himself. He had to discover the depths of Stephen's present iniquity.

"You tried to abduct this lady. Why?" he demanded in a harsh voice.

Stephen smiled malevolently. "She was under your protection, brother. Having her taken from under your nose will damage your reputation, will it not?'' He barked a laugh. ''But that was not my only reason. The lady appeared too profitable a prize to ignore. Her father will pay well for her return. I do not doubt he will rather part with wealth than swear allegiance to a foreign prince.''

Thomas shook his head in disbelief. ''Your ill-will I could bear,'' he declared fiercely, ''but your attempt to profit from another's misfortune I cannot tolerate.'' He drew a harsh breath. ''But your puny attempt at abduction failed, brother.''

''I will take her still.''

''I think not.''

Thomas spoke through his teeth. He had become all soldier. But so had Stephen. Margot watched in helpless dismay as the brothers faced each other with grim, snarling faces, and Stephen stepped back, drawing his sword.

''Do not think me an easy opponent,'' he gibed softly. ''I was no swordsman when I left Wenfrith, but since then life has taught me much. I have spent the last years with Sir John Hawkwood, and, incidentally, amassed quite a fortune, to which I intend to add. I shall be rich and powerful before I die.''

''A mercenary!'' sneered Thomas. ''A specialist in brutality, no doubt! Hawkwood's White Company must have welcomed you with open arms!''

A memory stirred in Margot's mind. She had already realised this was the man she'd noticed in Leicester, but now she knew she had first seen him in the encampment at Burgos, when his cold gaze, fixed on Thomas, had filled her with unnamed dread.

''Thomas!'' she cried, ''I've seen him before, in the camp at Burgos, staring at you! Even then I knew he was your enemy!''

Thomas didn't even glance at her, his gaze was locked with Stephen's. But his brows lifted. "So," he drawled, "you followed Hawkwood to fight under the Prince of Wales's colours!"

"Like you, and Cedric, and Dickon, I go where my commander leads."

"You know Dickon?" asked Thomas warily.

"Don't fret yourself, brother." Stephen gave another harsh bark of sardonic laughter. "I have quite given up my quest for Wenfrith. Richard is too well entrenched, and has too many heirs. I could have killed Dickon a dozen times over had I so wished. Who could fail to notice one so favoured by the Prince of Aquitaine? His godson, is he not?"

"Praise God you were prevented from killing him ere he left his mother's womb! And yes, Prince Edward graciously consented to sponsor the babe at his baptism."

"An honour indeed," observed Stephen with heavy sarcasm. "In verity, he was born with a silver spoon in his mouth! And you, brother. You are equally honoured by Lancaster's favour. For a *bastard*," he brought the word out with infinite scorn, "you have done well for yourself."

"By honourable means! Stephen," cried Thomas, his old bewilderment and distress rising again to inject unsteadiness into his voice, "how could you use me to poison our father, how could you seek to kill Richard and Eleanor? Had Richard not shown us both great kindness?"

"Charity!" spat Stephen venomously. "Charity, when I deserved to be the heir!"

"You are younger than Richard. Even if born in wedlock you would not have been the heir!"

"But I loved that manor," said Stephen with sudden

sincerity. "I wanted the land. Richard did not care for it, he preferred fighting in foreign parts!"

"For that you were prepared to kill your father and your brother?"

Men had killed for less, thought Margot ruefully, and Thomas knew it. Yet still he appeared not to understand. Or not able to believe.

Stephen shrugged. "Why not? Such things are done all the time. The sin was in being found out."

Thomas made a sound of utter disgust. "And now your roles are reversed! Richard remains at Wenfrith, the manor is prosperous and well run, while you wander the continent fighting with a Free Company!"

"For me 'twas the only way to riches," snorted Stephen. "The towns were pestilential, the countryside equally so, and I had no wish to hang, or mayhap rot in a dungeon, if I was discovered. 'Twas expedient to take ship for France."

"Where you found congenial company," spat Thomas contemptuously. "Men who make war to take what they want without mercy or respect."

Stephen shrugged, a mocking smile twisting his thin lips. "I joined Hawkwood as a lowly groom," he told his brother. "Now Stephen the Groom is one of his most able commanders. And very skilled in the arts of war, Tamkin. I have no desire to kill you—merely to cause your downfall. Do you still wish to cross swords with me?"

"You think me lily-livered? Nay, Stephen, even if I thought you could beat me—which I do not—I would still fight you for the wrong you did me, for murdering our father, for the attempt to kill Richard and Eleanor, for the suffering you caused Cedric, for leading Anne Radcliffe into disloyalty and death. Above all," he added deliberately, "I would defend Lady Marguerite from your brutality." He lifted his heavy sword with both hands, pointing it at Stephen's heart. "So, on guard, brother!"

Stephen laughed, a bitter, mocking laugh which sent a shiver through Margot. She had risen to her knees and, crawling sideways into the protection of a tree-trunk, watched with anxious eyes as the two men circled each other.

Stephen was the heavier man, but he was also older and hampered by the wound she had inflicted. He had already lost enough blood to weaken him.

Thomas, defending her for reasons she did not want to question, was at the peak of his powers, young, strong, lithe—but unprotected from the other's sword. Stephen's target was large, the whole of Thomas's body. While Thomas must seek to hit where Stephen's hauberk offered no defence.

The first clash was slow in coming as they took each other's measure. As though by common consent they moved away from the thrashing, wounded horse, trampling underfoot the brambles and nettles on the verges of the track, creating an arena in which to test their arms.

Stephen was the first to lunge, but Thomas skipped lightly back, evading his opponent's blade with ease.

Margot cowered in the shelter of the trunk, pressing her clenched fists against her cheeks in an agony of helpless anxiety. Not for herself. For Thomas. If Thomas was killed she didn't care what happened to her.

Their swords clashed and scraped again and again in a dogged, two-handed exchange of blows that had both men panting with exertion, before Thomas seized a chance to bring the edge of his sword down on Stephen's shoulder. The blade struck chain-mail and slid harmlessly away, though Stephen staggered back from the force of the blow, falling to one knee as his injured leg gave way under him. His ashen face was beaded with cold sweat, his lips curled back from his teeth in a snarl of agony.

Thomas seemed to realise for the first time that his opponent was wounded. With instinctive chivalry, he hesitated for a fraction of a moment before pressing home his advantage. That second was all Stephen needed. His hand shot to his belt. With a speed and force born of desperation he drew his dagger and flung the blade at Thomas.

Margot died inside as she watched the weapon find its mark. A stab of pain, fierce as if the dagger had pierced her own flesh, wrenched an anguished cry from her parched throat.

Thomas staggered with pain and shock, looked down to see the knife buried deep in his shoulder.

His left arm hung useless. His lips thinned as his right hand tightened its grip on his heavy sword.

With another snarl Stephen lurched to his feet and plunged forward, the point of his weapon aimed at Thomas's exposed heart.

Instinctively, Thomas heaved his blade up to parry the blow he could see coming. With a skill and strength born of many years of crossing steel with the best swordsmen in the world, he slid Stephen's lunge aside.

Both men now fought with desperation, Thomas grimly holding on to the knowledge that few men could best him in combat. Stephen certainly could not, not in fair fight. But he had not fought fairly, and that knowledge spurred Thomas to ignore his flagging energy, the pain in his shoulder, the weakening of the steely sinews of his right arm, and make a last, supreme effort. With a surge of suddenly renewed power, he swept Stephen's sword aside and sliced his own into his brother's exposed neck.

Stephen went down without a sound, while the blood gushed and made a pool on the ground. Thomas stood swaying over his fallen enemy, remaining upright only because he leant his weight on the hilt of his dripping sword.

Margot stirred and scrambled up on wobbly legs. Picking up her stained and torn skirts, her eyes averted from the horrifying sight of Stephen's almost severed head, she stumbled to Thomas's side.

He looked at her, licked dry lips and smiled weakly. "Are you hurt?"

"No, I'm not, but you are!" Margot studied his ashen face and her eyes darkened as new fear clutched at her heart. "Thomas, sit on that fallen trunk, let me see to your wound—"

"Thank you," muttered Thomas politely, and collapsed in a heap beside his brother.

With a cry of distress, Margot dropped to her knees. The pulse in his neck throbbed quite strongly and she breathed again. The dagger still stuck from his shoulder. With infinite gentleness she pulled it out. Thomas's tunic and surcoat, already red and sodden, dripped new blood. She had to stop the bleeding or he would surely die.

If only she had her kerchief! She had nothing with which to bind the wound except the chaisel of her smock. She delved beneath the voluminous skirts of her gown and used Thomas's clean dagger to start a tear in the fine material beneath. She hacked and tore ruthlessly until she had enough to make a pad, and a binding to keep it in place.

Teeth clenched grimly together, she cut away

Thomas's clothes and pushed the pad of linen hard against the wound. Surely betony or woundwort would be growing near by? With Thomas's head pillowed in her lap, she scanned the floor of the forest with anxious eyes, but could see no sign of any herb which might make a healing poultice. She could not leave Thomas while she searched further afield. The wound would have to be bound up without.

As her fingers fumbled with the last knot, Thomas's eyes opened. He struggled to sit up, and groaned, feeling his shoulder tenderly as he did so.

"Rest a moment," implored Margot, pressing his head back against her thighs. "You have lost much blood."

"I'm all right," insisted Thomas, though his voice was weak and he seemed to have some difficulty in focusing his eyes on her upside-down face. He frowned. "Did I lose consciousness?"

"Aye, for a while."

"God's blood! Am I such a weakling? To lose my sense when you are still in danger!" Despite her restraining hands, he struggled into a more upright position and gazed at the still form of his brother. She watched helplessly as anguish filled his eyes. In a moment it was gone, replaced by anger and deep concern. "Margot, his men will be searching for him. We must ride away from here…"

"Aye, but on what?" asked Margot wryly. Stephen's horse had struggled to its feet and was standing under a tree on three legs, head hanging, shivering. She nodded towards it. "That beast will die unless attended to, and there is no other."

A faint smile touched Thomas's lips. He whistled through his teeth. Margot had heard him do the same thing many a time, and Pegasus had responded. But surely, now, he was being unduly optimistic. She'd seen no sign of the stallion since the fight had started.

Her head jerked round as the undergrowth rustled. Pegasus emerged from the forest, blowing gently down his nostrils. At a further soft whistle he trotted over to stand beside his master.

"Oh, Pegasus!" Margot jumped to her feet and caught his reins, throwing her arms around his neck in her relief and gratitude. He tossed his head at the unfamiliar touch, but he knew her, and stood quietly at a word from Thomas.

With eager, fumbling fingers, Margot took Thomas's hide wine-flask from its strap and held the opened neck to his parched lips.

Thomas drank thirstily, supporting the skin with his good hand. When he had drunk his fill he handed it back to her with an imperative gesture.

"You drink, too. You look as though you need it."

His sight was clearer now. He could see the pallor of her face, the shaking of her hands. And the infinite concern in her fabulous eyes. For him? Or for her own safety?

Margot drank gratefully. The wine stimulated her flagging energy, but Thomas still looked as though he might pass out again at any moment.

"Can you mount?" she asked briskly.

He grimaced. "I can try. Perhaps if I use that log..."

He accepted her help to stand. Wiped and sheathed his sword. Staggered to the fallen tree, leaning on her shoulder.

It made an excellent mounting-block. Pegasus, as though sensing his master's need, stood rock still as Margot put all her strength behind helping Thomas up, wincing with pain as she straightened her elbow. Her entire body ached.

Thomas drooped over the horse's neck semi-conscious, barely aware when Margot climbed up behind the saddle.

She reached round his sagging form and took the reins. Pegasus shifted his feet, ready to move off at her command, but which way should she steer? Margot had no idea where they were, just that the chase had taken them deeper and deeper into the forest, miles from where they'd been when the attack had occurred.

She turned Pegasus's head back the way they'd come. Obediently, he walked on, bearing the double burden easily. Stephen's mount gave a pitiful whinny and limped after them.

Chapter Twelve

A maze of paths laced the woods and glades like an intricate spider's web. How long they wandered them Margot never knew. Time began to lose its meaning as she concentrated on keeping Thomas in his saddle. Pegasus, given his head, took his direction at random.

Had she been able to follow the rays of the westering sun, Margot thought she could probably have found her way back to Leicester. But the once clear sky had turned dark and ominous as thunder-clouds gathered.

Stephen's wounded horse dropped further and further behind. He gave one last, pitiful whinny before he stopped, to stand gazing after them with pleading eyes. Margot wished she'd extracted the quarrel from his hindquarters before mounting behind Thomas, because then the wound might have healed itself, but there hadn't been time. Even now she could spare nothing but compassion for the poor beast, such was her urgency to find shelter and safety before the clouds burst.

An unnatural stillness pervaded the forest as birds and beasts alike silently awaited the threatened storm, and the sudden, intrusive sound of distant human voices carried clearly. Margot's stomach lurched. She tugged on

Pegasus's reins, bringing him to a halt, soothing him in a hushed voice to keep him quiet.

Friends or enemies? She dared not proceed until she knew.

She manoeuvred Pegasus into the cover of a thicket, thankful that both she and Thomas were dressed in shades of green which blended into the background, as did Pegasus's darkish, dappled-grey coat.

The sudden shout brought her heart leaping to her throat. She heard Stephen's name ring out and glimpsed shadowy riders not more than a hundred paces distant, beyond a thin screen of bushes. They had discovered the wounded horse.

The men caught the lamed beast, examined its injury, searched for tracks, found none in the hard ground, and made off in the direction from which the animal had appeared.

Away from them. Relief washed over her. Margot urged Pegasus on, putting distance between the men and themselves.

She continued to allow the horse his head, prodding him forwards now and again when he hesitated, praying they were not travelling in a circle which would bring them face to face with their enemies. She had little choice but to trust the instincts of the horse, for, in the now oppressive, twilight world of the forest, her own sense of direction had failed completely.

Pegasus snorted and trembled as a distant flash of lightning cast eerie shadows through the branches of the trees. Seconds later came a rumble of thunder, and Margot hastily crossed herself as she tried to soothe the frightened animal. If only the storm would go away! But the distant rumbles continued, increasing her agitation. Thunder was a bad omen.

When Pegasus lifted his head and snickered, Margot's heart first skipped a beat, then began an urgent drumming. What had he sensed? Another horse? Danger?

But the grey did not seem alarmed. Rather, he lengthened his stride, ears pricked, and bore them swiftly to the place where he had caught the welcome scent of water.

He stood while Margot slid stiffly from his back. Thomas roused sufficiently to look around, see the stream, throw one leg over his horse's neck, and dismount. Margot went to steady him as he landed, but his falling weight was too much for her, and they finished in a heap on the riverbank as the first great drops of rain began to fall.

Margot hastily extricated herself from Thomas's sprawling weight.

"Are you hurt?" she asked anxiously. "Did you damage your shoulder again?"

"Nay." He sounded dispirited. "I don't know why I'm so cursedly weak. The loss of a little blood—"

"A lot of blood," put in Margot quietly. "Look at your tunic."

Thomas inspected the white linen bindings, now stained a bright red, the state of his clothes, and the careful way Margot had tucked his useless arm into the wide armhole of his sodden surcoat.

"I had not realised…"

"The dagger went deep." Her voice shook. "A few inches lower, and I believe it would have pierced your heart, Thomas."

Thomas responded to the quiver in her voice by saying, weakly but bracingly, "But it did not. Curse Stephen for the lying, dishonourable cur that he is! I should have known not to trust to his honour!"

Margot swallowed. "*Was*, Thomas. Stephen is dead."

"May God forgive him, for I cannot! Though God knows I would rather not have his blood on my conscience," he added sombrely.

Margot looked straight into his eyes, seeing his anguish clearly mirrored there. How could she ease his hurt?

"He wished you nothing but ill," she reminded him. "How can a man become so bitter? But he is gone now, Thomas, he can do no more harm, and you killed him in fair combat."

"On my part, at least," he agreed bitterly. "Aye, I know." He heaved a sigh. "What of his men?"

"They are probably still in the forest, searching. They passed quite near a while back. Pray they do not find us here."

"Aye. I shall prove a poor defender, my dear."

The slow smile of delight his unconscious endearment brought spread unbidden over Margot's features. She ignored the bitterness of his tone and smiled into his drawn, grey face. "Be thankful your wound is no worse," she comforted him. "Keep the shoulder still or you will start the bleeding again. Would you like some water? The stream looks clear enough."

Pegasus had already drunk his fill. Margot let the sparkling water bubble into Thomas's flask. A little wine remained, which would serve to purify it.

A flash, soon followed by a loud clap of thunder, heralded the downpour Margot had dreaded. Holding fast to a quivering Pegasus, she led him to a nearby tree and tethered him securely in the shelter of its overhanging branches. Normally he would not stray, but with the storm overhead she could not trust to his obedience.

She searched around desperately with her eyes, seeking shelter for themselves. The thick canopy of a nearby spreading oak seemed to offer the best protection, until she glimpsed what looked like the outline of a derelict building.

Her heart lifted. A quick foray confirmed their luck. She ran back to Thomas and put a hand under his good arm.

"Come," she instructed breathlessly. "I have found shelter. The rain is getting heavier. We cannot afford to get soaked."

Thomas grunted, gritted his teeth, and staggered to his feet. With Margot's support he managed to reach the abandoned woodsman's or maybe hermit's cot.

The mud and wattle walls were more or less intact, though the thatch had gone in places, eaten away by animals and birds. The lintel over the doorway had collapsed, bringing down the wall above, but the stout planking of the door still held together, hanging from the post by one rusty iron hinge.

Margot eased the drunken door aside. It was too dim to see much inside the hut, though a little light filtered through a small window-opening in one wall and, of course, through the doorway. An unpleasant smell of rotting vegetation and worse met her nostrils as they stepped over the threshold, which Margot ignored. Thomas needed shelter and rest. Nothing else was important.

Except security. Stephen's party was probably not the only band of cut-throats at large in the forest. The door would suffice, shut and barred.

"Wait here," she commanded Thomas. "I'll only be a moment."

"Don't get wet."

His cry followed her as she sped across to Pegasus to

fetch the saddle and bags. The horse would be happier without their weight, and the saddle would make a pillow for Thomas's head.

On her return she found Thomas slumped against the wall, his eyes closed. She threw down her burden and went outside again to gather a huge armful of ferns, still comparatively dry under the shelter of the trees. And, near the stream, she found comfrey growing.

Triumphant and only slightly damp, she spread the ferns and laid the saddle at their head.

"Come, Thomas, lie here. I must tend your wound again."

Thomas crawled over and subsided on the makeshift bed. He had hardly spoken a word in the last hours and, although he'd rallied a little recently, Margot could not help but worry. The wound was likely to be infected and, unless it was soon treated, Thomas would develop a fever, and then he'd most probably die.

Margot shivered at the thought. The downpour began in earnest as she retired to the darkest dry corner of the hut and lifted her skirts to tear more strips of linen from her ruined smock.

Armed with new dressings, the wine-skin and the comfrey leaves, Margot set about cleansing and rebinding Thomas's wound. He lay back, teeth gritted, while she worked in the dim light from the open door. Without the sun very little daylight filtered through the overhanging trees.

The bleeding had almost stopped, so cauterising would not be necessary, which was just as well since she had no fire going yet. Pressing crushed comfrey leaves against the raw flesh, she wadded and bound the shoulder again.

"I wish I had my veil," she grumbled when she'd finished. "It would make a sling for your arm."

"Be thankful it did snag on that bush." Thomas gave her a wan smile. "Had I not spotted your chaplet and then the veil way off the main track, I would have galloped straight on and not found you."

Weak tears of relief filled Margot's eyes. With the emergency over, some semblance of safety ensured, Thomas recovering, reaction set in. She bent her head to hide the wetness on her cheeks.

Thomas's good hand reached up to touch her tousled hair.

"Please don't cry, Margot."

His gruff voice, his gesture, both so tender, brought on a flood of tears she could not control.

"I'm sorry," she said thickly as the paroxysm passed. "I don't normally cry, I don't know what came over me."

"These are not normal circumstances." Thomas swore roundly, frustration with himself making him spit out angrily, "I should be looking after you, not lying here helpless as a kitten!"

That made Margot laugh, albeit a little shakily.

"I am quite recovered now!" she told him brightly. "The rain has stopped. I'll see what I can do about lighting a fire and finding us something to eat."

Having collected several armfuls of dryish twigs, she returned to dump them on the floor under the tiny window. The thinnest, most brittle, she set aside for kindling.

The activity restored her spirits. Humming under her breath, she rummaged in Thomas's saddle-bag for the tinder-box he kept there. She was adept at making sparks with flint and steel, and the thin, dry shavings caught quickly. She blew gently to encourage the flame to spread through the kindling, and was soon feeding the fire with more solid sticks. The smoke rose in a choking cloud as the surface dampness was driven off, but it found its way out of the window and the many holes in the thatch.

The forest had begun to come alive again. Small animals scuttled about in the undergrowth seeking an evening meal. Margot took Thomas's hunting bow and quiver, removed with the horse's saddle, and crouched in the doorway of the hut.

"What are you doing? Is there danger?"

She turned with a reassuring smile. "No danger. Since I've nothing to snare with, I shall try to shoot a coney. 'Tis the only way we shall eat this night! Would you enjoy roast rabbit for supper?"

"Can you use a bow?"

The doubt in his voice amused her. "Aye. I learned at Sedano. When Roberto was away, the castle's defence was in my hands, and I often led the hunt. The bolts are large for conies, but never mind."

A soft chuckle told her Thomas was feeling better. "Then good luck," he wished her cheerfully. "I confess to feeling that I could eat a horse!"

"Then perhaps two conies will be necessary!"

Margot wound the bow, loaded a quarrel and waited. The coney sat upright, brushing its whiskers with its front paws. Margot took careful aim and pulled the trigger.

She missed. But that shot told her where to aim the next time. She loosed again. The coney leapt into the air with a squeal and then lay still. It did not take her long to make her second kill.

She took the dead animals to the river, where she gutted and skinned them, threading the carcasses on sharpened sticks. On her way back she filled her skirt with early puff-balls, wild garlic, wild thyme, dandelion leaves and several tendrils of vine.

Finally, she picked up the stout branch she had previously chosen as a bar.

Pushing the door firmly shut, blanking out the last rays of daylight, she jammed the branch across it. Although the storm was over, the sky continued sullen, threatening. She had no way of knowing whether the sun had set or not. No way of telling the time, except by the very definite rumble of her stomach. It must be well past the normal hour for supper.

Working swiftly by the flickering light of the fire, she stuffed the rabbits with toadstools, garlic and thyme, tied the flesh with lengths of vine, and set the meat to roast over the fire, the sticks supported on stones.

While she worked, Thomas dropped off to sleep. She knelt beside him, nursing her own elbow, which had begun to throb. She unbuttoned the sleeve of her kirtle and pushed it up, to discover an ugly swelling. There was little she could do about that.

She touched Thomas's forehead with feather-light fingers. It felt quite cool. No fever yet.

Rising to her feet again, she went and squatted by the fire, nursing its flames, turning the meat. Before long the aroma of roast rabbit began to overcome the less pleasant stenches in the shelter.

"That smells good."

Startled from her thoughts, Margot turned to find Thomas regarding her from his bed of leaves. His bright eyes shimmered in the semi-darkness. His voice was stronger.

"I hope you're still hungry," grinned Margot. "It's just about cooked."

He answered her with a chuckle. "You are a resourceful woman, Margot. Most ladies would have thrown up their hands and given up by now. But you—not only have you found us shelter, but provided food as well!"

Her brows lifted quizzically. "Did we not decide once before that I am not upset by a little danger?"

This time he laughed outright, a hearty shout which reassured Margot more than anything else he had done since his injury. "Aye, we did!"

Neither of them mentioned her earlier tears. Margot still didn't understand what had brought on such an uncharacteristic display of weakness. Truth to tell, now the imminent danger was past she was rather enjoying their predicament. Safe in the hut, a night in the forest held no terrors for her, despite the possibility of wolves gathering to howl at their door.

Wolves. Might they attack Pegasus? She eyed the door, heightened by the gap betwixt it and the rotting roof. He could be brought into the shelter before they slept. She said nothing to Thomas as yet.

The meat was cooked. Using two flat stones and the dagger, she cut them into manageable pieces, laid them on beds of dandelion leaves, and carried the impromptu platters over, setting one carefully on Thomas's outstretched thighs.

Perhaps because they were both hungry, the stuffed meat tasted wonderful. Washed down with water and wine from Thomas's flask, it made a satisfying meal.

"I think," said Margot eventually, looking through the tiny window at stars emerging from behind dark clouds, "I'd better bring Pegasus inside. The door is high enough for him. Otherwise he will be at the mercy of wolves or thieves.''

''Aye. Bring the old boy in. He'll cause no trouble.''

Pegasus, though, was not at all keen on passing through the dark opening until Thomas called him. Then he snorted, shook his head, and sidled in at Margot's urging.

She re-barred the door. The space seemed very small with the horse inside.

''I'd better tie him up, but what to?'' she wondered.

''Leave him loose. He'll stand quietly.'' Thomas changed his tone to one of soothing, affectionate command. ''Stand by, Pegasus.''

The horse tossed his head, pawed the ground, snickered, moved into a corner away from the fire, and stood still. Margot spread an armful of ferns between his feet and gave him a pat.

''Good boy,'' praised Thomas. ''We had better sleep,'' he yawned, settling himself back on his bed of leaves.

''Yes.''

Margot had retained enough soft material to make a bed for herself. As she began to spread it, Thomas stayed her with a gesture.

''Margot, will you lie near me? The day has been hot, but we shall need each other's warmth before the night is through. Pegasus needs his blanket or he'll catch a chill, so we have no covering but our clothes, and they are thin. Besides, there is little enough room in here.''

All the emotions she had been suppressing for hours rose to choke Margot's throat. Lie near Thomas? Her nerves tingled with apprehension. Her heart speeded up as though she'd been running. How would it feel? Could she refuse?

Thomas had been weakened by loss of blood. He would suffer from any chill. It was surely her duty...

And her delight. She acknowledged her longing at last and nervously spread her litter beside him.

"Aye," she murmured, her voice a breathless husk.

"Sleep well," murmured Thomas drowsily, putting his good arm around her and drawing her stiff body closer so that his shoulder would pillow her head.

Margot gave a gasp of pain and shrank away.

"What is it?" asked Thomas sharply, then, seeing her holding her swollen elbow, realised what was amiss.

"Nothing. I bruised my elbow and it hurts if I rest on it. 'Twill be better by morn."

"Let me see."

Reluctantly, Margot allowed him to take hold of her arm. He drew the damaged joint near his eyes and scrutinised the swelling thoughtfully in the glow from the fire. "You're sure it's not broken?"

"Quite sure."

"Then perhaps this will make it better."

Gently, he drew her nearer and laid his lips on the inflamed flesh. They were cool, so reassuringly cool. Yet they sent fire streaking up her arm to consume her heart.

Thomas seemed not to notice her agitation. He released her arm and spread his own invitingly. "Arrange yourself comfortably, my lady," he suggested softly. "Put your head on my shoulder. There."

She felt so good in his arms. Too spent for passion, he examined with astonishment the sense of infinite contentment brought by just having her lying trustingly against him. Even if she was trembling with nerves.

She had undoubtedly saved his life that day. Gratitude reawoke in him the ever-present urge to protect. The feeling overwhelmed him, and his arm tightened around her shoulders.

If it cost him his life, he would defend Marguerite de Bellac against the world.

Margot, swamped in a gushing torrent of sweet sensation, felt his arm tighten and was not afraid. She nestled closer, closed her eyes with a soft sigh, and slept.

Pegasus woke her. Pegasus and the deafening sound of the birds' morning chorus as they joyously greeted the new day.

If wolves had howled she had not heard them. Her sleep had been deep and dreamless. Thomas had barely stirred, either, though his arm must be cramped under her weight.

Thomas. She moved, careful not to rest on her elbow or to wake him, slowly easing limbs stiff from lying on the hard ground. The sky outlined by the tiny window was gathering grey streaks, but as yet the light was not enough to disperse the shadows.

Margot leaned close over Thomas's sleeping face, a pale blur in the darkness. Tenderly, she touched his brow. It was cool, and she breathed a sigh of relief. It seemed that God had heeded her prayers.

She fingered the beads and cross at her waist and her lips moved in soundless thanksgiving. Crossing herself, she rose to her feet, feeling her way to the restless horse.

The hut stank like a stable, for Pegasus had not been continent. Escape from its close confines seemed inordinately attractive. Margot shifted the bar and put her head out into the clean air. Hearing and seeing nothing untoward, she led the animal down to the stream for water.

While waiting for Pegasus to drink, Margot found a

secluded spot in which to relieve herself, splashed her face and cleansed her hands, then drank some of the clear water herself. The sky had lightened and a faint tinge of red stained it in what must be the east. Soon they could be on their way.

Thomas awoke feeling rested and much stronger. His eyes strayed languidly around the dim interior of the hut, before, with a muttered curse, he struggled to prop himself on his good elbow, the better to see. His brows contracted into a scowl as he digested an unpalatable truth. Margot and Pegasus had gone.

For an instant he panicked. Had she decided to leave him and escape? Even as the thought crossed his mind he rejected it. He knew, with an inner, unshakable certainty, that he could trust Margot with his life. Had she not proved it, yesterday?

He scrambled to his feet and went to the door, sniffing the fresh air with relish. Pegasus had fouled their nest and it was good to escape its confines.

There they were. Down by the river. Dark shadows against the reddening sky. Relief, and a sweet, deep contentment swept over him. He watched for a moment while Margot sluiced her face and hands in the cold water. Then he dragged his eyes from her. He must take advantage of his momentary isolation to seek out a secluded corner for his own use. Thank God his legs felt as though they belonged to him again!

He did not go far, but Margot was back in the hut before him, packing the saddle-bags ready for departure.

"You've been out?" The relief in her eyes at the sight of him shone through the dimness. "You must be feeling better!"

"Almost back to normal. Thanks to you, Margot."

He moved close, reaching for her hand. "How can I ever thank you for your care?" he wondered.

He couldn't see it, but he could feel the blush rise in her face by the sudden, embarrassed squirm of the hand he held.

"You have no need of thanks," she murmured. "You fought to save me. What else could I do?"

"So perhaps we are indebted to each other. A bond, Margot." He laughed suddenly, boyishly. "We must never quarrel again!"

"We shall not, an you trust me at last!"

"With my life," he told her sincerely.

"Then eat these! They are not poisonous, I promise you!"

"More toadstools?" He took a handful from her with a wry laugh. "What a feast!"

"I would have caught fish to break our fast, but I had not the means, and the fire has died. With luck we may be back at the castle in time for dinner."

"In which direction did you think to go?" he asked, munching dutifully if a trifle warily.

"That is the east." Margot waved a hand at the rosy sky and took a bite from a puff-ball. "You know the forest better than I. What say you? Should we follow the stream?"

"I think I can find the way back from here. The water would no doubt lead us there eventually, but we can find a shorter route by heading west. Are you ready?"

"If you are. Can you mount?"

"Undoubtedly."

"I'll fetch Pegasus. He's a wonder horse."

Thomas chuckled. "I know, but don't tell him, he'll become uncontrollable!"

He mounted easily with the help of a log, and hauled Margot up behind him with his good arm.

All around the forest stirred. Rustles, grunts and squeaks preceded their progress. The sky lightened and Margot was reminded of their trek through the Pyrénées, where they'd always set out soon after dawn. How different was this journey! How she had fought against that leading-rein! Yet here she was, riding pillion without benefit of a saddle, revelling in her closeness to Thomas, quite happy to let him take control of their progress.

The sun had been moving steadily southward for a considerable time when they heard the first sounds of men and horses.

Thomas reined Pegasus in, gentling him with a word, and they both strained their ears to make out where the sounds were coming from.

"Whoever it is, they're spread out," muttered Thomas at last.

"A search-party."

"Aye, but whose?"

"They're coming nearer."

Thomas drew his sword. The sound grated along Margot's nerves like a rasp.

"If they want a fight, they can have it," he declared.

"But Thomas, your shoulder! And you only have a hunting saddle—"

"Stop worrying, woman!" Thomas grinned over his shoulder, his eyes sparkling with amusement and something more—anticipation. "I'll not confront them unless I'm forced. You dismount and take cover."

"I'll not leave you," muttered Margot, clinging fiercely.

His eyes suddenly reminded her of pools covered with

wintry ice. "Would you hamper me in a man's work?" he demanded coldly.

Margot slid to the ground, her face burning.

Unable to help herself, "Take cover yourself!" she pleaded.

He smiled, his eyes warm again. "Of course."

Pushing her way into a thicket of elderberry, she watched Thomas back Pegasus behind a screening hazelnut bush.

Silent, they waited.

The sounds drew nearer. Someone was making an excellent job of scouring the forest. The bark of hounds did little to reassure Margot. Stephen's men could hire a pack from any nearby manor. Though perhaps the dogs came from the castle. On balance, that seemed most likely, and her hopes rose.

Yet as the moments passed she found her hands damp with sweat, her heart thudding painfully in her chest. The waiting was unendurable. If something didn't happen soon her nerves would snap, she would behave like a dolt...

And then, a hundred yards away, a horse and rider emerged from the cover of the trees. The horse's head was up. It snickered.

Pegasus danced and answered. In his eagerness he moved forward, and Thomas did nothing to stop him.

Margot crashed through the undergrowth. "Juan!" she cried. "Thomas, it's Juan, riding Fleurette!"

"Aye, so I see!"

Completely relaxed as he was, the smile on Thomas's face became so broad that Margot couldn't help responding with a joyous laugh. "Praise God!" she cried. "Juan, how did you find us?"

But Juan, apart from crying *"Doña!"* in a triumphant

voice, was too busy sounding a loud blast on a horn to make reply.

He cantered up and threw himself off Fleurette's back, dropping to his knees at Margot's feet and feverishly grasping her hand.

After that, everything was chaos as men, horses and hounds gathered around them. More than half the garrison must be out, thought Margot dazedly. As well as many of the servants.

Questions were asked and answered, but Margot barely registered them. She stroked Fleurette's soft muzzle, leaned against her side, and struggled to regain her composure.

They were safe. Only then, when safety was assured, did she realise how anxious she had been. But Thomas was not out of danger yet. His shoulder required attention, he needed rest.

He had not dismounted and sat, completely in control, among his men. His face was pale and drawn, but otherwise he looked perfectly well. She doubted whether any, except those like Ned who crowded close to him, had noticed the wound or the dried blood still staining his clothes.

He gave his orders. Most of the men were to continue scouring the forest. He wanted them to recover Stephen's body if it still lay where it had fallen, and to make sure that his small army of mercenaries were no longer in the district. A couple of servants were detailed to gallop on ahead to give news of their safety. The remainder would escort them back at a more leisurely pace.

Margot would have preferred to ride pillion behind Thomas again, but Juan was already making a cradle for her foot with his hands, ready to throw her into her saddle. Thomas had moved away.

"I'm glad it was you who found us, Juan," she told the boy in Spanish.

"Fleurette found Pegasus," grinned Juan. "I realised she'd scented something, and let her have her head."

"You are very clever, both of you!"

"Nay, *doña*. 'Twas merely instinct!"

Margot laughed as she settled herself in the familiar saddle. It was certainly more comfortable than Pegasus's flanks, but lonely. She had a great need to touch Thomas to convince herself that he was still alive, that he was real.

But he rode off at the head of the depleted column, leaving her to trail behind among the retainers.

Depression settled over her. He had forgotten her already. The beautiful intimacy of the night might never have been. Now he was safely back among his own people he had no further need of her care or her company.

Back at the castle she had no chance to speak to him again. Her ladies immediately surrounded her and carried her off to her chamber and a bath. Thomas was similarly borne off by his attendants.

Once inside her room, Margot suddenly balked.

"Leave me," she ordered imperiously. "All of you but Kate."

"But, my lady, your bath—"

"Are you not exhausted, my lady?"

"*Doña*, you wish for me to go too?"

Margot ignored the chorus of protest. "Yes, Inés, all of you. I am not exhausted, and my bath can wait for an hour. Now go!"

Inés departed mutinously, Meg Throstle with injured dignity, and Beth Horsley with pursed lips and suspicious, narrowed eyes.

Margot did not care. Once they were alone she turned to Katherine.

"Sir Thomas has need of our help. Fetch the wound-salve and the dressings and come with me."

Followed by Kate, Margot swept to the Great Chamber. Inside, Thomas lay supine on the huge bed, surround by a group of anxious attendants.

"Ned, I told you to send everyone away. And to ensure that no word of my indisposition is let loose in the castle!"

Thomas's voice sounded weak, far away, as though it was a struggle for him to speak.

"I am sorry, but they would take no notice of me." Ned turned on the other men. "You heard Sir Thomas! Leave him, as he wishes, and say no word of this!"

"We must call the surgeon!" insisted the steward nervously. "He will let some blood to relieve the pressure on his brain and bring him back to his senses—"

"No!"

Margot's voice rang around the chamber, making everyone jump. "No," she repeated in a more normal voice, as she trod across the floor and pushed her way to Thomas's side. The welcome in his eyes as he saw her was reward enough for the nervous flutter in her stomach. Battling with these determined men would take courage.

"Can you not see the state of his clothes?" she demanded scathingly, looking round the ring of hostile faces with challenging eyes. "Do you not realise that enough blood has been let from his body in the last hours? He is exhausted, nothing more. Ned!"

"Aye, my lady?"

"See that all these people leave, as your master has commanded. You may remain and help Dame Katherine and myself to tend him." She turned to the others. "We have salve and bandages. You all know that I have cured many a cut and scratch, many a fever since I have been here. You may leave Sir Thomas in my hands with perfect confidence. And do not forget his command to remain silent."

"Aye, my lady."

They all backed out, bowing deferentially, though some faces held resentment.

Margot ignored them. "How do you feel?" she asked Thomas softly.

"Better for your presence." He managed a weak smile which brought tears to her eyes, tears she quickly blinked back. This was no time for sentiment or weakness. "I twisted my cursed shoulder in the yard," explained Thomas fretfully. "That brought on the faintness again."

"I do not wonder! Ned?" She called the young man to her. "Cut off Sir Thomas's surcoat, tunic and shirt. I cannot cleanse his wound properly unless they are removed. They are filthy, and caked with blood."

"Aye, lady, but..." Ned looked at her helplessly, his youthful face tinged with pink. "I cannot do it with you ladies here," he gabbled.

"Of course you can! We have both seen a man's bare chest before! Come, Ned, we need your help to lift him," she coaxed.

"Do as Lady Marguerite says, Ned."

Reluctantly, with many a sigh, Ned did as he was asked. The pain caused by the removal of the filthy clothes from under him was too much for Thomas. He relapsed into unconsciousness.

Margot studied the still form revealed, and a great, anxious tenderness overwhelmed her. So strong, so vital, his hard muscles visible even in his weakness. Yet so vulnerable. He had kept going despite everything during the journey back. Had reached his bed without showing his weakness. But once there he had finally succumbed to the effects of yesterday's wounding and today's new loss of blood.

The bandage around his shoulder was stained bright red again.

Chapter Thirteen

Although the deep puncture had re-opened, the surrounding flesh looked healthy enough. The fresh bleeding had practically stopped.

Vastly relieved, Margot told Ned to sponge down as much of Thomas's torso he could reach without moving him. By the time she was ready to spread salve over the wound, Thomas had come round and was able to prop himself up on the other elbow while she bound it again with clean linen.

"An you wish to recover your strength quickly, Sir Thomas, rest that arm," Margot advised. "Don't attempt to struggle into tight clothes. If you must dress, wear something loose."

"It seems I have little choice," returned Thomas wryly. "My shoulder is as stiff as a rusty hinge—I doubt I could move it sufficiently to get my arm into my normal garb." He flexed the joint experimentally, gave a grimace of pain, and sank back on the bed, perspiration beading his brow. "I'll dine here and Ned will find me something comfortable to wear to the Hall for supper."

Margot shook her head in despair. "You will not rest, will you?"

"Nay, lady, 'tis not that." Thomas tried to shrug, and winced instead. He ran his good hand across his forehead, wiping off the sweat. "But I cannot allow people here to believe me too weak to command this castle. 'Twould give rise to doubt and fear. My time here has been too short for me to have won the loyalty of everyone. There are those who would usurp my position."

Margot ran her tongue around suddenly dry lips. "Surely not," she protested. "You were appointed by the Duke. Who would dare…?"

"Ambitious men dare much," he retorted tiredly. "Nay, Margot, do not argue!" He grinned to soften the command and remove the worried frown from her face. He knew his position was less secure than it appeared, but that was no reason to upset her with his worries. "You would nurse me as a child! Do not forget that I am a grown man, and have a man's duty to perform!"

How could she forget that? thought Margot, her eyes drawn irresistibly to his broad chest. Goose-bumps came up as she imagined the *frisson* of running her fingers over the fine hairs dusting his silky skin. No, it wasn't revulsion, but something far more subtle. An awareness, a shrinking, and as yet unformed desire.

"I do not forget," she replied softly. "I will see you in the Great Hall."

"Then you had better be about your own concerns." He grinned wickedly. "Methinks you could do with a cleansing yourself. You exude a most appealing aroma of wood-smoke, roast meat, garlic and toadstools."

His tired eyes laughed into hers with intimate challenge, reminding her of the previous night.

Margot snorted, covering her confusion. "Not to mention horse and dung!" she responded lightly. "Come, Kate. We are no longer needed here!"

She tossed her head in mock indignation, but her lips twitched with an irrepressible smile as she led Katherine from the Great Chamber.

Her good humour carried her through her own ablutions. She barely noticed Meg's curiosity or Beth's animosity.

Kate and Inés helped her to dress, while the others inspected her discarded clothing, giving little cries of astonishment and dismay.

"Throw it away," instructed Margot carelessly. "I fear it is ruined beyond repair."

"It looks as though you've been rolling in the hay," observed Beth, the innuendo barely hidden behind an innocent smile.

"I slept on bracken and leaves," replied Margot with a lift of one bare shoulder. "There was naught else on which to lie."

Beth clicked her tongue. "And these tears—"

"Brambles and thorn." Damnation take the woman's insolence! "You saw how I was thrown over that bandit's horse. My chaplet and veil were whipped off by the bushes. Think you *your* clothes would have fared better under the circumstances?" challenged Margot coldly.

Beth lowered her eyes, but did not reply.

"How frightened you must have been!"

"Aye, Meg. 'Twas not a pleasant experience."

"I wonder who he was!"

Margot hesitated to reveal the identity of her attacker, so she did not respond to Meg's avid curiosity other than with a shrug. Thomas must be the one to decide whether he would admit to fighting and killing his brother. So far the body had not been recovered. His men had probably carried it away. A long way away, she fervently hoped.

A page brought meat, bread, cheese and wine from the kitchen, and Margot assuaged her ravenous appetite. She could not remember the last time she had felt so hungry!

Thomas appeared at the high table for supper, his face pale and drawn. Margot's eyes approved the loose tunic and wide-sleeved houppelande he wore. Apart from his lack of colour he showed no sign of indisposition.

He greeted her with a smile, which she returned. For a long moment their gazes locked while a flood of warmth and understanding flowed between them. Margot's heart began an excited flutter. At last, it seemed, they truly had become friends.

She watched him covertly. He ate well but, to Margot's concerned eye, quickly began to show signs of weariness. The furrows down his cheeks deepened and tiny lines of strain appeared around his eyes.

He left the table early, indicating that others should remain and enjoy the entertainment provided by minstrels and tumblers. He strode away, allowing no sign of weakness. Margot swallowed down the sudden lump in her throat, and wished she could join the train of personal squires and attendants who followed him from the Hall.

In little more than a week Thomas had recovered all his normal strength and vitality, though his shoulder remained painfully stiff. When Margot inspected it for the last time she gave a nod of satisfaction.

"It has healed well. Time is all it needs now. But do not tax it too hard as yet."

"I'll do nothing foolish," he promised her.

For once they were alone in his chamber. Margot had dismissed her ladies before making her routine visit to check on his wound. Thomas's pages were at their lessons, his older attendants scattered about the castle at their duties. After Ned had helped him on with his tunic, Thomas had sent him on an errand to Leicester. Ned would doubtless find his way into a tavern, and it would be some hours before he could bring himself to leave the entertainments provided there.

Margot waited, enjoying the rare moments of quiet intimacy, knowing that Thomas had arranged it so. The bustling castle allowed few chances to be alone, fewer still to share solitude with someone special. Even now, some inmate, servant or master could break in upon them, demanding Thomas's attention.

Thomas lifted down a small coffer resting in a wall-niche, placed it on a table, opened the carved lid and took something from it. He turned, smiling, and came back to where Margot sat on a stool by the hearth.

He dropped to one knee beside her.

"I never meant to keep this," he explained softly. "Now seems a good time to return what is yours."

Margot gasped when she saw her gold filigree necklace gleaming on his palm, the gems flashing in a myriad colours in the rays of the sun.

"Thomas! But 'tis yours by right of ransom. You do not have to return it to me! There must be some lady you would wish to have it."

During those first days at Leicester she had dreaded seeing her favourite piece of jewellery clasped around Beth's neck. More recently she had forgotten about it. Now she waited breathlessly for Thomas's response.

"Nay, Margot. I think you know there is not. Were it not already yours, I would wish to bestow it on you.

You saved my life. And I believe that now we are friends. Let me place it where it belongs.''

Margot shivered as his fingers brushed her nape, fumbling slightly with the unfamiliar fastening. When he had done, he shifted back to face her. His fingers traced the delicate workmanship where it rested against her creamy skin, then lingered on a large agate glowing palely in a field of green flirt silk just at the point where it dipped into the valley between her breasts.

''Exquisite,'' he smiled, the *double entendre* quite blatant.

Margot quelled the uneasy ripple of sensation which rushed through her at his look and touch.

''Worthy of a greater beauty than mine,'' she responded tightly.

''Not so. You have beauty, Margot,'' he insisted, ''beauty of soul, which radiates from your face. 'Tis of a more lasting kind than that which is only skin deep.'' He laughed slightly, as though embarrassed at voicing such a sentiment. ''And I believe I have told you before that you do not lack attraction. Do not denigrate your charms, my dear.''

He reached out to grip her shoulders. Margot's breath caught. She began to shake, but both knew it was not with fear.

Soberly, Thomas's eyes searched hers. ''You have heard the gossip running through the castle?'' he asked quietly.

''Aye. To spend a night alone in the forest with a man—''

''Even a wounded man! Aye, Margot, I fear your reputation has suffered because you remained with me to save my life. Had you fled and saved yourself, no doubt you would have been praised as a virtuous heroine!''

"Fools! But what care I for their scandal? I have little reputation to lose, being neither virgin nor wife."

"Even so, it would quieten their wagging tongues if we were betrothed."

Margot gasped. Her lips moved, but no sound emerged.

"What say you, Margot?" The sudden hesitancy in his eyes caught at her heart. He drew a sharp breath before he spoke again. "Dare I ask you to do me the greatest of honours, to become my wife?"

"Oh, no!"

The instinctive response was dragged from Margot's throat as conflicting emotions shattered the last vestiges of her calm.

Thomas's fingers tightened their grip, almost cruel under the intensity of his shock. Margot saw the hurt pride, the painful acceptance of rejection which flashed across his face before he noticed the agony written on hers.

His fingers slackened. "Margot?" he whispered. "Why say you 'no'?"

Margot had to swallow deeply before she could find any voice. "For no reason to do with your birth or position!" she proclaimed hoarsely. "You must know that! But, oh, Thomas, my love…" She faltered, flushing furiously, ashamed of showing her feelings so openly. Thomas had not said he loved her. But she must make him understand, must not allow him to think her indifferent to his suit…

Seeing the suddenly arrested look on his face, she gulped down a bolstering breath of air. "I am barren," she gabbled, "and…and…"

Thomas's hand moved to cup her nape. "Afraid?" he questioned.

Margot nodded, her eyes wide, her breathing difficult.

"I will show you that you have nothing to fear."

He leapt to his feet, crossed to bar the door to the Great Chamber, and returned to her with swift strides.

She saw the purpose behind the gentle, humorous expression on his face, the banked-down fires burning in the depths of his smiling eyes, and understanding of his intention burst upon her.

She began to shake again. "Thomas, to lock ourselves in will only add fuel to the fires of speculation," she protested in panic.

"Which we will confound," he promised tenderly.

He lifted her to her feet. She did not resist. It was as though she had no control, no sense of reality as his clever fingers removed her veil, searched among the coils of her hair for the pins, and loosened her plaits until they hung down her back. He worked slowly, carefully, until her hair hung in a loose cloud around her shoulders, his touch on her scalp, the tug on the roots as he untangled her braids somehow both soothing and unbelievably exciting. Only after he had luxuriated in the feel of the free length of her hair running through his fingers did he encircle her with his arms and pull her close.

She felt his heart thudding against her breast, the awesome hardness of his need pressing against her belly. He kissed each eye softly, tenderly. His lips traced the contours of her chin. They wandered off towards her ear and, with a little moan of protest, Margot searched blindly to capture his lips with her own.

He met her demand with a sweet, sensuous pressure, a warm, languid exploration which sent heated shockwaves rippling through her body. His lips parted, hovered over hers as though in invitation. And Margot, risking everything on a sudden surge of longing, let her tongue seek the soft, teasing curl of his.

The sudden sensation of melting sweetness which drained the strength from her limbs took her by surprise, though she should have expected it. It brought back memories of another time, another place, when she had panicked, when Thomas...

But Thomas was forewarned. He curbed his growing need, sublimating it in the desire to please her, to remove forever the memory of her cursed husband, the grip of fear which had kept her passionate nature locked in some unreachable recess of her being. He wanted to set her womanhood free, to bring her unawakened body to its complete fulfilment, and find his own rapturous release in the process.

Gently, coaxingly he let his tongue fence with hers, drinking of the sweetness of her mouth. He felt her surrender, and, although he tightened his arms to give her support, was careful not to let them demand.

When he lifted her from the floor, Margot wound her arms trustingly about his neck. He grunted as his shoulder took the strain, but carried her easily to the huge bed and laid her reverently upon its satin coverlet. Then he drew the rich, thick hangings and stretched his muscular length beside her.

He kissed her again and again until her lips were swollen and throbbing and her body a jumbled mass of sensation. Only then did he let his mouth wander down to her neck, nuzzling the filigree necklace aside to find the pulse fluttering like a trapped bird in her throat.

The buttons along the sleeves of her kirtle were tiny and awkward. He undid them one by one, every success marked by a kiss on her wrists. He could feel the ever-quickening pulse-beat under his lips, but knew also that tension had taken hold of her as he began to remove her dress.

She was still fearful. He had not conquered yet. He turned her over with infinite gentleness and undid the lacing down the back of her kirtle, kissing the silky skin above her smock with warm, sensuous lips, rewarding her shudders of pleasure with lingering strokes of his sensitive fingers as they massaged each separate vertebrae through the fine material.

When he lifted her skirts she made no protest, other than a small, inarticulate sound, although neither did she assist him to remove the garment. She behaved like a doll in his hands as he raised and turned her body, inching the silk over her head. His fingers ran caressingly up her legs to untie her garters and push down the fine silken hose. The latchets of her slippers took but a moment to unfasten.

Now she lay in the thin smock, beautifully embroidered and scented with fragrant herbs. He smoothed it over her subtle curves, marvelling at the swell of her small breasts, the taut nipples already straining against the fabric—erotic proof of her arousal—the gentle curves of hip and thigh revealed in the absence of the cumbersome folds of her gown.

His breath caught and a surge of blood flowed to his loins. He fought down his desire, desperate not to move too quickly, astonished that it mattered so much to him that Margot should enjoy his lovemaking, should respond to it, should lose her fear, should reach her own peak of pleasure.

He would need all his skill and control to wipe out her bad memories, to prove himself a considerate, expert lover, to show her the joy to be found in the union of a man with a woman. He drew a harsh breath and mastered his throbbing body. He could not let go yet. Not before he'd accomplished the task he'd set himself.

He did not seek to remove the last remnants of her modesty. Through the fine fabric her tender breasts fitted so well in his palms. His thumbs brushed over her taut nipples, bringing a sighing groan of pleasure. But not until he lowered his mouth and took the peak in his mouth, drawing on it through the thin chaisel of her smock, did she suddenly come alive under his hands.

Fear became swamped by the thrills running through her body. Thomas's caresses sent spears of fire shafting down to a point low in her belly, and Margot could not restrain her groans of pleasure.

Under the feel of his little kisses, the stroking pressure of his fingers on her spine, her body had become a mass of shivering nerve-endings, her blood a fiery stream in her veins. She couldn't believe the pleasure, yet even so couldn't prevent herself from tensing up, waiting for the pain to begin. So she lay breathless under his assault, helpless to stop him, not wanting to, really, although the entire episode was madness. The rumours, the talk, the innuendoes could only grow. Yet she did not care. Her reputation was already compromised. What matter if it became a little more tarnished? She had no intention of marrying, no ambition to hold a place at Court.

But she did want to know Thomas's possession. To know what it would be like to lie in the arms of the man she loved. To prove to herself that all men were not like Roberto. That sex, that universally necessary activity, was not always the degrading and painful business she had known in the past.

When Thomas's mouth found her nipple, the exquisite pain of his slow, languorous sucking seared to the depths of her soul. It was as though her whole being exploded with joy. Pain she had feared, but not this pain!

Exultantly she cried aloud, and her arms wound tightly about his body, binding him tightly to her.

He lifted his head. In a fever of anxiety, Margot took hold of his hair, refusing to let him move away, crying out again as his mouth closed on new territory, leaving the first pulsating breast encased in fine linen made transparent by moisture. Her nipple shone pinkly through the clinging fabric, huge, defiant, throbbing.

She eyed it in disbelief as his fingers took it in their tender grasp, twisting, teasing, brushing, while his mouth worked magic on its twin.

Her fingers tangled in his vibrant hair, she couldn't keep still, her hips began to writhe impatiently. Thomas raised his head, smiled into her feverish eyes and shifted his position, tugging at the hem of her smock. The warm moisture left by his mouth had cooled swiftly, leaving the material clinging uncomfortably to her breasts. With a breathless laugh, Margot lifted her hips and helped him to remove the last vestige of modesty.

The necklace still hung round her neck. Thomas's breath caught in wonder. She looked like a Barbarian princess.

Her hands tugged tentatively at his clothing and Thomas needed no further urging to discard tunic, hose and shirt. Margot nestled against his naked chest, discovering the exquisite friction of fine hair brushing against her breasts his lips had so thoroughly sensitised.

Gently, he extricated himself from her feverish clasp so that his hands and lips could trace every soft curve of her body, search out each secret place, each source of ravishing pleasure.

Margot revelled in his lovemaking, held hard to his

hair when no other part of him was within her reach, abandoned every prudent thought, discarded inhibitions like tattered garments. When, at length, Thomas probed her womanhood, the gush of warm response produced by his clever fingers made her melt with love and gratitude. How gentle he was! Yet his mastery was so sure, so unbelievably precious!

Instinct told her she could return the pleasure. She reached blindly for the hard flesh lying against her thigh. As she felt him swell and throb in her grasp the realisation of her feminine power filled her with delicious exultation.

Her touch was too much for Thomas. He gave a great shudder and moved over her, covering her body with his nakedness. He buried his face in her neck, breathing deeply. Clinging grimly to the last shreds of his control, mastering his response, he slid inside her warm, moist sheath, unable to deny himself the rapture of complete conquest. He'd not intended the ultimate seduction, had thought he could show her pleasure, banish her fear, make her ready to commit herself to him and then stop, waiting for his own release until after they were wed, for Margot could not be taken lightly, as he'd taken his women in the past.

But he hadn't expected to wake a sleeping wanton, to find himself enmeshed in silken limbs, seduced by provocative hands and hungry lips.

Eyes shut, breathing suspended, he thrust gently to her core, though every nerve in his body demanded urgent, forceful possession.

He lay quiet, savouring his own delight, the aroma of roses and woman she exuded, allowing her time to accept the invasion he had not originally intended. He knew both elation and guilt in that moment. This conquest was like to change his life, but there was no going back now.

Concentrating on ravishing her mouth in anticipation of the final progress to completion, he lay inside her, sensing the melting laxity which had overtaken her limbs.

He began to move. Soon, so very soon, she was rising to meet his thrusts, her little cries of pleasure and passion music to his ears.

He raised her to a peak of expectation, then stopped to kiss and stroke. Her fingers bit into his back and his shoulder was beginning to feel the strain, but when he moved again nothing could mar his sense of triumph as he felt her muscles grip, the tremors begin, and knew that at last he could allow himself release.

Margot had known nothing like the tingling, shimmering pleasure which racked her body, the mindless sea of sensation in which she floated after Thomas's last, fierce thrusts. She bore his beloved weight as a trophy, breathing in the male smell of his heated skin while his spent body shuddered over hers.

She could not believe what had happened. Revelation was a poor word to describe the bliss of those ecstatic moments shared with Thomas. So this was what it could be like! The spectre of Roberto's perverted usage rose for an instant to throw a shadow over her new knowledge, but she laughed it in the face. She was free of that trauma at last, and she lifted grateful lips to kiss the man who had banished it.

"Thank you, Thomas," she whispered.

He stirred, reluctant to break the spell which held him in thrall.

"I deserve no thanks, Margot." His voice shook. "I

must beg your forgiveness. I had not intended to use you so. I meant only to demonstrate…''

"Had you not, that would have been cause to beg my forgiveness! Thomas, I wanted you to take me. Surely you knew that?''

"Perhaps, but I should have been stronger. Margot, you must not think yourself held lightly in my esteem. A man does not dishonour the woman he wishes to marry. But—'' he gave an embarrassed laugh ''—I confess I was unable to resist making you mine!''

"Or I to let you.'' She smiled mistily and ran a tender hand down his cheek before her lips sought his. His response was instant. Good God! He was hard again already!

Feeling full of feminine power, Margot wriggled under his weight, lifting her hips as her body opened like a flower seeking the brilliance of the noonday sun. She strained towards him. "Do it again,'' she whispered.

Her words shattered the last remnants of his restraint. With an inarticulate groan of need, Thomas thrust, hard and deep, heard her cry, and thought it was a protest.

He held still, pulsing urgently inside her. "I'm sorry, sweeting,'' he groaned, "I didn't mean to hurt you!''

As he began to withdraw, Margot's arms closed fiercely around him, her legs locked behind his buttocks.

"No! Don't go!'' she implored, straining to take him deeper, to fill herself with him.

"I won't.'' His relief was powerful, the knowledge that he had won, had conquered her fear, a potent aphrodisiac. "Don't move!''

"Why not?''

"Because if you do I can't last.''

"Oh!''

She lay still beneath him, feeling him pulse with need.

Tenderness welled up within her and she began to kiss his shoulders, sprinkling them with hot, wet kisses that made him groan.

When he began to move again she thought she must have been translated to the realms of Glory. Nothing, not even Heaven, could be so perfect. Thomas took his time, leading her to a place where time ceased to exist, where reality ended and glorious sensation filled the world.

He exploded within her. Together they spiralled dizzily up, up, to soar in realms where only eagles flew. But, as she descended earthwards again and her brain began to focus, Margot knew the truth must be faced. Tears she could not control began to flood down her cheeks.

Thomas felt the moisture. "Margot? Sweeting? Tears? What ails you, Margot?"

"Your seed is wasted on me, Thomas. Your glorious seed will never beget a child from my body."

"Sweetheart, it doesn't matter!"

"It does to me!" She did not want to break the sweet rapport between them, but she could not let him foster false hopes. "Thomas, I cannot wed you."

He lurched to his good elbow to look down on her with confused, disbelieving eyes. "You must! After this you have no choice!"

She buried her hot face in his neck, feeling the prick of the gold and stones as her necklace pressed against her breast, reminding her it was not the only thing to come between them. "I will not burden you with a barren wife, Thomas," she told him in a voice strangled by tears. "It would not be fair. Before long you would begin to resent your lack of heirs and blame me—"

"Never!"

She lifted her head and smiled sadly at his vehemence.

He protested too much. Her wavering resolution became firm.

"All men set store by their ability to breed. I know you have a bastard son, but you cannot acknowledge him. I could not condemn you to the frustration of an unfruitful marriage."

"You know Robert is mine?" He looked shocked, and paused. "Did Beth tell you?" he asked suddenly, wrathfully.

So her guess had been right. The confirmation brought a renewed stab of agony, which she masked with a smile as she stroked his arm.

"She had no need. The relationship between you and the boy speaks for itself. Would you treat any other child—apart, perhaps, from your nephews—in the way you do Robin? Giving him a pony, teaching him to ride it, showing him how to handle a toy sword..."

"I had not known I made it so obvious," he said stiffly, the colour on his cheekbones high. "Do others suspect?"

"That I cannot say. I do not indulge in gossip, Thomas. Perhaps my eyes are more perceptive than most."

Where you are concerned, she added silently.

He wiped the tears from her cheeks with tender fingers. "You know, then, that I have someone to whom I can leave any fortune I may amass."

"But no son you can acknowledge." Her voice cracked and new tears filled her eyes. "You need a legitimate heir, Thomas. You will not change my mind."

Thomas did not know what to do. She was suddenly remote, tragic. He wanted to take her in his arms, to comfort her, persuade her, but she was unreachable. He drew back the curtains, rolled from the bed, and began to draw on his hose.

"You said you loved me," he attacked as he fastened his breech-belt.

"Did I, Thomas?"

Margot lifted the smock over her head and then her kirtle, turning for Thomas to fasten the lacing. The touch of his fingers almost weakened her resolve, but she knew that to accept him as her husband could lead only to disaster. He did not love her. He desired her, liked her, respected her; but that was not love.

"You know you did." Agony was wrenching his gut, but he managed to speak calmly. "You did not mean it?"

She would not feed his ego or give him false hope. She did not dare, in case she weakened. She kept her back turned to hide the grief in her eyes. "A slip of the tongue, Sir Thomas," she said briskly, "I believe I feel for you what you feel for me, respect, affection—desire."

"The foundation for a sound marriage," he said softly, sliding his hands down her arms in a way that sent tremors shivering through her body.

"Says he who has sworn never to wed a maid he does not love!" she retorted scathingly, working furiously on the buttons at her wrist. "See, Thomas, I throw your own words back at you. You do not truly wish to marry me."

"How can you say that?" He turned her to face him, took her by the shoulders and shook her slightly. His gaze was fierce, intent on hers. "I want you most desperately, Margot. After today I shall burn for you..."

She evaded the demand in his eyes by concentrating on fastening the belt around her slender hips.

"You will find some woman on whom to slake your thirst," she rejoined sadly, and slipped from his grasp to stoop to fasten her slippers.

"No." He gave a brief, self-derisory laugh. The prize he had worked so hard to win seemed about to slip from his grasp. "I know now why I have wanted no other woman for months. You seeped into my blood without my knowledge, Margot. Change your mind, my dear heart."

She gazed into his earnest eyes and was almost persuaded. Certainly, he did desire her, and that was heady knowledge. Teetering on the brink of capitulation, a mental picture of Robin flying into his father's arms rose to confound her.

She loved Thomas too much to condemn him to a childless future. Just in time, she found the strength to shake her head.

She took a moment more to think before she stood to meet his challenging stare.

"But we need not deny ourselves the pleasures we have just discovered," she suggested, her lips curving in an unconsciously seductive smile, her eyes languorous with promise. "As well be hanged for murder as for being wrongly accused."

The shocked expression on his handsome face almost unnerved her.

"No!" he exploded. "I will not settle for a tawdry affair!"

"Then you had better ask Beth Horsley back to your bed," retorted Margot tartly, her face suddenly tight.

She might have slapped him in the face. He took a step backwards and his expression hardened.

"Can you not see, Margot, it is because you are so different from Lady Horsley that I cannot contemplate such a liaison? Your reputation would be ruined!"

"I am deeply grateful that it concerns you, Thomas. Personally, I do not care. I am willing—nay anxious—" how anxious he would never believe "—to have you as my lover, to know again the joy of being held in your arms, of feeling truly a woman.''

As he still stared silently at her, she burst out, ''I do not expect you to understand, Thomas, but you have given me freedom, freedom from the bondage of fear, freedom to enjoy the delights which are every woman's right!'' She threw out her hands in a last, desperate appeal. ''Please do not deny me the enjoyment of my new-found liberty! Unless—'' She hesitated, all the animation wiped from her lovely face. Her voice trembled. ''Unless I do not give you pleasure?''

He swore roundly and grasped her by the shoulders to shake her. ''Do not doubt that! Why else would I insist on wedding you, woman?''

''For many reasons, Thomas.'' She spoke regretfully. ''Your sense of honour is strong. But I will not marry you, my dear. The decision is yours.''

She devoured his face with eyes full of naked love.

But Thomas was too incensed to see it. He glared at her for a long time until the sudden lightening of his expression, the gleam of humour which returned to his eyes, told her that his anger had passed.

He would have his prize after all. But not in the way he had anticipated.

''You mean it, don't you?'' He laughed suddenly and let his arms drop. ''You are full of surprises, Margot. Perhaps that is why—'' He broke off, and began again. ''Very well, then. But do not blame me if you become the butt of spiteful tongues. I have sought to defend your honour.''

''I will not blame you, Thomas.''

She traced the curving line of his mouth with a tender finger. It had not taken much to deflect him from the idea of marriage. She had been right to refuse.

She smiled bravely, her eyes deep, dark, sad pools.

And Thomas gathered her against his still bare chest and kissed her fiercely, as though he would prove the extent of his passion.

"My lady," he said, in a voice so deepened by emotion Margot barely recognised it, "you do me more honour than I deserve. I shall seek no other arms while yours are ready to receive me."

Margot realised rather hysterically that she had just become his leman. She must guard her heart. It was involved enough already, without her showing it to him or to the world.

When he found someone else to love she would suffer heartbreak. That would be the inevitable price of her self-indulgence.

She patted her hand playfully against the golden-tipped hairs dusting his broad chest.

"Do not make promises you may be unable to keep," she warned lightly. "Unbar the door, Thomas. People will be wondering where we are!"

His arms released her reluctantly as he moved to do as she asked. His eyes continued to brood on her as he lifted the bar.

"I will come to you soon," he promised gravely.

Her smile, her light step as she left him, all contradicted the great longing welling up within her, threatening to overthrow her resolve.

She had only to say the word and Thomas would seek permission to marry her even now. But, for his sake, it was a word she could not allow herself to speak.

Chapter Fourteen

Thomas had changed his mind. Margot was certain of it. Days had passed and he had not come to her. She waited, inwardly suffused with embarrassed shame whenever she recalled her wanton behaviour. Smiled distantly and responded coolly to his polite conversation, always conducted in public. It took Inés's innocent chatter to release her from her cage of humiliation.

"Sir Thomas sent Edwin to Suffolk with Lady Horsley's duty letter," she told her mistress, eyeing her warily before rushing on in rapid Spanish. "He instructed him to let slip to Sir Robert's servants all the scandal concerning his bitch of a wife!"

Margot kept her expression neutral with difficulty. In one exhilarating moment Thomas's recent neglect was explained. She instantly excused all those nights spent waiting and wondering, only to drop off to sleep at dawn, frustrated and depressed, fearing that the gleam in his eyes, the pressure of his hand when their paths crossed, were merely pretences disguising an interest already dead.

Having digested Inés's information during a somewhat lengthy silence, Margot assumed an air of disinterested scorn to cover her real emotions.

"But not, I imagine, that concerning himself?" she enquired tartly.

Inés went on with slightly less assurance. "No. But that died some time ago now."

"Perhaps they have found a new source of tittle-tattle?" suggested Margot drily.

Inés shifted uncomfortably, refused to meet Margot's eyes, and ignored the suggestion. "I think it was a good idea and so did Edwin," she muttered defensively. "I know how much you hated having that woman near you, *doña*, and she was a constant burr under the hauberk of Sir Thomas. It seemed a wonderful way to be rid of her. And no more than the English whore deserved!"

"You may be right, Inés," sighed Margot, unable to maintain her air of indifference. "I confess her departure gives me great pleasure. But, if you value your skin, do not allow this piece of gossip to go beyond yourself and Edwin."

"Oh, no, *doña!* Sir Thomas warned Edwin." Inés blushed suddenly, twisting her fingers in nervous embarrassment. "*Doña,* Edwin and I—we would seek your permission to wed."

Her tiring-maid's normally bold face was suffused with a shy flush. Margot forced down a stab of pure envy.

"When I am free, I shall be leaving here," she reminded her quietly. "Will you wish to remain with Edwin?"

"Oh, *doña*, I shall not want to leave you, but I love Edwin and my place will be with him…"

"Then of course you must stay." Margot managed to raise a genuine smile. "I have no reason to prevent your marriage, Inés, apart from selfishly wishing to keep you with me. What of Sir Thomas?''

''He gave Edwin his permission before he departed for Suffolk.''

''Then there seems nothing to stand in your way.'' She drew Inés towards her and kissed her forehead. ''I wish you both great happiness.''

And she did, sincerely. But she found the prospect of losing the girl's services and companionship depressing. She could think of no one she fancied to replace her.

''And you, *doña?*'' They had grown close since leaving Castile, two women thrown together in a strange world of unknown dangers. So Inés risked the intimate enquiry. She was no fool. She knew where her mistress's heart lay.

''Me, Inés?''

''Yes. You and Sir Thomas… Were you to wed, Edwin and I could both remain in our present service.''

Shocked at the girl's perception, Margot's instinct was to resort to denial. But Inés deserved better than that. Despite her initial fears of the unknown, she had turned into a faithful, thoughtful retainer, almost a friend. Besides, when…if…she and Thomas…Inés would have to know.

''I cannot marry Sir Thomas,'' she said softly, frowning, ''but I may take him as my lover— That shocks you, Inés?''

''Fornication is a mortal sin, *doña!*'' wailed the girl.

''Then I shall have to seek absolution.'' Margot drew a breath and added her own verdict. ''It would be a worse sin to wed with him knowing I can give him no heir.''

Inés was silenced.

* * *

When Sir Robert Horsley, grey, balding, gaunt, short of breath and stiff with rheumatism, came hotfoot to Leicester to reclaim his wife and son, Margot was therefore prepared. His jealous rage led him to challenge the young knight with whom Beth had been amusing herself over the last weeks, an unequal contest the prospect of which caused ripples of excitement, amusement and shocked anticipation to rustle through the ranks of the household. Thomas handled the situation with masterly efficiency. The duel was forbidden, the young knight sent away for a few days, the old man's ruffled feathers soothed, and the Horsleys packed off to sort out their marital differences away from the hothouse atmosphere of the castle's court.

Margot viewed Beth's suppressed fury with equanimity, but was moved to reluctant sympathy by the sight of her chastened, obedient departure with the decaying, mannerless man who was her husband. Beth's future life would not be an easy one.

Parting with little Robin wrenched at her heart, but she knew the boy would come to no harm. He had Amy to love him, and Sir Robert clearly doted on his heir.

Watching Thomas wave a too-casual farewell to his son, her tears refused to be denied. He would probably not see Robert again for many a long year.

Once Beth's departure was accomplished, Thomas lost no time in sending Margot a discreet message to announce his intention of seeking her bed. Inés was with her, and let him in. Her ladies had already retired behind the barred door of their chamber, and would remain unaware—or so Margot hoped—of Thomas's presence. Inés, on her pallet in the wardrobe, would be a discreet attendant within call. She waved the girl away.

The tall, heart-stoppingly handsome figure, swathed in a vast cloak which did nothing to disguise his potent masculinity, came striding towards her as she sat waiting.

"So," she greeted him, "you have come at last!"

He dropped to one knee beside her and took her hand. The flickering candle lit his hair, threw shadows across the dear, familiar features. The warm clasp of his fingers almost undid her. Margot longed to throw herself into his arms, but resisted the race of passion his mere touch released. He deserved to wait a little longer, however good his reasons for neglecting her for so long.

"I could not come sooner."

"Why, pray?"

"You know full well! Do not tease me so, Margot! It was for your sake! I could not submit you any longer to the venomous presence of Beth Horsley, nor conduct our liaison with her on the other side of a door!"

"Beth? She had troubles enough of her own. I wonder how her husband discovered her infidelity?" asked Margot, keeping her voice and expression neutral by a supreme act of will.

Thomas eyed her searchingly, his expression earnest. "I arranged Beth's departure." He awaited her reaction. When none came, save a raising of her eyebrows, he burst out. "I could bear her presence no longer, and when I contemplated her listening, mayhap tending you after—"

He broke off. "We are free of her, Margot. Free to enjoy our union without jealous eyes watching our every move."

"I have wanted her to go for so long!" admitted Margot, unable to tease him a moment longer. She gave in to her longing and slipped to the floor beside Thomas, clasping him as his arms closed hungrily around her. "You should have told me what you were doing," she chided. "I had begun to think you had changed your mind and would never come to me!"

"Apologies, my heart." He stroked the mass of hair from her smooth, alabaster-like forehead. "The task was distasteful and I did not want you tainted by knowledge or association. Does that sound foolish?"

"Aye, but chivalrous, too." She pushed aside the heavy cloth of his cloak and inserted her arms beneath, discovering that only a thin shirt stood between her caressing hands and his smooth, silky skin. "I would have slept better this last week had I but known your mind!"

He laughed softly. "One way or another, it seems I am destined to be responsible for depriving you of rest!"

She felt his urgency burgeon against her, and knew with delight that sleep was still a distant prospect. She turned to him with joyous submission as their lips fused.

"I want you," he whispered hoarsely, and Margot eagerly led him to her bed.

It was almost as though this was their first time. Both knew the other intimately, but the separation had made the memory of that other time dim, had erased the images of fear and uncertainty, leaving only the anticipation of ecstasy, of mutual satisfaction.

Thomas realised all Margot's dreams of delight, while she filled him with such tender, urgent passion he knew he was enmeshed in her allure for as long as she would allow him to sip of her cup.

Lying entwined in the sated aftermath of loving, Margot felt bold enough to broach the subject of his son.

"What of Robin?" she asked Thomas sadly. "You will miss him."

"Aye, but I was becoming too fond of the boy. You

showed me that. 'Twas not wise. He will do well enough, and I shall delight in his achievements—from a distance.''

''How sad!''

''Nay, Margot. My happiness does not lie with a son I cannot recognise. It lies here, with you.''

His arms tightened. He sounded sincere. Margot's heart overflowed with love. With a little cry, she burrowed more closely against his warm, silky skin, her hands seeking out all the hidden secrets of his body.

He groaned, his breathing quickened, and she felt his passion rise again, more strongly than ever. The knowledge of her own power overwhelmed her. She, the frigid, skinny, plain Margot de Bellac could rouse a splendid male creature like Thomas d'Evreux to such heights of passion he had difficulty in retaining control! And she revelled in it!

The exultant knowledge acted as a spur and Margot set herself to give him the fullness of pleasure he had given her, caressing with hands and lips until, at last, he could stand it no longer.

''Margot!'' he gasped. ''You're killing me! I can't wait...''

He took her fiercely, deeply, satisfyingly. Margot responded with all the frustrated sexuality of the years with Roberto, recognising, just as their bodies merged in shimmering ecstasy and she lost all power of coherent thought, the essential difference between overwhelming passion and unbridled, perverted lust.

Such a liaison, however discreetly conducted, could not remain unremarked upon for long. Margot's new, quietly glowing radiance would have betrayed them without the proud possessiveness Thomas found it impossible to hide.

Whispers followed them wherever they went. Thomas had suffered his share of notoriety in the past, and the innuendoes bounced off his back like arrows from his armour. He knew it to be born of curiosity and boredom rather than spite. In a curious way he gained respect and authority in the wake of his important conquest. There seemed little fear now that any would challenge his position as castellan.

But for Margot the experience was different and, despite her protestations of indifference, hard to bear. For blame did attach to a woman who defied the Church's strictures, and people were not slow to make their censure felt.

She held her head high and ignored the sly looks and disapproval which followed her wherever she went. Her confessor was so severe in his condemnation that she stopped going to confession and mass. It was her own immortal soul she was risking, and there would be time enough for her to embrace holy chastity when Thomas tired of her. She could feel no shame in giving herself to the man she loved. The pleasure they shared was surely God-given and no sin.

Thomas sought her company so assiduously, made love to her with such an exquisite blend of subtlety and arrogance, that she began to wonder whether he was actually in love with her. If so, her happiness would be complete. But, although he called her ''love'' in an affectionate way, he had never said he loved her, not even in the heat of passion.

But that did not stop her from dreaming. Supremely happy and content in his arms, Margot voiced a thought which stilled Thomas's wandering hand in surprise.

"The Duke of Lancaster would never countenance a union between us," she murmured idly.

His fingers gripped her slender hip. "Are you considering my offer anew, my sweet?"

His voice was tense. With hope or fear?

"Nay." Realising where her rambling thoughts and desires had taken her, Margot was quick to deny her lapse and erect another barrier against what she knew instinctively would be a mistake. "Never forget that I am still a hostage, my dear. Our marriage would take away my value as a bargaining counter."

Thomas stirred angrily. "It is high time your father swore his oath of allegiance and set you free! Until that day comes your future is at risk, married to me or not. Even as your husband I doubt I could save you from whatever punishment the Prince of Wales thought fit to decree. But the Count your father will surely act to save you!"

"I wish I could be so certain." For the first time Margot felt able to voice her fears, to admit to the desolation of believing herself abandoned. "You do not know my father," she whispered, with a shiver of dread. "I do not believe he feels much affection for me. I have not seen him since I wed."

Thomas gathered her closer. "I cannot believe the Duke would countenance too severe a punishment." He tried to look into her eyes, but the darkness in the enclosed privacy of the huge bed defeated him. "Is that why you took me for your lover?" he asked gruffly. "To seek happiness while you may?"

His hold had become almost painful in its intensity. Margot snuggled closer, caressing the smooth musculature of his powerful shoulders. His arms represented at least a semblance of security.

"Perhaps."

Lying alone after Thomas had crept away in the chilly autumnal dawn, Margot considered his question anew.

Was it because of the threat still hanging over her head that she had found the courage to take what she wanted from life while she could?

Perhaps.

Roberto had robbed her of so much of her youth, had destroyed so many of her dreams.

Thomas had crossed the drawbridge to her besieged and battered emotions. Her love for him had given her the impetus, a strong enough desire to flout convention and the teachings of a lifetime and snatch at all the happiness she could find in the face of a distinctly uncertain future.

King Pedro of Castile attempted to murder his prisoners and went back on all his promises. Bitterly disillusioned, the Duke of Lancaster returned from Castile with the remnants of the thousand archers he had raised from his domains. Rumour had it that not one in five of the English force which had set out on the venture survived to tell the tale. Battle losses had been few, but sickness swept the ranks as all summer the victors waited in vain on the sweltering Burgos plain to receive the million crowns Pedro had promised as reward for their services.

Gaunt and weakened by dysentery, that scourge of soldiers throughout the world—but not dead, as were so many of his followers—the Prince of Wales led his depleted and unpaid army back to Bordeaux with nothing but a handful of jewels as his reward, knowing he would be forced to raise new taxation from his unwilling duchy of Aquitaine in order to meet his war debts.

"Sir Cedric would surely have been among the dead had he remained," mused Margot. She reached up with a loving gesture to smooth back the rumpled waves on Thomas's brow. "And how glad I am that you were forced to return when you did!"

Thomas had just told her the unpalatable news. He grimaced ruefully, captured her hand and kissed it.

"Part of me still wishes I had been able to remain—or to return again with the Duke. I deserted my duty. Living softly here, enjoying your bed—I feel guilty!"

"Now you are talking nonsense!" She patted his injured shoulder with her free hand, and noticed the slight wince he could not hide. "Your duty was here, and you were wounded executing it! Was that soft?" She hit the shoulder with a clenched fist, not hard, but hard enough to make him draw in a sudden breath of pain. "You suffer from the wound even yet. You have no cause to feel guilt, Thomas!"

He grimaced again. "No doubt you are right! I'll try to be grateful for my mercies."

"Stephen's body was never found," pondered Margot, remembering.

"Nay. His ruffians disappeared, too, no doubt to fight over that fortune he boasted of having amassed."

"That should surely have been yours!"

He shook his head in fierce negation. "I want no part of any such spoils!"

She kissed his smooth cheek in quick sympathy. "You are right! We have so much for which to be thankful."

"Aye. Praise God, Dickon is well. He is in Bordeaux with Prince Edward, but will shortly return to Wenfrith to see his family."

"The Lady Eleanor will be delighted. Was it only yesterday that I received this letter from her?" asked Margot, fumbling in her scrip for the folded parchment.

"It was, and already you have regaled me with the contents several times!"

Thomas grinned, and Margot pouted. "Well, the news is worth repeating, is it not? Isobel is to be married in the spring, and Sir Cedric and Matilda are already wed! I saw that attachment growing when we were there."

"At one time I thought you and Cedric were attracted."

"And I could not understand your stiff-necked disapproval!"

"I thought you ill-matched."

"Was that all?" asked Margot provocatively. Thomas grinned ruefully, and a dull flush spread under his skin. She smiled. "There was never aught between Cedric and me except affection and friendship."

"You did not pine to have him in your bed?" he countered outrageously.

"Nay, Thomas." She chuckled and pushed him away. "You are merely fishing for compliments! I shall not give you the satisfaction of telling you that you are the only man I have ever wanted in my bed!"

"Margot, my love!" He saw the luminous tenderness in her eyes, the lift of her lips as she smiled. He drew a sharp breath, his nostrils flaring. "How I wish I did not have to spend the next hour with my steward, arranging for the Duke's coming! But since he brings his family and retinue there is much to prepare!"

If Margot had a moment's unease at the thought of Thomas seeing the Duchess again, she suppressed it. Blanche represented an ideal. She, Margot, was his reality, the fact written in every passionate line of his face.

"And I must visit the hospital," she told him rather breathlessly. "But you will come tonight?"

He kissed her seductively upturned lips, sending her senses spinning. "Nothing shall prevent me."

The next few days saw the castle in turmoil. The entire fortress was cleansed and sweetened from stable to Great Hall. Walls were whitened, roof beams blackened, stone flags scrubbed and strewn with fresh rushes, window glass cleaned until it sparkled in the low-slung sun. Cart after cart drew up in the yard to deliver mountains of food and fodder, tuns of ale and casks of wine. Thomas had not a moment to spare during the day, and arrived in the Hainault chamber so weary he could scarce summon up the energy for passion.

Margot did not mind. His presence was enough. She smoothed the tired lines from his face, kissed his drooping eyelids, and gladly took on the role of wife rather than lover.

If only it could be so in truth!

The Duke arrived amid a blare of trumpets and a commotion worthy of the King himself. He and his Duchess swept into the small hall of the living quarters at the head of a gaggle of courtiers, attendants, children and nurses. Thomas made his obeisance and Margot noted the reverence with which he kissed the Duchess's hand.

Margot waited to be presented. The Duke acknowledged her with princely charm, while his wife offered a gracious greeting.

Margot was slightly disappointed in Lady Blanche at first, thinking her rather insipid in looks with her almost silvery hair, light blue eyes and pale complexion. But when she smiled her charm and goodness were instantly evident. Margot understood why men acclaimed her fair beauty and fought to serve her.

The Duchess departed with her attendants with much swishing of brocade and satin over the newly scattered rushes. The freshly beaten tapestries swayed in the breeze of their passing. The children dutifully followed with their nurses: Philippa, a sallow, flaxen-haired child of eight, Elizabeth, a noisy termagant with brown hair and green eyes just half her sister's age, and the baby, Harry, six months old, reminding Margot of how long she had been in England, a hostage in a silken cage.

The Duke had his arm around Thomas's shoulders. Margot knew she had been forgotten, and retired discreetly to the Hainault chamber.

Thus she was not aware of yet another arrival until a knock on her door heralded the entry of Thomas, escorting a young lady and her nurse.

"My lady."

He bowed low, studiously correct in his manner.

Margot curtsied in response. "Sir Thomas?"

Thomas urged the girl forward, and she came, her golden hair a ray of sunshine in the shadowy room, her blue eyes as clear as a sunlit sky.

"My lady, may I present Demoiselle Celia de Boursey? She is His Grace's ward, and on his orders has travelled from the manor of the knight entrusted with her present guardianship." He turned to his companion with a smile. "*Demoiselle,* this is Lady Marguerite de Bellac, with whom you will be sharing this chamber."

The girl acknowledged the introduction with an enchanting smile and returned Margot's curtsy with slender grace.

Margot felt as though she'd been kicked in the stomach. Share the Hainault chamber? With this ravishing child?

She suddenly felt a hundred years old, plain and dowdy. She schooled her voice with a supreme effort. "Did you say *share*, Sir Thomas?"

"I regret the necessity, my lady, but the castle is overfull, and the steward assures me there is no other chamber in which Demoiselle de Boursey can bed." He met her eyes, allowing some of the frustration he was feeling to communicate itself to her. "I myself am sharing a chamber with several of my fellow knights," he added, "and am lucky not to be spreading my pallet in the Great Hall or even in a passage!"

Margot nodded, reassured by the look in his eyes, the darkening of her own the only sign of her shock. "I quite understand. Such a large company puts a severe strain on the accommodation. You are welcome, my dear."

She gave the youngster a friendly smile, and nodded to her nurse, who curtsied in response.

"Your nurse will find space in my ladies' room, or she can sleep on a pallet in here if you prefer."

Privacy was hardly important any more.

"Oh, Nan doesn't mind where she sleeps," retorted the girl cheerfully. "Do you, Nan?"

She turned and flung childish arms round the older woman's neck, and Nan smiled indulgently.

"Not at all, my lamb."

Celia danced round to smile winsomely up at Thomas. "Please tell them to bring my coffers."

"I believe they are on their way, *demoiselle*."

Thomas bowed and retired, the dazzled expression on his face bringing a sudden sickness to Margot's stomach.

Celia took off her expensive grey woollen cloak, revealing a travelling gown of sapphire wool shot with threads of silver. She draped the cloak over a coffer before moving over to inspect the bed.

"It seems reasonably soft, and quite big enough for two," she remarked, adding thoughtfully, "I am used to sleeping alone on a mattress filled with swansdown."

"Then I trust we shall not disturb each other, *demoiselle*. We have no choice but to make the best of the situation."

Celia's facile smile faded and her eyes became wary as they met Margot's. Margot immediately regretted the acerbic note she had allowed to enter her voice. She smiled as warmly as she could manage.

"When your coffers come, my maid, Inés, will help Nan to arrange things to your liking. Will you take a bath after your journey?"

Celia pulled a face, wrinkling her small nose. "Thank you, no. I dislike intensely immersing myself in water. It cools so quickly, and shrivels the skin. Nan can sponge me down."

She wandered over and sat on Margot's stool while Nan went down on stiff knees to remove her riding shoes.

"As you like. I am sure you do not need me to tell you to make yourself at home," responded Margot wearily.

How was she going to endure this girl's charming, self-centred company for several days? Perhaps weeks. Any appearance of maturity she had was skin-deep, not even that. It derived from her costly gown and the natural arrogance, which kept peeping through her engaging charm. "How old are you?" she asked impulsively.

"I am told I have seen fifteen summers, my lady," retorted the girl. "I am quite old enough to wed. That is why I am here," she confided importantly. "His Grace has chosen a husband for me."

"Really? And who might that be?"

"I do not know, yet. But I am ordered here to meet the knight in question."

"What if you do not like him?" enquired Margot, wondering whether this maid would have more say in her choice of partner than she had had at a similar age.

Celia shrugged. "I do not think the Duke would force me, though it scarcely matters, does it? Wives see so little of their husbands, and once I am married and with child I shall be able to return to my manors as and when I like." She giggled. "But I have been told he is young and handsome, so I can see no reason why I should object to the match. And since I have a considerable fortune," she went on complacently, "I cannot think that *he* will have cause for complaint."

Whoever it is will need a strong hand on *your* bridle, thought Margot grimly. But a fortune could make almost any woman attractive in the eyes of an ambitious man. Not that Celia needed a dower to make her desirable. Quite the reverse.

With the Duke and Duchess seated in the huge, canopied chairs of honour at the high table, Margot and Thomas were moved down to lesser places. Margot could not object, but found herself placed on the Duchess's right among a knot of courtiers, while Thomas sat down the table on the far side of the Duke, with Celia on his left.

Why wasn't Celia placed among the Duchess's ladies? wondered Margot resentfully. Celia had no right to such an important position at table—except perhaps as the Duke's ward. And why put her next to Thomas?

She agonised all through the interminable meal and

the entertainment which followed, trying to appear affable to her neighbours and finding it well-nigh impossible. Her strained attention was fixed immovably on Thomas and the youthful figure beguiling him with vivacious, mischievous charm. The girl's blue eyes sparkled, her clear voice sliced bell-like through the general bedlam of the noisy Hall, so that, although she could not pick out the words or catch more than the occasional glimpse of them when others moved, Margot was uncomfortably aware that her chatter was making Thomas laugh and smile down indulgently into a charming little face framed by silky golden tresses.

A face and colouring which must realise his ideal of the perfect woman.

But the child had come to marry some unknown knight. Thomas might look, but he could not take.

Though no betrothal had been sealed. Celia was still free to accept another offer. Margot felt the foundations of her happiness begin to tremble.

Even when the boards were cleared and people began to move about, dancing, playing games or carousing with their friends, it was a long time before Thomas left Celia's side. Even then it was because Celia had joined the dance with another partner.

Margot saw him coming towards her and suddenly couldn't bear for all the castle household to see them meet. What must everyone be thinking after noting their forced separation, after, no doubt, crowing over Thomas's besotted behaviour towards the lovely Celia?

She jumped to her feet, intent on flight, when John of Gaunt called Thomas, who threw an apologetic glance in her direction before diverting his steps.

Margot, breathing a sigh of relief, had begun to make

a dignified exit when Gaunt's imperious tones floated to her ears and her feet became rooted to the spot.

"What think you of my ward, Tom? Would she suit you as a wife?"

Margot's eyes flew to Thomas's face. An assortment of expressions shifted fleetingly across it, from sheer amazement through consternation to dawning interest, before his expression became inscrutable.

"Me, Your Grace?"

"Aye, you Tom." The Duke waved a dismissive hand as Thomas opened his mouth. "I know your background, none better, and I shall be prepared to overlook it if my ward is. There is no title involved, though her estates are considerable. What say you?"

"I—" Thomas's knuckles whitened as he gripped the hilt of his knife. He swallowed. "Your Grace, may I have time to consider the matter? I confess your suggestion has taken me by surprise."

"God's blood, Tom, she is fair to look upon and young enough to be trained to your ways! The marriage would be much to your benefit. What ails you, man?"

"Your Grace does me too much honour. Nevertheless, I would beg your indulgence. I had not thought to marry."

John laughed, as though at some entertaining memory. "You're a lusty lad, that I can vouch! You should be eager to take a wife—or are you afraid that to wed would spoil your present sport?" he speculated slyly.

Thomas smiled, a thin smile that did not reach his eyes. His jaw clenched before he spoke.

"Perhaps, lord. I have always valued my freedom."

Margot's hands became fists at her sides and she bit her lip as colour flooded her face. She was suddenly aware that a silence had fallen in the immediate vicinity, and that those spectators who knew them were watching both her and Thomas with ill-concealed amusement and varying amounts of malice.

"Oh, very well." John shrugged somewhat irritably. "Get to know the maid. I'll have to mention the matter to her, for she is expecting to meet her future husband. Court her, Tom. When you have made up your mind, let me know. But don't take too long."

Thomas bowed. As Margot regained control of her legs and fled from the Great Hall, she heard him say, "Very well, Your Grace."

She was shivering violently as she crossed the yard to reach her room but, although she drew her mantle closely around herself, she was barely aware of the cold.

She heard someone follow her from the Hall, and darted down an alleyway between the buildings, where no torch burned to alleviate the darkness. A rat scuttled out of her way.

Her ladies would feel obliged to leave with her, but she wanted to see no one, she had to be alone to absorb the shock, to compose her emotions before she faced anyone at all, let alone Celia.

She would have to sleep in the same bed as the girl. Searing, shocking pain ripped through her and she retched, covering her mouth with her hand. Any moment now she would vomit.

"Margot! Margot, my love!"

Thomas had followed her. She felt herself gathered into his arms, her heaving body pressed against his, heard soothing words murmured into her ear.

Her face buried itself in his neck. She breathed in the clean male scent of him, felt his heart beating steadily under her hand, and a measure of outward calm cloaked the turmoil raging inside her.

"Hush, Margot! It's all right."

He shifted them into deeper shadow as someone carrying a torch passed the end of the passage.

Margot lifted her head in time to see the flare of the disappearing light. "Is it?" Her stomach still churned, but she managed to keep her voice steady and cool. "Then why are we hiding?"

"You came in here, I merely followed. I thought," said Thomas grimly, "that you wished to conceal your distress."

"Perhaps I did. But you were simply avoiding being seen with me. No, don't deny it!" she said sharply as Thomas began to protest. "It will be like that now, won't it, Thomas? If we want to talk alone we shall have to find some corner where we will not be noticed!"

"Only until John departs. He will not stay above a month."

"While you court Celia de Boursey! For heaven's sake, Thomas, I'm forced to share my bed with that girl!"

"Would that I could change places with her!"

Margot struggled out of his arms. He let them fall to his sides. She could not see the expression on his face.

"Or with me?" she asked sadly. "Oh, don't pretend, Thomas. You are taken with her, what man wouldn't be? She is your idea of the ideal woman—fair, beautiful, kind—yes, I think she is essentially kind, despite her youthful self-centredness. She would make you a fine wife, Thomas, could bear you many sons."

The words almost choked her, but they must be said.

Thomas remained silent. It was too dark for her to see the expression on his face.

Margot's shoulders sagged. "God go with you, Thomas."

She moved to walk round him, back to the shadowy light of the yard.

"Margot!" His fierce grip on her arm halted her as she passed. "It is not as you think," he gritted. "But I must humour John. I cannot throw his generosity back in his face without due consideration!"

"Of course not. I understand completely. And I think you should seriously consider his proposition, Thomas."

If he had drawn her back into his arms and kissed her then, Margot would have believed his interest in Celia de Boursey to be entirely diplomatic. But he did not. And for his sake she must set him free.

But she was hurting so much she wanted him to hurt, too. She tilted her chin defiantly.

"The Duke of Lancaster's patronage is like to make a great noble of you yet, Thomas," she said coldly. "I only hope that Celia shows the same generosity of spirit. And now, if you will kindly release me, I will return to my chamber."

He dropped her arm as though it were red hot. His voice rang cold and inflexible. "As you wish, my lady."

Margot swept away, his words echoing hollowly in her ears.

When, over the next few days, he sought the girl out, took her riding, danced with her and spent hours teaching her to play the lute—an accomplishment she found it singularly difficult to acquire—Margot knew in her heart that Thomas was lost to her.

But wasn't that what she wanted? Oh, yes! But the knowledge that she was doing the right thing in thrusting him into marriage with Celia did nothing to ease the pain of her own loss.

Chapter Fifteen

Sharing her chamber and bed with Celia de Boursey subjected Margot to an exquisite form of torture.

Celia showed unfeigned delight at the Duke's choice of bridegroom for her. She enthused over Thomas's looks, his charm, his bravery, until Margot wanted to scream. There could be little doubt that Celia de Boursey approved the match, though whether she yet knew of Thomas's base birth Margot had no way of telling. Celia never touched on that subject.

Daily Margot waited for the blow to fall, for the Duke to announce the betrothal ceremony and feast. If only she could escape! Never had her invisible fetters seemed so heavy, never had she chafed so bitterly against her confinement. But no word came from Aquitaine to signal her release.

She repressed every instinct to scratch and claw at Celia, to lash out with her tongue and prick the bubble of the girl's complacency. It wasn't that she disliked Celia, frivolous and youthfully selfish as she was. In other circumstances she might even have welcomed the girl's friendship.

At night, in the big bed, she tried not to disturb Celia

with her tossing and turning, thankful that the girl had a healthy knack of dropping into a deep sleep the moment her head touched the down-filled pillow. Margot doubted that even a violent storm would wake her.

Bitter regret added to her restless inability to sleep. If only she had not given in to her base instinct to hit back at Thomas. Then at least she could have faced him without shame. But to attack him where he was most vulnerable had been unforgivable. She could expect nothing but scorn from him.

Inés and Edwin were to be married in the porch of Saint Mary de Castro. Margot prepared to attend the ceremony knowing that a meeting with Thomas was inevitable. He would not fail to support Edwin any more than she would desert Inés.

But they need not speak, she assured herself desperately.

Margot had given Inés one of her newest gowns and its matching mantle as a wedding gift, and the radiant girl, black hair streaming down her back as a sign of her maidenhood, proud as a peacock in sky-blue embroidered taffeta trimmed with squirrel fur, looked every inch a proud and spirited Spaniard.

Margot hid her misery as best she could. At that moment she would cheerfully have changed places with Inés if she could have been going to the arms of her own lover.

As the little procession approached she saw Thomas standing beside Edwin. It appeared he had been generous to his groom, for Edwin was decked from head to toe in brand new apparel. He held his perky felt hat in his hand because his head, like his bride's, was crowned with a bridal chaplet of laurel leaves entwined with rather bedraggled flowers gleaned earlier from the wintry pleas-

ance and fields. Encased in a scarlet tunic and saffron
tights covered by a voluminous blue houppelande, his
tall, lanky figure outshone Thomas's, dressed as his was
in more sober russet and tan, and protected from the
wind by a mantelet of warm burel trimmed with fox. But
his master's presence overshadowed him in every other
way—at least in Margot's sight, though Inés rightly had
eyes only for Edwin.

Thomas looked pale under the remnants of his bronze.
He acknowledged her without a flicker of emotion in his
blank grey eyes. Where was the laughter, where the teasing twinkle? Margot, who had been avoiding him for
days, knew her worst fears were confirmed; he did despise her. Her stomach plummeted to her thin leather
shoes, through which the cold ground struck a chill
which seemed to penetrate right to her bones.

By the time the short ceremony was over and Inés and
Edwin had exchanged their vows, Margot's teeth were
chattering. Her tunic, cote-hardie and miniver-lined mantle were warm enough, but the cold encompassing her
body was not entirely due to the weather.

"My lady, you look chilled and ill. 'Tis as well we
return to the warmth of the Hall."

Thomas's emotionless voice in her ear was the last
straw. She rounded on him angrily.

"I am quite well, I thank you, Sir Thomas. Once we
have drunk the bridal toast, I shall seek the warmth of
my chamber. No doubt I shall have it to myself, since
Demoiselle de Boursey will be enjoying your attentions
elsewhere."

A gleam of some sort of emotion flickered in his eyes,
but was gone so quickly that Margot could not identify
it. He ignored her thrust.

"It would be well if you took my hand, my lady. As

chief supporters, we should follow the bride and groom together.''

It was her duty. Reluctantly, Margot placed her trembling, gloved fingers in Thomas's. They felt fragile held in his tense grip, the only indication that he, too, was on edge. Her eyes seemed glued to their clasped hands, held out in the manner decreed by their stately progress across the yard to the Great Hall. Once inside she snatched her fingers away, and caught a sardonic gleam of amusement in Thomas's eyes.

Back in her chamber, she allowed Kate and Meg to divest her of her finery and dress her in a warm chambergown before dismissing them. She craved solitude, the chance to let her emotions run riot. As they curtsied and left, she sank down on a pile of cushions near the blazing fire and gazed into its heart.

Inés would return to her duties later. Where would the bride and groom go when they left the celebrations in the Hall? she wondered idly. To Edwin's pallet in the crowded room he shared with others? Or to a soft hidden bed of hay in the stables? She could have wished them a swansdown mattress on which to consummate their marriage vows, yet Margot knew they would not miss it. The leaping flames seemed to taunt her with a vision of warmth and intimacy which could never again be hers.

Celia had been in the Hall awaiting Thomas's return, and immediately appropriated his attention, speeding Margot's early escape from the jollity.

At the thought of them together still, Margot buried her hot face against her drawn-up knees. With her arms clasped tightly about her legs, she rocked back and forth in an agony of despair.

I must not resent her, Margot told herself fiercely. God

forgive me, I am compounding fornication with the sin of jealousy! And I have no cause! Did I not know he would marry one day? Did I not face the fact that I would suffer for my indulgence?

Sunk in an anguished muddle of incoherent thought, Margot's mind roamed. Memories of Thomas, of their fights, their loving, flitted across her vision like the myriad coloured patterns thrown by stained-glass windows lit by the sun.

Perhaps she dozed. But she jerked back to full consciousness with a course of action clear in her mind. It was the only one left to her.

Next morning, possessed of a new inner strength and a calm determination, she requested an audience with the Duke of Lancaster.

Royal Prince he might be, but he had a rare gift of understanding and compassion. He could no doubt be autocratic, arrogant, harsh and ruthless, but that day he heard Margot's request with a sympathy which led her to believe he was privy to at least some of the castle gossip concerning herself and Thomas.

"My lady," he said, raising her from her knees where she had fallen in gratitude, "after the months you have spent here in comparative freedom, I have no fear that you will attempt to leave England. D'Evreux trusts you, that in itself is recommendation enough. But I must provide you with an escort, and they will remain to protect you at Idenford. Go in peace, with God's blessings. If news reaches me from Aquitaine, I will send to you immediately. I will instruct that an escort be ready on the morrow, at dawn."

Margot guessed the escort would be charged to see that she did not attempt to cross the Channel. The Duke professed to trust her, but she could not blame him for declining to gamble on his instincts.

She kissed the gracious hand extended and left him, with a feeling of emptiness inside. She would be leaving behind everything she loved when she rode out of Leicester in the morning.

Kate was upset at the news, though Meg took it calmly enough. Celia gave a smug little smile.

"You have been kindness itself, Lady Margot, but I confess I shall be glad to have the bed to myself! And you must be delighted to be granted so much freedom!"

"Oh, I am," responded Margot drily.

Inés, torn between duties, sincere affection for her mistress and love of her new husband, tearfully offered to accompany Margot on her journey.

"Nay, Inés," responded Margot, her smile as bleak as her foreseeable future, "your place is with your husband. The Duchess Blanche has already chosen a tiring-woman to accompany me—a widow who comes from Kent and is pleased to return to her childhood haunts. She will serve me well, never fear."

Inés would soon forget her and settle to her new life. If only she could view the prospect of a lonely existence in a strange land on a small manor in a remote corner of Kent with similar equanimity! Whenever she thought of her own future—and, however hard she tried to occupy her mind elsewhere, it returned with the sure instincts of a homing-pigeon to a prospect she was trying to ignore—her stomach began to churn and her hands to shake. Yet pride forbade her showing her inner desolation.

Thomas knew she was to depart, for he had the ordering of the guard. After supper in the Great Hall he cornered her.

His cheekbones stood out prominently, the creases scored his cheeks more deeply than ever. His eyes held a hint of strain. He planted himself before her, hands on hips, every inch of him aggressive manhood set to dominate.

"You are leaving. Why?"

"I have been given permission to inspect my manor. I requested to be allowed to do so once before."

"So you did. But—"

She intervened quickly, before he could splinter the fragile credibility of a reason both knew to be an excuse.

"I have no wish to linger here and, even with the new steward installed, my manor needs my presence. I am grateful to you, Sir Thomas, for your trust has convinced the Duke that I will not attempt to escape to France."

"Margot, you shall not leave!"

He was not pleading, he was ordering. She had not expected him to care. She quelled the leap in her pulses, and defensively reacted to his insufferable arrogance.

"I have the Duke's permission," she reminded him coldly. "You cannot stop me. Why should I remain while you court Celia de Boursey?" she added tartly. "Wed the maid, Thomas. You never truly wished to marry me."

His nostrils flared. "That I dispute!"

"Had you been truly committed to the idea you would have tried harder to persuade me, Thomas. But, admit it, you were glad to settle for an affair. Which is over. There is no one—nothing to hold me here now."

He bowed, his face in the flaring torchlight pale, haughty and slightly sneering. She'd never seen him sneer before, and shock quivered along her nerves.

"Whatever you say, my lady. But neither do I desire to wed Celia de Boursey."

"Hah!" Margot's scorn made him flinch. Her small triumph left her feeling guilty. She pushed the emotion aside. "That is plain for all to see!"

"Nevertheless, it is the truth," he declared tersely.

"Then show a little less enthusiasm, Sir Thomas. Tell the Duke you have no liking for his ward or her inheritance!"

He smiled grimly. Thomas did not lack for courage, but His Grace the Duke of Lancaster was no mean man to cross, even if one was on intimate terms with him.

Margot slipped her shaking hands under the wide sleeves of her cote-hardie, making the fur tippets shake as she massaged the prickles on her upper arms.

"God go with you, Thomas." She wished her voice were less husky. "I wish you happiness."

She moved abruptly, sweeping past him, blinking rapidly to deny the stupid tears which welled into her eyes, hugging her arms about her body in an unconscious attempt to gain comfort. She had done what she must.

Yet she could not resist a last glimpse. As she left the crowded Hall she saw Thomas standing where she had left him, a strange, proud stillness about him; and it must have been something to do with the light or the sheen of the moisture clouding her sight, because Thomas was the last person to let a small rebuff penetrate his self-assurance, but he looked so alone and vulnerable she longed to put her arms around him and offer him comfort.

Even as she watched, Celia glided up to claim his attention. He moved abruptly, as though his mind had been recalled from elsewhere. Then he smiled his devastating smile, placed her hand on his arm, and led her into the dance.

* * *

The journey south passed in an endless blur of misery. Cold, damp days followed chilly, sometimes scratchy nights spent in whatever shelter—lousy and flea-bitten or not—the escort could commandeer in the Duke's name. Travelling with six guards, the commander only a sergeant, was less prestigious than being in the exalted company of the Duke or even that of a knight who not only served a royal master, but was also of some consequence himself. Margot let it all slide past her, riding in grim silence except when Juan sidled up to her, on the hack she had purchased for him, to entertain her with jokes and chatter.

Her new tiring-woman, Alice, was normally a quiet woman, skilled and obedient, but as the journey proceeded and the weather worsened she became a silent bundle of damp wool, dejectedly huddled on the back of a sturdy nag from the Duke's stables.

"'Twill snow before long, mark my words," said the sergeant. Nothing upset him or the men under his command, used as they were to far worse than a bit of cold and damp, and mud above the horses' hocks.

"If it freezes tonight the roads will be more passable on the morrow," responded his corporal cheerfully.

Margot silently wondered how Fleurette would fare on hard, ridged surfaces where her dainty hoofs could slither and slide into troughs and pot-holes. If she broke a leg Margot would never forgive herself for setting out on this journey at such a bad time of the year.

Yet if she hadn't taken herself away from the constant presence of Celia, the frequent sightings of Thomas, she would have gone mad.

The men raised their voices in song to cheer the plodding progress, geared as it was to the speed of the laden pack-animals and the drover who walked behind them constantly prodding with his goad. Margot's unruly mind wandered to the morning of her departure.

He'd come to see her off, handing her the stirrup-cup before lifting her gloved hand to his lips in a courtly gesture of farewell.

His touch had burned through the fur, and Margot had wanted nothing more than to slide from Fleurette's back and fling herself into his arms, to beg him to ask her again to stay.

But courtly, remote, he'd smiled into her face without a hint of regret as he'd made his farewells. Margot had crushed down her wild desire, schooled her features into an answering cool smile, masked the turbulence in her eyes with lowered lids, and hurriedly turned Fleurette towards the gate.

Leaving him was like cutting out her heart. Had she fought, she could have won the battle with Celia. Thomas had a passionate interest in her body, he'd offered to marry her, and if she'd used a few womanly wiles she could have kept him.

For what? she asked herself viciously. To deprive him of a presumably fruitful wife, Celia's youthful adoration, and all the possessions she brought with her? To offer in exchange her own heart and soul, her useless body, no hope of an heir and a profitless manor in Kent? What a paltry bargain!

It had taken all her will-power not to weaken at the last moment. She suspected that had she remained at Leicester she would have given in and thrown down the gauntlet, fought Celia for the man she loved. Snatched at a few years of bliss knowing it to be wrong, that no lasting happiness could be theirs if she was selfish enough to grab at it.

Would have succumbed to the temptation to ward off

the fearful suffering, pushing it into the future, where perhaps it wouldn't hurt so much...

Unconsciously, she straightened her back. She had always faced up to the unpleasant aspects of life. Accepted them and made the best of a bad bargain. And Idenford beckoned. Her own manor. Mayhap not a home yet, but a place where she belonged, where, by all accounts, she was needed. A messenger had ridden ahead to warn the new steward of her arrival. Her revenues had improved since the man, Gideon, had taken over. She wondered what she would find. One more uncomfortable night, and she would know.

It would be easier to banish thoughts of Thomas once she arrived and could involve herself whole-heartedly in the life of the manor. Idenford would demand so much of her attention that she would have no time to think of him or of anything else...

Chapter Sixteen

Margot threw herself into her new life with a determination that belied her true feelings. As the weeks passed, she found that most days she managed to push thoughts of Thomas to the back of her mind. Only at night did his image return to haunt her.

The snow came, and nothing could be done in the fields. Sheep were dug out of drifts and penned. Oxen were brought into the byres. Logs were cut and split for kindling.

Everyone would enjoy a holiday over the twelve days of Christmas, and filled the days of enforced idleness with preparations for the festival. It was on Christmas Eve, as Margot was preparing for supper, that Alice suddenly erupted into the solar.

"My lady! 'Tis Sir Thomas d'Evreux! Whatever can have brought him here? In this weather! And at Christmas, too!"

Margot's face had drained of all colour. She swayed and put out a hand to steady herself against the wall.

Alice rushed forward. "My lady! Are you all right?"

"Aye, don't fuss." Margot breathed in deeply, her nostrils flaring, then dropped her hand and moved resolutely towards the doorway, though the extra air in her lungs had done nothing to stop her head from spinning, and her legs threatened to collapse under her. "I must go to greet our guests."

She didn't realise how shocked she looked, how distraught she sounded. Alice eyed her mistress with a sympathy Margot would have found surprising had she noticed it. But she trod down the stairs blindly, holding tightly to the rail, the hem of her dark red working-gown clutched in a shaking hand. Once she reached the Hall she dropped the coarse wool, blinked rapidly to focus her eyes and, fingers threaded tightly together at her waist, moved carefully forward.

Thomas stood by the fire, his back half turned, conversing with a white-robed friar. Straight as a lance, his head thrown back, the fringes of hair showing under his riding cap burnished by the torchlight, the sight of him, so dear, so near, almost undid Margot's hard-won composure. For an instant her steps faltered as she drank in anew his particular, masculine presence, heard again his crisp, well-modulated voice.

Ned, facing his master across the fire, saw her first. A smile of greeting lit his youthful face.

Thomas swung round instantly, his heavy riding cape creating a draught to waft billows of smoke between them, his gilded spurs jangling in the semi-hush which had fallen over the Hall.

He bowed. "My lady!" His expression gave nothing away. "I thank you for the generous hospitality extended by your manor."

"Any traveller is welcome to shelter here, Sir Thomas," responded Margot formally, curtsying on trembling legs, and wondered at the coolness of her voice, when inside her breast burnt a furnace of emotion. "To what do we owe the honour of your presence?"

He indicated the spare figure at his side. "Brother Hugo is a Priest, as well as a Monk. I will explain our presence later."

Margot and the man of God exchanged wary greetings. Margot thought the Friar eyed her with unwarranted curiosity.

"Is Edwin with you?" asked Margot politely.

"Nay. I left him at Leicester with his wife."

"Is Inés well? And happy?"

"Aye to both, I believe."

He paused, but Margot had run out of small talk.

"Is there a place where we may be private?" he demanded.

If Margot had hoped for some sign of feeling, some softening of his curt, uninformative manner, she was disappointed. After only a moment's hesitation, "The solar," she suggested.

"Excellent."

Thomas moved towards her, stepping over the great yule log waiting to be fed to the fire on Christmas Day. Margot had watched it dragged in earlier, stout enough to last the twelve days of Christmas. Would Thomas remain that long? Could she bear it if he did? Her leaping joy at seeing him had disappeared in the face of his distant manner. Her first hope, that he had come to reclaim her affections, had died. What *had* brought him?

She urged her own limbs into delayed action, turning to lead the way, praying that the tremor in the hands lifting her skirts would not be noticed as she mounted the stairs and passed through the door into her solar.

Alice dipped in a reverential curtsy. After a brief acknowledgement, Thomas dismissed her with a wave of his hand.

"You may leave us."

"Nay—"

He cut Margot's protest short. "Go!" he commanded Alice decisively. "Close the door behind you!"

With a helpless look at her mistress, Alice obeyed.

"Sir," protested Margot grimly, "you are not master here! I'll thank you not to take that tone with my servitors!"

Thomas lifted an arrogant eyebrow. His aggressive male presence filled the small chamber, and Margot's knees began to shake again. She stood her ground grimly.

"My lady, I bring news from Aquitiane."

Margot's eyes leapt to his as her stomach lurched. A breath was squeezed from her lungs as though she'd been punched in the midriff. She searched to find her voice.

"What news?" she managed.

"Bad, I fear." His tone still held no emotion, and Margot wondered how he could stand there and deliver his blow so dispassionately. "Your father refuses to renew allegiance to Prince Edward. Trastamara and the French are harrying the borders of Aquitaine near the Limousin. He is a foolish and obstinate man."

"Then my life is forfeit."

The words came out huskily, hopelessly, as she gave way to her rising panic and sank down on the stool, dropping her head to gaze sightlessly at hands clenched tightly in her lap to disguise their shaking.

A sense of inevitability kept her immobile. Such defiance on the part of Bertrand de Bellac, Comte de Limousin, was tantamount to treason. It had sealed her fate.

She would be incarcerated, perhaps in the Tower of London, either to rot away or to be sent to the block.

"You have come to escort me to London," she articulated with difficulty.

"Not necessarily."

His voice was clipped. Margot looked up slowly, blinking. Hope began as a tiny spark, lightening the darkness of her eyes. "What is my choice?"

Thomas shrugged, thus momentarily lifting the heavy folds of his cape from the Persian carpet. "You are of no further value to the Prince of Wales. He is not a vindictive man. In recognition of his brother's aid in Castile, he has handed you over fully to the Duke's custody, to make whatever profit he may from you, to do with as he wills."

"I am at John of Gaunt's mercy?" she gasped.

He dipped his head in affirmation.

"But of what possible value can I be to him?" she demanded desperately.

Thomas moved to stare out over the wintry landscape, over land which belonged to her. "The Duke has named his terms for your release."

"And what are they?" she choked. Premonition had almost closed her throat.

"Idenford is held directly of the Crown." He turned abruptly to face her. "Your tenure is forfeit. The manor will revert forthwith, and become part of the Lancastrian domains."

Margot's chin came up in instinctive denial. She drew in a quick, shaken breath. "But I have nowhere else to go!" she gasped. Her voice came out harsh with panic. "I refuse to return to my father!"

A muscle in Thomas's jaw moved. "There will be no

need. That was only part of the bargain. John has given you to me.''

''*What?*''

Margot leapt to her feet. Power surged into her limbs as colour flooded her pale cheeks. ''He confiscates my land and then disposes of my person? By what right?''

''By right of conquest, my lady.''

The blood drained from her face, leaving it chalk-white. ''King Pedro hands me to Edward of Woodstock, Edward presents me to John of Gaunt, and now John has passed me on to you! I might as well be a horse!'' Indignation died as the hopelessness of her situation sank in. Her voice dropped to a whisper. ''I am to be in bondage to you for the remainder of my life?'' she asked wearily.

''Aye.'' He smiled, but only with his lips. ''I had hoped that such fetters would not greatly distress you.''

Margot began to shake. Her mind whirled, but one thought stuck out from the jumble. ''I have no desire to be at any man's mercy!'' she blazed, sudden anger bolstering her fragile strength. ''Think you to keep me as your leman? I utterly refuse!''

''I have no desire to bed you as my mistress, my lady.''

His voice was flat. So he didn't want her any more. The false strength poured from her. She collapsed ignominiously on her stool. ''Then what do you want of me? What of your wife?'' she demanded shakily.

''Wife?'' He was surprised out of his impassivity. ''I have no wife, nor yet a betrothed.'' He paused a moment, watching the relief flit unknown into her troubled eyes. ''The Friar is here to wed us.''

''Wed?'' she mouthed stupidly.

''Aye,'' he confirmed grimly. ''Wed. Marry. You will

become my wife. I have a licence given me by the Bishop of Leicester. Come, I will escort you to the Church, so that the ceremony may be performed without delay.''

The room began to spin. She felt blindly for the edge of the stool and held on tightly with both hands. "N-now?"

What a stupid thing to say! Why not a loud, resounding ''No!''? But her numbed brain refused to transmit her pride, only her need.

"Aye, the sooner the better. We can then enjoy the Christmas festivities together, and travel to Acklane after twelfth night. You may remain there, or accompany me back to Leicester, as you will.''

The room righted itself and Margot stared into his impassive face. Not one word of tenderness or love had passed his lips. Had the Duke forced him into this marriage. Why?

"Why, Thomas?'' she asked thickly. "Why did you agree to this…this arrangement?''

"Would you rather rot in some dungeon?'' he demanded curtly.

"No.'' Forced or not, the thing she wanted, needed most in the world was to wed Thomas. Without him, her life was nothing. The peace of Idenford was boring, tranquillity a lost art, contentment as distant as the stars. And it seemed he'd had her welfare in mind when agreeing to the Duke's proposition. He must still have some feeling for her. However little it was, whatever her past resolutions, she would have to make it enough. She met his opaque eyes bravely.

"It seems I have little choice. I accept the terms.''

Was that relief in his eyes? She couldn't be sure. But if it was, why did he look so grim? Why was he behaving as though it was taking all his not inconsiderable determination to see this thing through? Her heart sank. What future could they have together if he was so reluctant for the match? She began to regret her easy acquiescence.

"Then let us go."

"I must change my gown—"

He made an impatient gesture. "Your dress is of no importance. We are keeping the good Friar waiting. He wishes to travel back to the Priory at Rye today."

"He will not reach it before nightfall." The protest was automatic. It would make no impression on this purposeful man.

"That does not concern him. My lady?"

He opened the door and moved aside, waiting for her to pass. Margot stood for a moment, on the point of rebellion. He could not force her!

"Come!" His voice was brusque. If he felt any sympathy for her predicament it did not show. "Delay cannot help you. Make up your mind that there is no escape."

She tossed an angry, rebellious head. "I did not think you could be so unfeeling. So dishonourable!"

Admiration for her spirit brought a gleam to Thomas's eyes. A gleam she mistook for scorn.

"Dishonourable? Nay, my lady, do not think to taunt me with that accusation. I am acting entirely within the chivalric code. Unfeeling? But then, you never understood my inmost sentiments, did you?"

"I think I understood them perfectly!"

With a defiant flourish, she picked up a thick cloak and prepared to accompany her future husband to the Church.

The ceremony at the stout door was short, a straight

exchange of vows with no trimmings. By the laws of God and man they returned to the manor house man and wife.

Margot felt light-headed. It had all been so unemotional. So quick. She did not feel married. She hadn't been dressed for it. Unreality was compounded by a sense of profound relief she couldn't banish, mixed with equal proportions of anxiety and anticipation.

She mounted the dais to take her place at the high table with her new husband beside her. This could not be happening! After those weeks of shared joy and intimacy at Leicester, how was it that Thomas seemed like a stranger sitting at her side?

Yet, despite his rigid control, she realised with a tingling of her nerves that he was not unaware of her. Just as her body responded to his every look, his every touch, so his eyes darkened when he watched her; there had been a tremor in his strong fingers as he'd placed the heavy, wrought gold ring upon her finger, and now a thin film of sweat beaded his upper lip. They had spoken of bonds and fetters earlier but tension stronger than iron held them enmeshed in an invisible magnetic net, pulling them together despite the deliberate inches separating their thighs, and the coolness of Thomas's manner.

Margot could not think ahead. Could not face up to what the night might bring. Part of her longed for Thomas. To be held again in his arms would be bliss beyond belief. Her senses told her he would be no laggard lover, yet, if he was a reluctant bridegroom, ripe promise could quickly turn to ashes in her grasp. Before she could give way to the relief and happiness burgeoning in her breast she must know how much pressure the Duke had brought to bear on her new husband. Why he had changed his mind and ordered Thomas to wed her, rather than Celia de Boursey.

The answer came to her like a hammer-blow, bringing a rushing in her ears and a darkening of her sight. The succulent lamprey turned to ashes in her mouth.

She had become a burden the Duke wanted to unload. He did not wish her ill. So, perhaps mistaking his act for one of kindness, he had shifted it to Thomas's shoulders.

And Thomas had been forced to comply or lose his favoured position in the Duke's service. Poor man. Her eyes slid sideways to glimpse his beloved, familiar features. No wonder he appeared grim and distant.

She pecked at the food set before her, but drank deeply of the spiced mead. Thomas did not seem to be suffering any pangs of anxiety or regret. Despite the palpable tension radiating from his body, he ate with his usual hearty appetite. He also drank several cups of wine, more than was his usual practice. Was he, too, seeking spurious courage?

He was far from drunk when he touched her arm and suggested they retire before the merrymaking degenerated into debauchery.

Margot rose obediently. Thomas held power over her now. The power to give infinite happiness or crushing misery.

As they left the Hall he waved their attendants away. There would be no bedding ceremony that night. The Priest had gone. Margot smiled grimly to herself. What use to bless a bridal bed that could not host a fruitful union?

Even Ned and Alice were ordered to remain in the Hall.

"We will wait upon ourselves," Thomas told them briefly. "Disturb us at your peril!"

"Aye, lord."

Ned's eyes twinkled into Margot's. He and everyone else knew exactly what was about to happen, and bawdy shouts rang about their heads as they mounted the stairs.

Margot closed her ears to their lewd remarks and sought to calm her churning stomach. She did not want to be sick. Not yet.

Thomas closed the door behind them and slotted the bolt into place. Noise filtered up from below, but the atmosphere in the solar was hushed. He remained where he was, back against the wooden planks, and smiled. His first real smile since his arrival.

"Come here, wife."

Margot, already tense, felt ready to snap. She searched his face and saw something there that widened her eyes in disbelief. Tenderness, amusement and, yes, the old flare of desire smouldering in those darkly fringed grey eyes.

It was as though she were on the end of a string. She could no more resist the pull of those eyes than Fleurette had been able to buck the leading-rein. Her feet took her across the floor until she stood inches away, her gaze locked with his as her tension ebbed and she began to drown in those silvery, shimmering pools.

His fingers stroked a coil of her hair, then slid down to trace the line of her jaw and rest against her neck.

Margot trembled.

"Do I have to seduce you again, woman?" His voice deepened, became a husky growl. "Or do you burn for me as I burn for you?"

His arms came around her and his lips swooped in a swift, sure movement, capturing hers. He plucked at them seductively several times before hers softened in helpless response. The empty ache of longing, so long suppressed, surged up, swamping her reason. With a moan Margot opened her mouth, giving him kiss for kiss, tasting, stroking, demanding with lips and tongue, lost in a sweet need she could not control.

Thomas lifted his head, and his eyes laughed into hers.

"Well," he observed, "that answers one of my questions!"

Margot pulled her scattered senses together. Damn him! He had been testing her reactions while remaining supremely in command of his own!

She tugged herself away and turned her back.

"Oh, yes," she said, putting as much derision as she could muster in her voice. "Stirring the senses is easy, once you have found the key. But you would not willingly wed with a landless, barren widow almost as old as yourself." She spun back to face him. "And what of love, Thomas? If desire is all that drives you, this union will soon become little better than the one I suffered before."

Thomas regarded her flushed face for a moment, his own broodingly inscrutable. Then he pushed himself away from the door and strode over to the fire. It was little more than smouldering ashes in the hearth, and he stooped to feed on more twigs and logs. Margot waited in an agony of suspense for him to answer her. He took his time. Not until the fire was burning to his satisfaction did he straighten up.

His eyes traversed the tapestries, the bed, the carpets warming the floor. "You have made this a comfortable chamber, Margot. I am sorry you will have to forfeit this manor, but your things will fit well at Acklane."

"Thomas!" She was almost in tears. "Do not change

the subject! Why did you not marry Celia? Did the Duke change his mind as to your suitability as a spouse for his ward?''

"Nay. But Celia discovered that a bastard has few notions of chivalry once he has gained his objective. She was so clearly delighted with the arrangement, I presumed upon my position as her future betrothed.'' He grinned impudently. "I abused it most regrettably. She did not like my ordering her about, controlling her frivolous ways, and she fought most valiantly to defend her maidenhead.''

"Thomas!''

Margot's shocked cry made him shout with laugher. "There are more ways to skin a cat than one, my dear!''

"But what if she'd not resisted your advances?'' demanded Margot, appalled, and not a little disturbed by her instinctive jealousy. "Would you have taken her?''

"Nay, Margot, you know me better than that! I do not deflower virgins, even willing ones! But I judged her, correctly as it turned out, to be not only virginal but cold and prudish beneath her appealing ways. As my wife, she would have bored me to tears within the month. I wanted to be rid of Celia without offending the Duke. I succeeded.''

"But was he not upset at your treatment of his ward?'' choked Margot.

"She did not tell him. 'Twould have hurt her pride. She suddenly discovered that I was not good enough to deserve her high-bred hand.''

"Then...'' She swallowed painfully. "How was it that the Duke offered you my hand, instead?''

"I asked him for it,'' said Thomas simply.

That simple statement got to her more directly than any flowery explanation could. Her pulses began to race.

"Why?" she whispered.

"Because, my love, you had refused me before, and accused me of not truly wanting you as my wife. Since no declaration of mine seemed able to convince you, I decided to give you no choice in the matter."

Margot digested this in silence. Her unwavering gaze was fixed on his face, her eloquent eyes mirroring doubt and confusion. Thomas swore softly, but stood his ground, one hand raised to clasp an empty torch-bracket on the wall.

"Margot, my dear love!" His voice deepened and roughened. He couldn't help that, or the way his knuckles showed white where he grasped the metal, an outward manifestation of the grip he held on himself. But she had to believe him, to come to him freely, or his gamble would be lost. "Margot," he repeated, "I discovered that I could not do without you. I missed you most desperately. No!"

His grip tightened as he saw her stiffen, and his other hand clenched on the hilt of his sword so that it wouldn't reach out to her. "Not just for the exquisite passion we shared, but for your presence. Leicester Castle was empty without you, as would be my life if you were not part of it." He hesitated, then told her softly, "That is why I wanted to marry a landless, barren widow of almost my own age, to use your own words."

"But who is also the daughter of a Count."

Margot couldn't help interjecting the suspicion nagging deep in her mind.

"Even so," he acknowledged equably, and she could detect no shadow of guilt or unease in his steady grey eyes. "That, too, I cannot change even if I would. But you—" he watched her face intently "—you are content to have as husband a bastard who owes his wealth to the generosity of others?''

"And his position of trust to his integrity and courage? Husband.'' Margot stepped forward to trace the line of his curving lips with the tip of her finger. He captured it between his teeth, sending a shaft of fire up her arm. "Are you trying to tell me that you love me?'' she whispered.

"I've never felt for any other woman as I feel for you, Marguerite d'Evreux.'' He spoke her new name caressingly, and a shiver of delight slithered down Margot's spine. He laughed, self-mockingly. "I thought my ideal woman would look like Eleanor or Blanche, but it seems I was wrong. I loved Blanche as a young man idolises a goddess, a woman out of reach, the wife of his liegelord. You, my darling, are the only woman I have ever longed to share my life with. If that is love, then I love you.''

She made one last bid to see into his heart. "You have ignored my chief reason for refusing your suit before.''

"Your lack of fruitfulness?'' He frowned. "Aye, Margot. I'll not deny your barren state gave me pause for thought, but I've realised that no children borne by another woman could compensate for losing you.''

Margot breathed a sigh of pure happiness and moved against him, her arms winding round his tense, waiting body. Still he didn't move, though he allowed his hovering mouth to be claimed by her parted lips. She tasted her fill, releasing all the pent-up longing of the past weeks, pressing ever closer, rubbing her soft body against the hard proof of his response.

"Thomas!'' she whispered desperately. "What is wrong? Why are you hanging on to that bracket as though it were a lifeline?''

"Because, my love, I have to stop myself from reaching out for you. I have to be sure you are coming to me freely, with your mind and soul, not just your body. I know I can persuade you if I hold you in my arms. I proved that earlier." He laughed shortly. "That would not be enough. I am greedy. I want all of you. Unreservedly."

"You have me! All of me! Oh, Thomas, my love! Hold me! Love me!"

With a groan, he unleashed his body at last, crushing her to him with almost brutal intensity.

Margot gave a gurgle of contentment and clung as fiercely, claiming him as her own.

At Leicester she had thought their lovemaking could not be surpassed. But she had been wrong. Now they were husband and wife, their union blessed by God. All sense of guilt had been wiped out. Secure in his love, she revelled in his tenderness, his mastery, his fierce passion, and answered it with a boldness, a demand he found irresistible.

"Wife," he murmured hoarsely into her neck, "I think I shall die if I do not take you this instant!"

"I am yours," she breathed in response. Her body throbbed unbearably with need. "Now and always. Oh! Thomas!"

She almost swooned with the intensity of her pleasure as they united. This time, no one and nothing could come between them.

"My husband! My love!" she shuddered as their bodies moved in perfect harmony. "I love you!" Her arms tightened convulsively around him. "I've loved you for so long!"

"You tried to deny it," he chided. "Why, sweeting?"

"You did not love me."

Arrested, he stopped his movements. "I think I did, though I didn't know it." They lay quietly, joined together, as he made an honest endeavour to be truthful.

"For a very short while I was tempted by Celia and her fortune, since you wouldn't have me. But I couldn't get you out of my system, my heart. You had denied your love with words, but your actions branded you liar. So I wagered on the fact that you *did* love me when I asked John for your hand." He gave a sudden, fierce thrust which sent shivering ecstasy thrilling along Margot's nerves. "And now I have you! Till death parts us!"

She drew him closer, deeper, wishing that her body would truly melt and merge with his. And, as they scaled the peaks of delight, it seemed for a time as though it did.

Time and again that night Thomas proved his virility and love. Margot responded with all the loving passion at her command. Near dawn, sated, exhausted, they dropped into slumber.

Margot woke first, roused by the sound of a distant bell calling the manor to mass. Thomas's arm lay warmly, possessively across her waist. She raised herself on one elbow to gaze down lovingly on his relaxed features. Seldom had she been able to indulge her desire to watch him unawares at Leicester. Thomas had left her bed in the dark.

Now the grey light of Christmas morning filtered through the hangings to give his sleeping face a youthful, unlined air of peace. She couldn't resist the temptation to kiss his curving lips.

His arms were about her in an instant. He rolled her over. Margot's head spun and her stomach heaved.

"Thomas," she gasped urgently, trying to escape his clinging arms, "I'm sorry, I must..."

She leaned from the bed to find the skin bucket hidden behind the draperies. She bent over it and retched.

"Sweetheart!" Thomas was behind her, his warm body cradling hers as the sickness overwhelmed her again. He was trembling. "Margot, my love, what is it? Are you ill?"

"Nay."

The wave had passed, and she sat up. Thomas reached for chamber-gowns, because the morning air was cold.

He carefully wrapped her shivering body in her gown before tucking the covers about her with anxious, clumsy hands. Only then did he sling his own gown about his shoulders.

"Margot!" His voice was sharp with fear. Thomas, afraid? "Tell me what ails you! Was it the food yester-eve?"

"Nay, love." Margot's white face broke into the most beautiful smile he'd ever seen. "Your child is growing in my belly," she told him softly.

"Margot?"

The incredulous joy on his face told her all she wanted to know. But almost instantly a new set of emotions tightened the line of his mouth and filled his eyes with anger.

"You are carrying my child and did not tell me?" he grated. "Why?"

Margot brought the covers up tightly under her chin, shrinking under the force of his attack.

"You were so far away. And I thought you betrothed, possibly married."

"But did nothing to find out? Despite the fact that your chief reason for rejecting my suit was supposed to be your inability to breed, which had been disproved?"

"I did not think you loved me. I wanted you to be happy."

"And for that paltry reason you would condemn my child to bastardy? I thought you loved me. I do not understand."

"Paltry? Your happiness, paltry? Perhaps it was because I loved you *too* well, Thomas. Do you think it was easy for me to deny my instinct to send for you? But even for the sake of the child I could not endure to have you resent your bondage to me and seek your pleasures elsewhere."

"And what gave you the ridiculous notion that I would feel so?" he groaned.

"I don't know." She looked at him helplessly. What had made her so certain that he didn't love her? Because, for so many years, she had thought herself unlovable? Had been unable to recognise the emotion when it stared her in the face?

He'd given up Robert for her. That thought led to another. "You didn't object to leaving Robin with his mother—"

He cut her off curtly. "Robin has a name and an inheritance!"

"Our child would have inherited all I possessed!" Margot insisted.

"You did not possess the name of its father!"

Suddenly, the anger left him and a weary kind of desperation took its place. "Margot, you knew how I felt about bastardy. And this child would be *yours*. Whatever you might have thought, I cared for you deeply. Other women, including Beth Horsley, were no more than conveniences," he admitted, faint embarrassment burning his cheekbones. "You meant so much more—yes, more

than I realised at the time, I admit that. But your child—
our child—would have been especially precious to me.''

"Would have been, my love?'' Margot reached up to
trace the scar which still marred the perfection of his
broad shoulders. ''Surely he...she...will be?''

"Of course! Margot, Margot,'' he groaned, giving in
to the insistent demand of his heart to understand, to
forgive, ''to think what we almost missed...''

"'Twas Roberto's fault I did not conceive before, not
mine,'' she explained softly. ''Or so the midwife says.
I will bear you many lusty heirs, my dearest husband.''

"You waited until now to tell me!'' Sudden agony
twisted his beloved features. ''Margot, you let me...''

"No harm was done, my dearest, nor will be.'' Her
beautiful eyes shone up at him, twin stars to lead him to
the haven of her love. ''I wanted—want you so much.
But most of all I needed to know that you loved me for
myself, as I love you. If I'd told you last night, I would
never have been completely sure. Now I am. You have
set my heart free.''

He said not a word. Simply lifted her from the pillows,
wrapped her in his arms, and buried his face in the fra-
grance of her hair.

* * * * *

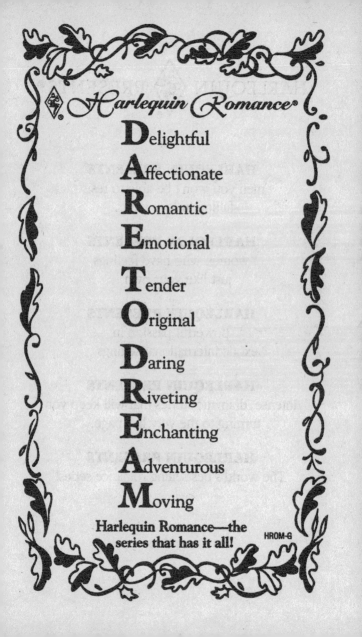

Harlequin Romance®

Delightful

Affectionate

Romantic

Emotional

Tender

Original

Daring

Riveting

Enchanting

Adventurous

Moving

Harlequin Romance—the
series that has it all!

HROM-G

HARLEQUIN  PRESENTS®

HARLEQUIN PRESENTS
men you won't be able to resist
falling in love with...

HARLEQUIN PRESENTS
women who have feelings
just like your own...

HARLEQUIN PRESENTS
powerful passion in
exotic international settings...

HARLEQUIN PRESENTS
intense, dramatic stories that will keep you
turning to the very last page...

HARLEQUIN PRESENTS
The world's bestselling romance series!

Harlequin®
Historical

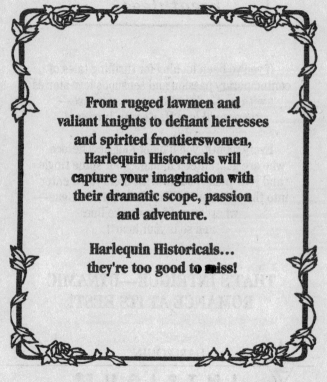

From rugged lawmen and
valiant knights to defiant heiresses
and spirited frontierswomen,
Harlequin Historicals will
capture your imagination with
their dramatic scope, passion
and adventure.

Harlequin Historicals…
they're too good to miss!

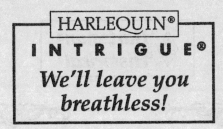

HARLEQUIN®
I N T R I G U E®
We'll leave you breathless!

If you've been looking for thrilling tales of
contemporary passion and sensuous love stories
with taut, edge-of-the-seat suspense—
then you'll *love* **Harlequin Intrigue!**

Every month, you'll meet four new heroes
who are guaranteed to make your spine tingle
and your pulse pound. With them you'll enter
into the exciting world of Harlequin Intrigue—
where your life is on the line
and so is your heart!

THAT'S INTRIGUE—DYNAMIC
ROMANCE AT ITS BEST!

HARLEQUIN®
I N T R I G U E®

LOOK FOR OUR FOUR FABULOUS MEN!

Each month some of today's bestselling authors bring
four new fabulous men to Harlequin American Romance.
Whether they're rebel ranchers, millionaire power brokers
or sexy single dads, they're all gallant princes—and
they're all ready to sweep you into lighthearted fantasies
and contemporary fairy tales where anything is possible
and where all your dreams come true!

You don't even have to make a wish...
Harlequin American Romance will grant your every desire!

Look for Harlequin American Romance
wherever Harlequin books are sold!

HARLEQUIN SUPERROMANCE®

...there's more to the story!

Superromance. A *big* satisfying read about unforgettable characters. Each month we offer *four* very different stories that range from family drama to adventure and mystery, from highly emotional stories to romantic comedies—and much more! Stories about people you'll believe in and care about. Stories too compelling to put down....

Our authors are among today's *best* romance writers. You'll find familiar names and talented newcomers. Many of them are award winners—and you'll see why!

If you want the biggest and best in romance fiction, you'll get it from Superromance!

Available wherever Harlequin books are sold.

Look us up on-line at: http://www.romance.net

HS-GEN

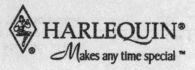

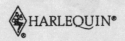

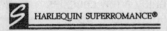
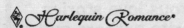

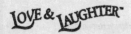